Sitting ducks

Encizo silently crept up to the corner of the storage building. He raised the H&K chopper in one fist and flattened his back against the wall as he slowly inched forward. He went on full alert when he saw shadows flickering on the pavement.

A man suddenly stepped from around the corner, a man with a hawkbill nose and dark, wild eyes. He had a pistol in his hand, the barrel pointed upward. Though he had obviously not expected to find trouble this close, his hand was tight on the trigger.

Encizo had a split-second advantage, and his hand flashed out to deliver a numbing karate chop. But even as he connected with his target he caught a blur of movement to his left.

He had the drop on the enemy he'd stalked, but somebody had the drop on him.

Mack Bolan's
PHOENIX FORCE®

PHOENIX FORCE®

GAR WILSON

GULF OF FIRE

A GOLD EAGLE BOOK FROM
WORLDWIDE®

TORONTO • NEW YORK • LONDON • PARIS
AMSTERDAM • STOCKHOLM • HAMBURG
ATHENS • MILAN • TOKYO • SYDNEY

First edition September 1989

ISBN 0-373-61343-1

Special thanks and acknowledgment to
William Fieldhouse for his contribution to this work.

Printed in U.S.A.

1

The Stars and Stripes banner of the United States of America snapped briskly in the strong breeze. It rode atop the flagstaff at the stem of the supertanker. The huge oil freighter was a Kuwaiti ship, but it was under the protection of the U.S. Navy as it began the hazardous voyage along the Persian Gulf.

Commander Anthony Draeger stood at the foredeck of the USS *Conway*. The frigate was following the supertanker. Another warship also trailed behind the oil ship, and two more frigates cut the waves before the tanker. Draeger peered through his binoculars to observe the Kuwaiti crew moving about the decks of the enormous center vessel. He shifted the aim of his binoculars to scan the gulf beyond.

It seemed peaceful that morning. The sky was a bit overcast, and cloud cover blocked out much of the sun's rays. The relatively cool weather was a relief after spending months in the usually sweltering heat in the gulf. The temperature often exceeded one hundred degrees. A few gulls circled the air above the blue-green waters. Waves rocked gently and the sea appeared fairly calm.

Then Draeger noticed an object on the distant horizon. It was out of effective range of his binoculars, but the vessel was certainly a warship. Battleship gray with gun mounts and a high mast, it cruised in the opposite direction from the convoy.

"I think it's Iranian, sir," Lieutenant Lear remarked, lowering his own pair of binoculars. The junior officer approached Draeger. "I can't tell for sure, but it looks like one of the smaller destroyers they favor."

"Probably one of the military vessels Uncle Sam sold to the Shah when Iran was still supposed to be an ally," Draeger remarked, slipping on his sunglasses. "That seems like a long, long time ago."

Ten years had passed since Mohammad Reza Pahlavi fled Iran after riots and unrest forced the Shah to run for his life. The Ayatollah Ruhollah Khomeini and his Shiite extremist followers established the Islamic Republic of Iran. The new regime immediately earned an infamous reputation with the American people. They were not apt to forget the takeover of the U.S. embassy in Tehran or that the current Iranian government had held fifty-three Americans hostages for more than a year.

Relations between the U.S. and Iran remained tense, often hostile. No one appreciated this more than the American military forces stationed in the Persian Gulf.

Iran was at war with its Arab neighbor, Iraq, and there seemed little hope the conflict would end in the near future. To date, the war had been a stalemate. Iraq's military was better trained and better armed than the Ayatollah's forces, but Iran had more manpower and its soldiers were fiercely motivated to fight the so-called jihad or "holy war."

The Persian Gulf had become a battlefield in the Iran-Iraq war. Both sides had mined the waters. Aircraft and vessels clashed in combat in the gulf. The situation was a powder keg which could erupt at any second. As is usually the case, the victims of the war were not always soldiers or citizens of the nations involved in the conflict.

The United States would have been glad to keep away from the Iran-Iraq war, but the threat to oil transports from other countries who were not engaged in the war forced the U.S. to get involved in escorting supertankers through the gulf. Kuwait was particularly vulnerable due to its geography. A small, prosperous country no larger than the state of New Jersey, Kuwait was bordered by Iraq to the north.

Uncle Sam agreed to help Kuwait get its supertankers safely through the dangerous gulf waters. Commander Draeger and his frigate were part of the naval forces assigned to escort duty.

There had already been American lives lost in this deadly bodyguard business. Thirty-seven servicemen aboard the *Stark* were killed on May 17, 1987, when two Iraqi missiles struck the frigate. President Hussein officially apologized for this "accident." Three more servicemen died in a helicopter crash on July 30th the same year. Americans and Iranians had exchanged fire on several occasions. It was a frightening situation that promised to get worse before it was over.

The *Conway* had participated in escort duty for other supertankers over the past few months. Thus far Draeger and his men had been spared any confrontations in the gulf. The commander hoped their luck would hold out until they could return home to the United States.

Draeger was a combat veteran from the Vietnam conflict. He had considered that to be a crazy war, too, but at least the majority of the North Vietnamese had not been suicidal fanatics. Many of the Iranian Shiite zealots were willing to sacrifice their own lives in order to take an infidel or two with them. Draeger wondered if the entire population of Iran wanted to be martyrs.

Tehran officials publicly announced that they would send "suicide attack boats" to assault U.S. ships in the gulf. Draeger had seen some film footage of such Iranian action. Three men in a small, swift boat armed with automatic weapons and explosives. However, Draeger had not actually seen any suicide boats since he arrived at the gulf. He had heard some tried to attack U.S. vessels in the gulf during the big skirmish between Iranian and American forces in April of 1988.

Draeger recalled that the Iranian government had the gall to scream foul when an Iranian fishing vessel got shot up after venturing too close to a U.S. ship. He figured the State

Department should have told Tehran to go to hell, because they had no one to blame for that incident except themselves. Khomeini and his cronies made statements about attacking U.S. vessels with small unconventional craft, and then they complained when the net effect was to escalate the risk to any Iranian vessel that approached the American ships in the gulf. Tehran was annoyed because the U.S. Navy took the threat seriously.

One more month of borderline madness in the Persian Gulf and the *Conway* would be on its way back to the "world." This would be the last assignment for Commander Draeger. He had been in the Navy for thirty years. His entire adult life actually, since he first enlisted at the age of seventeen. It was time to pack it in. Three decades in the military was enough for any man.

Draeger did not regret his navy career, but it had carried a price. He saw his wife and kids only three months out of the year. His oldest daughter had graduated college, married and had an infant son of her own. Draeger had never even met Katie's husband, let alone set eyes on his grandson.

Well, Draeger reckoned he would have the rest of his life to try to catch up on lost time. Maybe he would have to explain why he had not been there when his kids needed him. Maybe he would have to prove he loved his wife and appreciated how she had stood by him for twenty-six years of a marriage, one which had endured a lot of strain due to his career. Whatever was needed to make things right with himself and his family, he would do it.

First they had to baby-sit the Kuwaiti supertanker through the gulf. The frigate escorts formed a "four-corner" pattern around the oil freighter. The shadow of a Bell UH-1D helicopter fell across the foredeck next to Draeger. Two Bell gunships hovered over the convoy. If any potential opponents came within two hundred leagues, the escort personnel would spot it either from the ships or from the eagle-eye view of the copters. The frigates were equipped with both sonar and radar to detect virtually any sort of aggressor attacking from the air, on the sea or beneath it.

Those Iranians will have to pick another target, Draeger thought as he peered out at the tranquil ocean and the sky, quiet except for the noise of the gunship rotor blades. The convoy was prepared for anything. Fighter aircraft, submarines, suicide boats, Silkworm missiles, they were ready for any or all types of attack. Draeger's confidence grew as the voyage continued.

The roar of a large projectile slicing through air came so suddenly, so unexpectedly, that Draeger barely glimpsed the long cometlike tail that streaked from the rocket. The missile crashed into the bridge above Draeger and exploded with a thunderous clap. The radio tower and fly bridge were torn apart by the blast. Flames sprang up from the wreckage, and the *Conway* trembled from the force of the explosion.

Shouts filled the air as frantic men bolted across the decks. Mangled, blood-drenched corpses littered the area near the blast. Others stumbled about, wounded and blinded, gasping for breath and clawing at their throats as if choking to death. Draeger was too stunned by the unexpected attack to notice the deep gash in his left thigh. A piece of shrapnel had slashed into his upper leg. He glanced down at the bubbling crimson stain on the pant leg of his white uniform.

"Goddamn it!" Draeger exclaimed. "Where the hell did it come from?"

He looked about desperately, as if searching for a clue to determine where the rocket had come from. He squinted up at the Bell helicopters as a second rocket streaked toward the sky. It struck one of the gunships. The chopper exploded in a brilliant burst of blinding light and flying debris—metal, Plexiglas and torn bodies.

Draeger finally spotted the source of the attack. Four men stood at the stem of the Kuwaiti supertanker. Two held tubular objects braced across their shoulders. Another man fired a compact machine pistol at other crew members

aboard the tanker. The fourth figure was busy reloading one
of the rocket launchers.

The injured continued to stumble around in a daze on the
decks of the *Conway*. Some collapsed, gasping and thrash-
ing about in apparent agony. Draeger did not see any
wounds or blood stains on most of the victims. He could not
understand what was wrong with them until the strong scent
of something sickeningly sweet drifted along the breeze to
his nostrils. It smelled like almond extract....

"Oh, Jesus!" Draeger exclaimed when he realized what
this meant.

He clasped both hands over his nose and mouth, but it
was already too late. His head began to throb, and his nervous system seemed to be soaked in volcanic lava, then
convulsions overtook him. As he lost control of his muscles and sank to his knees, he was not sure if he really heard
another explosion and the chattering roar of automatic
weapons. Perhaps it was just his imagination, or the mon-
strous thunder inside his own head.

He felt his brain dying. It was mercifully swift, and the
terrible awareness of death lasted a matter of scant seconds. Commander Draeger's body sprawled across the deck
and shivered slightly in a final throe of death.

The escort duty in the Persian Gulf had indeed been his
last assignment.

2

Smoke clouds floated from the burning hull of the USS *Conway*, and the bodies of the dead and dying littered the decks of the crippled vessel. The fiery wreckage of a Bell gunship was scattered across the surface of the water, the charred bodies of slain airmen floating among the debris.

The other UH-1D chopper circled above the Kuwaiti supertanker and opened fire with twin machine guns. The 7.62 mm rounds slashed the stem of the oil tanker. Two of the terrorists toppled backward to the deck of the tanker, their torsos ripped open by multiple bullet holes. A mounted machine gun aboard another U.S. frigate sprayed the Kuwaiti vessel with another salvo of high-velocity slugs. Bullets sparked along the handrail and against the rim of the stem. Other projectiles tore into human flesh and brought down the two remaining terrorists.

The five men of Phoenix Force watched the carnage unfold on a wide-screen television in the Stony Man War Room. There was no sound with the videotape, but the supercommandos of Phoenix Force knew the noises of combat all too well. The wails of the wounded, the roar of explosions, the furnace doors of hell itself yawning open to spill out the agonies of the damned. Phoenix Force knew the sheer terror and confusion of the battlefield, the stench of burning flesh and the salty-copper smell of fresh blood leaking from ravaged flesh.

"As you can see," Hal Brognola commented, pointing at the screen with an unlighted cigar between the V of two fingers, "the rest of the escort immediately retaliated. They managed to take out the terrorists twenty seconds after the attack began. Some Kuwaiti personnel appeared on the decks of the supertanker...yeah, next frame."

The videotape continued from an elevated, overhead view, spliced on from helicopter camera footage. The Kuwaiti vessel was clearly displayed from this angle as several Arab crew members rushed toward the fallen terrorists. Three fired pistols at the enemy gunmen to be certain the opponents were dead. Two crewmen suddenly spun about and performed a grisly dance across the deck, then collapsed as survivors dived for cover.

"They were accidentally fired upon by the *Fredrick*—the frigate nearest the *Conway*," Brognola continued. "Two Kuwaiti sailors were killed. Others were wounded, but none are serious. There is a much higher body count for the American servicemen. Eighty-seven men aboard the USS *Conway*, and all eight crew members of the destroyed Bell gunship were killed. Twenty-two other servicemen from the *Conway* are on the critical list and only have a fifty-fifty chance of recovery."

"It looked as though some of the victims on the *Conway* were choking to death as they stumbled across the decks," Yakov Katzenelenbogen remarked. The middle-aged Israeli still watched the television screen as the scene once again returned to the bodies scattered across the decks of the unfortunate frigate. "Their skin is discolored and their lips are blue. They resemble drowned corpses that are still walking about. I've seen that before. Appears to me those men have inhaled some sort of poisonous fumes."

Katz had indeed seen death in nearly every form imaginable. He had been a veteran warrior, espionage agent, antiterrorist commander and military officer during a career that spanned more than four decades. Katz had fought the Nazis when he was a teenager in Europe during World War Two. He battled the British and Arabs during Israel's war for independence. Katz lost his right arm and his only son during desert combat in the Six Day War, but this did not stop him from becoming the top field operative for Mossad intelligence assignments.

The soft-spoken, gray-haired gentleman with the mild blue eyes and a kindly smile hardly gave the impression that he was one of the best-trained and most-experienced experts in warfare and intrigue in the world. Yet Katz had been chosen to be the unit commander for Phoenix Force because he was the best man for the job. Only the best, the very best, comprised the ranks of Phoenix Force.

"That's what I figured too," Calvin James added. The tall, lanky black man nodded in agreement as he glanced from the TV screen to Brognola. "Making a diagnosis from watching TV is iffy at best, but I'd say neurotoxic poison, probably cyanide gas."

"Bingo," Brognola confirmed as he stuck the cigar in his mouth and struck a wooden match to light the stogie. "You're both right," he agreed, then examined his cigar in disgust and stubbed it out.

James grunted softly. He was a former hospital corpsman with the elite SEALs unit in the U.S. Navy during the Vietnam War. A product of the tough streets of Chicago, James had pursued a career in medicine and chemistry after he left the service, but fate steered him away from science to join the San Francisco police department. He had been a crack SWAT team officer when he was recruited for his first mission with Phoenix Force. James had been with the commando unit ever since.

"Cyanide gas," Gary Manning said, shaking his head with dismay. "I heard both Iran and Iraq have been using poison gas along the border. Cyanide gas and mustard gas. That's becoming one very ugly war."

"All wars are ugly," Katz agreed. "The Iran-Iraq conflict is becoming downright hideous."

"What they did to the men aboard that frigate and the gunship was certainly grotesque," Manning stated. "The United States isn't at war with Iran or Iraq. Those men were on escort duty, not involved in combat. Attacking them was inexcusable. Unforgivable.''

Manning was a big man, built like a lumberjack from his native Canada. A rugged, hardworking individual with enough physical and mental stamina for half a dozen men, Manning was one of the top explosives and demolitions experts in the world. He was also a superb rifle marksman and skilled in virtually every form of combat. But it sickened him to see good men slaughtered by fanatics.

"Who said anything about forgiving them?" Brognola remarked as he switched off the videotape recorder. "I'm sure you guys recognized the weapons used by the terrorists?"

"The rocket launchers were Soviet-made RPG models or similar copies of the Russian antitank weapon," Rafael Encizo replied. "The machine pistol used to hold off the Kuwaiti crew looked like a Czech-made Skorpion. Both Iran and Iraq have been using Communist Bloc weapons. Iraq is a socialist military nation, supported by the Soviet Union. Iran still has a lot of American arms left over from the Shah's regime, but has also obtained arms from Libya, Syria and North Korea—all of which use Soviet-style weaponry."

"I see you've been keeping up with world events," Brognola commented, eyebrows raised with surprise. "That must be hard, because you guys spend so much time in the field, out of the country on missions. Staying up-to-date with the news must be tough."

"Considering our line of work," Encizo replied with a thin smile, "we have a professional interest in keeping up with the news. Especially news about hot spots in the world. We've been talking about the Persian Gulf for a long time, Hal. In fact, we're sort of surprised it's taken this long for Phoenix Force to get a mission there."

Encizo shrugged as if an assignment to the most dangerous war zone in the world—at that particular moment in history, at least—was no big deal. In actual fact, Encizo knew better. The muscular, strikingly handsome Cuban veteran warrior realized that anything Phoenix Force was assigned to had to be a big deal. Every mission meant the five commandos would have to risk their lives against enormous odds. Of course, it was the sort of warfare Encizo was accustomed to.

He was a survivor of Castro's purge after the Communist takeover in Cuba. Encizo's family had been practically wiped out by Castro's soldiers. He had joined a band of freedom fighters to try to resist the Communists, but the effort proved hopeless, and he was forced to flee the country. Encizo later returned to Cuba as one of the combatants of the Bay of Pigs invasion. He was captured, beaten and tortured in Castro's notorious El Principe political prison. Encizo managed to escape and returned to the United States.

The Cuban had fought in many little-known battlefields since the Bay of Pigs. Encizo was working as an insurance investigator specializing in maritime claims when he was recruited into Phoenix Force. The attraction of being part of a five-man team of Davids pitted against the organized Goliaths of international terrorism was too much for Encizo to resist.

"Well, we know more about the weapons used by the terrorists than about the killers themselves," Brognola declared, dropping into a chair at the head of the conference table of the Stony Man War Room. "What little we do know isn't much help. Of course, the Soviet Bloc weapons could have come from just about any gunrunning source in gulf. Or from either Iran or Iraq..."

"Bloody hell," David McCarter snorted as he rose from his seat and began to pace along the green-carpeted floor. "You know who the most likely suspect is as well as the rest of us do. The boys in Washington know it, and so do those useless diplomats at the United Nations. It's either Iran or some Shiite Muslim extremist group linked to the Ayatollah's jihad. Who else would have any reason to pull a stunt like this?"

The tall, lean Briton had little use for beating about the proverbial bush. He was a man of action. A bundle of nervous energy with a short fuse, the British ace was more at home in a battlefield than on the streets of his native London. He was a veteran of the famed SAS and had participated in numerous military actions, including the spectacular raid on the Iranian embassy in London in 1980.

McCarter lived for adventure. He was unashamed of his addiction and welcomed any opportunity to charge into combat. Phoenix Force gave him more opportunities than any other source available. McCarter had been born to be part of such a special commando unit. One might think he had spent his entire life preparing for it, and, in a sense, he had.

"It's dangerous to jump to conclusions, David," Katz stated, taking a pack of Camel cigarettes from a shirt pocket. "You know that by now. Nonetheless, you have a good point. The only deliberate attacks on noncombatant vessels in the Persian Gulf have been by Iranian forces. If I remember correctly, Iranian forces attacked tankers at port in Saudi Arabia in 1984. That's when the United States sold four hundred Stinger antiaircraft missiles to the Saudis."

"Sometimes your memory is kind'a scary, Yakov," Brognola admitted, looking at the Israeli with undisguised admiration.

Katz smiled and lighted his cigarette before replying. "In this case I have good reason to recall the incident fairly well," Katz explained. "I was contacted by some former Mossad colleagues who wanted me to use whatever influence I might have with covert Washington sources to prevent the Stingers being sold to the Saudis. Israel gets quite nervous about sophisticated weapons being put in Arab hands. Tel Aviv need not have worried. The Saudis were only concerned with protecting themselves, not attacking Israel. They shot down two Iranian fighters that tried to attack a tanker in port shortly after the Stinger sale was made."

"Yeah," Encizo added with a grin. "And a U.S. AWAC plane helped them direct the missiles to the targets. Makes you proud to be an American."

"The United States and the Saudis aren't alone when it comes to having reasons to dislike the current Iranian government," Manning added. "They even had the gall to attack a Soviet freighter a couple years ago. The Ayatollah seems to be determined to piss off the entire world, and he's off to a pretty good start."

"Well, if the Iranian government is responsible for this incident," Calvin James remarked, stabbing a finger at the television screen, "they've finally committed an act of war against the United States. Maybe I should say they've done it *again*. When they seized our embassy in Tehran and held American citizens hostage, they had technically launched an attack on United States soil. Uncle Sam and the administration in power at the time shouldn't have tolerated that crap. If the Iranians are gonna attack our ships in the gulf, then they'd better get ready to kiss their collective asses goodbye."

"The footage you saw here is still confidential," Brognola declared. "The President realizes he can't keep something like this a secret, but he's hoping to sit on the story for a couple days before making any official announcement. The media knows the escort was attacked, of course, and information will be given to the public in bits and pieces. If we're lucky, there will be enough time to bring some facts to light before the figurative shit hits the political fan. Right now we don't know if this is an act of state-sponsored terrorism by Iran or some independent group. All four terrorists were killed, so there is no information forthcoming from that quarter."

"They haven't been identified?" Katz inquired, holding his cigarette between the steel hooks of a trident prosthesis device attached to the stump of his right arm.

"Oh, they were members of the Kuwaiti crew aboard the supertanker," Brognola confirmed. "Supposedly honest, hardworking employees. The Kuwaitis seem to be as startled and upset about this as we are. They're also worried that it might set the United States and American business against them. Kuwait depends on foreign sales for its economy. It is also a good friend to the West, especially to the United States."

"Kuwait deserves credit for trying to conduct sane business and maintain neutral relations with its neighbors in the middle of general insanity, which has become the usual state of affairs in the Middle East," Katz stated. "Oh, at one time they helped finance other Arab countries at war with Israel, but that's ancient history now. Kuwait tried to stay out of the Iran-Iraq war, but geography hasn't been in its favor."

"True," Brognola said with a nod. "Kuwait has also invested tens of billions of dollars in American businesses, real estate and stocks—including some stocks which probably would have taken a dive when the stock market took that big plunge on October 14, 1987. A number of U.S. firms may have gone belly up if it hadn't been for foreign investors like the Kuwaitis."

"That's one of the reasons the U.S. was escorting the Kuwaiti tankers," Manning, who had been a business executive for a firm based in Canada, remarked. "Not just because America needs the oil, but it values friendship with Kuwait. The Middle East is a very volatile region. If it has any chance of avoiding major war in the future, it will be because of moderate Arab nations like Kuwait."

"Along with the United Arab Emirates, Qatar, Saudi Arabia and, of course, Oman," David McCarter added. "Every one of them is located in the Persian Gulf region. The future of all those countries could be in jeopardy if the Iran-Iraq war continues to escalate. Bloody pity, too. Some people in the West tend to view the Arab world as a bunch of wild-eyed fanatics and terrorists. They think of Qaddafi in Libya or Assad in Syria, or even lump in the Ayatollah—although Iran *isn't* an Arab nation. Yet there are a number of strong Arab nations that aren't associated with terrorism of any kind, and only a narrow-minded bigot would have anything against them."

"I know you were stationed in Oman in the seventies when you were with the Special Air Service," James began with a shrug. "I'll agree you know more about it than I do, David, but Oman is still a monarchy, not a democracy. In fact, I think all the countries you mentioned are run either by sheikhs or sultans. Those royal families have gotten superrich from selling oil, man. An elite few who are pulling all the strings in their countries."

"Before you put horns and pointed tails on any of those royal families of the moderate Arab countries, you ought to consider what they've done for their people with a lot of that oil money," McCarter insisted. "Free medical care, free schools, free telephone services, and most of those countries don't have any bleeding income taxes. Some of the highest standards of living in the world are found in those nations . . ."

"Okay, okay," Encizo began, waving a hand in the air. "Let's get off the debate on world politics. I figure we'll all get a chance to see how these moderate nations work firsthand anyway. Right, Hal?"

"You've got it," Brognola said with a nod. "You guys are going to Kuwait just as soon as you can get there. The United States could wind up in a full-scale war with Iran in the very near future. We've come real close to it ever since the Ayatollah took over, but we damn sure don't want it to happen unless there's absolutely no way to avoid it."

"It might take longer than two days," Katz said with a sigh. "You can't put a time limit on this sort of thing. CIA, NSA and no doubt a lot of other intelligence organizations are certainly already involved in the investigations. If they haven't turned up anything, there's a chance we won't be able to, either."

"You guys can get results faster than anyone I know," Brognola stated. "Maybe I'm just getting used to expecting miracles from Phoenix Force. You've provided too many in the past."

"Come on, Hal," Manning said, shaking his head. "Let's keep in the real world, okay? We're just five men. We have abilities and we do our job pretty damn well, but none of us can walk on water or feed the multitudes with a loaf of bread and a couple of fishes."

"Look, Gary," the Fed answered, "this is a desperate situation. The United States can't turn its back on its Arab allies in the gulf, and Iran shouldn't be allowed to freeze up the trade in the Persian Gulf. We can't let Americans get butchered and look the other way. You guys know this. That's what Phoenix Force and the whole Stony Man setup is all about. If that attack on the *Conway* was state-sponsored terrorism, we have to know for sure. If it isn't, you fellas had better find out who the hell is responsible and stop 'em cold, before America winds up sending thousands of troops off to fight a war based on a misunderstanding."

"There's a very good chance that's gonna happen anyway," Encizo remarked grimly. "This may or may not be the incident to set it off, but the trouble has been brewing for a whole decade now. Nobody should be too surprised if it boils over into the biggest conflict since World War Two."

"That's a cheerful thought, Rafael," Brognola replied grimly. "You may be right, but you know the terrible price of war better than most. It's vital we know for sure what the hell is going on in the Persian Gulf. One way or the other."

"I assume we'll be working with some personnel from CIA or NSA already stationed in the Middle East," Katz stated.

"CIA case officer Brackman will meet you in Kuwait," the Fed confirmed. "The Kuwaiti security people will also be there, as well as a special officer with SIS British Intelligence. I think you know him, David. Colonel Hillerman?"

"Damn right I know him," McCarter said with surprise. "Hillerman was my commanding officer in Oman during the SAS campaigns in the Omani Dhofar dispute. Haven't seen the old war-horse since London about four years ago. He was still a major at the time—still with military intelligence, too. I wonder when he joined the Security Intelligence Service?"

"Ask him in person," Katz declared as he crushed out his cigarette in an ashtray. "We've got a mission. Let's get on with it."

3

The mosque stood between the rock walls of the mountains, guarded and concealed by the stony monuments of nature. It was unlike the mosques of the cities and villages and was a hidden place of worship for a very few. The chosen faithful attended it, the bizarre Shiite order that proudly called itself the Purple Warriors of Righteousness.

Qabda stood at the pillars of the mosque. Towering above him was the great tear-shaped dome, purple, and with a gold crescent symbol of Islam atop the cupola. Purple was the color of royalty. Qabda wore a purple turban, red *keffiyeh* headpiece and a white robe. White was purity. Red was the color of blood, the color of martyrdom and death.

More than a hundred loyal followers knelt before Qabda, heads bowed to touch their brows to the prayer rugs. He was their undisputed leader and spiritual commander. He virtually owned them—mind, body and spirit.

Qabda stood with his back straight and head raised. His slender body stood more than six feet tall and he appeared majestic above the prostrate figures of his followers. They regarded him as their absolute ruler. He felt humbled by his role. He did not not consider himself a prophet in the sense that Mohammad was a prophet or even the Ayatollah, whom the Shiite sect regarded as Allah's voice on earth. Yet Qabda did believe he was inspired and driven by a divine force.

It was indeed rare for a comparatively young man to command such respect from Shiite zealots, but the thirty-eight-year-old sect leader was no ordinary man. No one knew his real name or his nationality. He had traveled through Kuwait, Saudi Arabia, the United Arab Emirates and Oman, quietly recruiting followers from the more militant ranks of Shiite Muslims.

His message had appealed to the young fanatics who saw Iran as an opportunity for the rebirth of the Islamic empire and the Ayatollah as the guiding light for the new Shiite revolution. Qabda selected those who wanted to be part of the jihad. He fueled their resentment toward Sunni and other Islamic orders they felt had oppressed them. Nearly all minority groups consider themselves to be picked upon by the majority, and the Shiites in predominantly Sunni Muslim nations were no exception.

"Allahu akbar!" Qabda called out to his congregation. *"La illaha illallah!"*

The warriors chanted in reply and repeated the universal creed of Islam. "Allah is great! There is no god but Allah!"

"Four of our brothers have died as martyrs for the jihad," Qabda announced, gazing at his minions. "We shall mourn them not, although we shall surely miss their friendship and devotion. The loss is not theirs, my brothers. We have lost four good and true men, but they have gone on to the promised paradise."

Heads bobbed in agreement. Qabda raised his hands to shoulder-level and extended his arms as if to embrace the crowd.

"In the suras of the sacred Koran we are told of the wonderous paradise which waits for the true believers," Qabda continued. "They shall dwell forever in beautiful gardens with rivers flowing and trees of fruit aplenty. Peace and prosperity shall be theirs for the rest of eternity. They lived as righteous men and brave warriors. We have reason to envy them, for they have been rewarded by Allah Himself. May we all be as fortunate to be martyrs for this holy war."

The followers muttered their agreement and whispered the names of their slain comrades. Some began to weep, not because they grieved for the dead men, but because they were overcome with joy. Their friends had found paradise. Soon all the members of the Purple Warriors of Righteousness would have the opportunity to do likewise.

"The Koran tells us how to deal with the infidels," Qabda stated. "When we meet an unbeliever, we are to smite his neck. We are to slaughter the infidels and bind up the survivors, to either free them later from mercy, or for ransom. The Ayatollah did this with the American hostages in Tehran. Our Shiite brothers in Lebanon have done likewise. Again the Koran tells us Allah shall give us signs. Only an unbeliever, in league with Satan, would dismiss these signs."

Qabda smiled broadly as he turned slowly to examine the effect of his words on his audience. Their beaming faces pleased him. Truly, no army could fail with such dedicated, true believers in its ranks.

"The United States of America is generally regarded as the most powerful nation in the world today," Qabda said, enjoying his lecture more with every word. "Yet those Yankee infidels have been unable to take any sort of action against Iran or the Shiite commandos in Palestine. Why? Because money and technology are meaningless when pitted against the very armies of Allah. The will of God is greater than science, governments or the other feeble trappings of man."

Qabda stepped down from the stairs of the mosque to walk among his fellow terrorists. He continued to smile as he spoke.

"How can we fail with Allah on our side?" Qabda inquired. "The Koran states that twenty believers are a match for two hundred infidels. A hundred can defeat a thousand unbelievers because they are ignorant of Allah and know not the truth. This is the time for our glory, my brothers."

The young men smiled in response, their faces glowing with the excitement of their mission. Truly they had the best of both worlds. The jihad offered them an opportunity to serve God and deliver destruction and death to those toward whom they had developed personal antagonisms. They believed their religion was the only correct one. The followers of all other forms—Christianity, Judaism, Sunni and other branches of Islam—were infidels, misguided unbelievers who walked with Satan. They were being given permission to strike out at these "corrupt enemies of Allah." In fact, they understood that to be their sacred duty.

A shrewd leader understood that the excitement of killing and plundering appealed as much as the claims of a peaceful paradise in the afterlife. They were supercharged young men who enjoyed what they did. The violence, danger and bloodshed satisfied them, although they gave lip service to the claim that it was regrettable to have to use such tactics, but circumstances made it necessary. Any one of them would have found a tranquil garden paradise a boring hell for eternity.

Qabda strolled through the ranks. Occasionally he placed a kindly hand on the shoulders of his followers as he passed. The terrorist leader moved toward a tray of burning charcoals at the rear of the congregation while he continued to speak.

"Even now," Qabda declared, "another team of our brothers is prepared to strike once more against the infidels. The enemy will feel the terror of divine judgment. They will know the power of Allah's wrath delivered by us—His servants. The victory will be God's kingdom on earth restored and, for us, the acceptance into paradise."

Qabda stepped near the charcoal and gazed at the gray smoke columns that rose from the burning nuggets. He slowly moved a hand over the coals. The others watched with fascination.

"We must sacrifice, my brothers," Qabda stated, lowering his hand into the metal tray. "We must be hardened to suffering. That of others as well as our own. There will be much pain..."

He placed his hand on the burning charcoal, his palm touching the hot surface. The stench of charred flesh immediately rose from the metal tray. Qabda's expression remained calm. He smiled slightly as he stared down at his blistered hand. The fingers closed around a piece of glowing charcoal.

"We must all endure suffering to be worthy of paradise!" With those words, he held the burning charcoal high for all to see. His voice remained steady. He seemed immune to pain as he continued, "We must accept pain for ourselves if we are to cause it for others. Justice demands a balance. Allah is all-seeing, all-knowing. He knows of our sacrifices. They will not be in vain."

Qabda turned and tossed the chunk of charcoal into the tray. He barely glanced at his burned and blistered hand as he faced the congregation once more.

"Flesh is nothing," he told them. "The spirit will endure forever. The soul will either know the fires of hell or the pleasures of paradise. We may suffer in this life, but eternity will be our reward for fighting God's war on earth."

The Purple Warriors of Righteousness bobbed their heads in agreement. Some drew knives and cut deep grooves into their own arms and hands. Blood dripped from the self-inflicted wounds as they raised their arms to proudly display the crimson tattoos. Others gathered up a sort of flail that resembled a cat-o'-nine-tails, with chains instead of leather straps.

Men began flogging themselves, striking their own backs repeatedly with the chains. Qabda picked up a flail with his unburned hand and gripped the wooden handle firmly. He swung the instrument over his shoulder and lashed the chains across his back, then repeated the procedure over his other shoulder.

The ritual of self-abuse lasted for several minutes. They chanted and recited passages of the Koran as they flogged themselves. But Qabda did not allow it to continue too long. He realized the self-punishment helped to toughen the men—mentally more than physically. It helped build up a frenzy for violence and a desire to unleash their anger on other persons. The practice also increased the men's confidence. They believed the floggings made them stronger and able to face death without fear. He knew that to be false. Death was a strange and mysterious thing. Facing a grand mystery always included some degree of fear.

However, Qabda did not want the men to injure themselves in their zeal. He put down his flail and walked back to the entrance of the mosque and from there called to his followers and ordered them to cease. Flails fell to the ground. Many chains were stained with blood. The terrorists breathed heavily, their faces glittering with sweat, yet their eyes remained filled with enthusiasm.

"Listen, my brothers! It is important not to be overcome with expressing your eagerness for sacred battle. Rest now, rest and meditate on the wondrous privilege Allah has bestowed unto us. We will be the favored martyred faithful in paradise, the holy warriors who returned the world to Allah and delivered the infidels to fires of hell."

NINE U.S. WARSHIPS were in port near Muscat, the capital of the sultanate of Oman. The USS *Harrimon* was one of the vessels which waited in dock for orders to make the hazardous journey up through the Strait of Hormuz to the Persian Gulf. The next escort operation for transporting another Kuwaiti supertanker had been postponed due to the recent attack by terrorists in the gulf. The ships in port in Oman took advantage of the chance to conduct some general maintenance and granted most crew members brief shore liberty in Muscat.

The Gulf of Oman had thus far been spared any turmoil from the Iran-Iraq war. The American vessels were relatively safe in the current port, although the southern coast of Iran extended across the opposite shore of the Gulf of Oman. That knowledge caused some concern among the Americans. Iran had yet to carry out any hostilities against

Oman, but the U.S. was still despised by the Ayatollah and his jihad followers. As a result, any location in the Middle East and the Near East was potentially dangerous territory for American citizens, military or civilian.

The night was warm but not uncomfortably hot as the sailors stood their watch aboard the *Harrimon*. The city lights of Muscat burned brightly in the distance. Comparatively few lights for a major city, but the Omanis were not noted as being night people. The men on the decks of the frigate did not know how much fun their shipmates were having in Muscat. They knew alcohol to be scarce in Islamic countries, forbidden by the Koran, and understood that Arab women are not inclined to give their bodies to a man before marriage—especially to foreigners.

Of course, Oman had established a long, generally agreeable relationship with the West, especially Great Britain. Most of the foreign vessels in port were British. The English seamen would probably know where to go for a good time in Muscat. The sailors on watch at the decks of the *Harrimon* discussed the possibility of questioning some of their British counterparts when they got their liberty the next day.

The docks were quiet, although numerous vessels were in port. These included several Omani oil tankers and some local patrol boats. Oman had increased its military forces due to concern about Iran and the Soviet-Afghanistan conflict. A few Omani warships were also in dock, and others cruised the waters beyond.

Seaman First Class Gorshin noticed the headlights of a vehicle approach along the pier. It was not a U.S. military rig, so he did not pay much attention. Guys on guard duty tended to worry more about inspections than actual threats unless they were stationed in a confirmed combat zone. The vehicle appeared to be a British Land Rover or perhaps an Omani version.

Then Gorshin saw one of the men in the Land Rover stand up in the back of the vehicle with a long tube across his shoulder. Some sort of bazooka or LAW, the sailor realized in a moment of sheer terror. The Rover came to a halt as the man with the Soviet RPG rocket launcher pointed his weapon directly at the port side of the *Harrimon*.

"Jesus Christ!" Gorshin screamed to the other sailors on watch. "Hit the deck!"

The rocket streaked from the muzzle of the RPG. It slashed through the night with a tail of white smoke trailing behind it. The projectile smashed into the helicopter hangar, dead center of the *Harrimon*. The warhead exploded. Metal and glass were violently strewn across the deck as the chopper within the hangar was torn to pieces. The tanks blew, and a second explosion followed the first. Flames spilled across the deck as gasoline ignited from the blast.

Gorshin clung to the deck, his M-16 rifle clutched in his fist. The weapon was not loaded. Stupid fuckin' regulations, he thought as he pawed at the ammo pouch on his belt. The sentries had been ordered not to load their rifles. Goddamn brass was worried about somebody getting shot by accident or upsetting the civilians or some such bullshit. Somebody should have been worried about assholes with rocket launchers....

Gorshin smelled something that turned his stomach. A sickly sweet aroma, like cough syrup mixed in with a bag of almonds. The sailor was still puzzled by the smell as he shoved the magazine into the well of his M-16 and pulled back the charging handle. He did not hear the bolt snap home. His body had suddenly convulsed in a wild fit along the deck of the USS *Harrimon*. Within seconds he was dead.

Flames rose as the figures of other sailors stumbled across the decks. The two terrorists in the Land Rover cheered. The dying shapes with the backdrop of the fire resembled damned souls condemned to the pits of hell. It was a vision they could identify. Qabda's claims were true, they thought with intoxicating delight. The infidels would be punished and the righteous would become martyrs....

Two sailors on shore patrol suddenly charged across the pier and opened fire with pistols. Some British seamen from a neighboring vessel also hit the enemy Land Rover with a wave of automatic rifle rounds. The bullets slashed a cross fire that ripped into the terrorists. The man with RPG was killed instantly, but the other extremist rose up from behind the steering wheel. He was already bleeding heavily from wounds in his torso, but he raised his arms overhead and looked up at the heavens above.

"Allahu akbar!" he shouted before another bullet crashed into his skull.

4

From the air Kuwait displayed a staggering view of contrasts. The men of Phoenix Force and other passengers aboard Flight 247 peered down at the enormous network of pipelines that crisscrossed the oil-rich desert and extended to the startling skyline of Kuwait city. Skyscrapers, apartment complexes and office buildings seemed to rise up from the sand dunes like a fantastic mirage. An ultramodern city in the middle of a desert.

The plane trip had already been interesting and a bit threatening. The flight had passed over Saudi Arabia and drawn the attention of suspicious Saudi military forces stationed near Jubayl. The newly completed multibillion dollar industrial complex and port city was zealously guarded by the Saudis because they feared it might be a target for terrorists or warring factions of the Iran-Iraq war. Fighter jets had streaked across the sky near the commercial flight, and ground observation posts had ordered the pilot to identify his craft and warned Flight 247 to avoid getting any closer to Jubayl than necessary.

Paranoia was growing in the Middle East. It had always been plentiful in this part of the world, but the fierce gulf conflict had escalated terrorism among the smaller gulf nations. The Saudi government certainly had reason for concern. Shiite terrorism has been a major problem in Saudi Arabia ever since fanatics seized the Grand Mosque in Mecca in November 1979. Further bloodshed erupted in August 1987 when Iranian Shiite pilgrims clashed with riot police in Mecca during the Ramadan pilgrimage to the most holy city of Islam.

Flight 247 passed Saudi Arabia without incident, but it was still a reminder for all on board that the Middle East was filled with tension and potentially ripe to explode without warning. The plane continued on to Kuwaiti air space and soon approached the international airport at the outskirts of Kuwait city. After a smooth and uneventful landing, the passengers and crew alike uttered a sigh of relief. Anytime a plane took off or landed safely in the Middle East was reason enough to be thankful.

The airport was enormous, very modern and extremely efficient. Four men waited for Phoenix Force to deplane. They waved the commandos through customs, saving them from going through the usual inspection. Three of the men in the reception committee were strangers to Phoenix Force, but the fourth was quite familiar to David McCarter. The British commando had no trouble recognizing Nathan Hillerman.

The former SAS officer was a stocky, gruff man, fifteen years older since Sergeant McCarter served with him during the Omani Dhofar War. Hillerman appeared to be somewhat thicker at the waist, his hairline had receded a bit more, and he had grown a shaggy salt-and-pepper mustache. He wore a tan suit, almost khaki brown, with a white shirt and narrow houndstooth tie. Hillerman leaned on a walnut cane as he watched Phoenix Force approach. McCarter grinned at his former commander. Hillerman nodded in reply.

A tall, thin black man stood next to Hillerman. His light blue, single-breasted suit was American in style, and a pair of wire-rim glasses were perched on the bridge of his nose. Phoenix Force recognized Anton Brackman from the file on the CIA case officer in Stony Man headquarters.

The other two members of the group meeting the commando team were Arabs, clad in the pure white robes and the *keffiyeh* headcloth favored by native Kuwaitis. The taller of the pair sported a trimmed black beard and dark glasses. His companion was several inches shorter and heavier, with a pencil-thin mustache. As he interlaced his pudgy fingers on his broad chest, sunlight glittered on the gold band of his Rolex wristwatch. "Welcome to Kuwait, gentlemen," he greeted with a polite nod. "Are you the Anderson party?"

"No need for passwords and codes," Hillerman told him. The Briton looked directly at McCarter. "I know one of these gents personally. What name are you going by these days?"

"The passport says my last name is Stark," McCarter replied. "What should we call you, sir?"

"Same as before, except they promoted me to colonel," Hillerman answered. "We can go into more detailed introductions later. Right now you can just call us Brackman, Mohammad, Ahmed and Hillerman."

"I'm Ahmed," the paunchy Arab declared. "I suggest we leave quickly. A demonstration is in progress here at the airport. It is not wise for us to linger."

"A demonstration?" Gary Manning inquired. The Canadian warrior carried an aluminum case, nearly a meter long, in one hand and a briefcase in the other. "What kind of demonstration?"

"An unpleasant one," Ahmed answered. "Please, gentlemen. Shall we go now?"

"Sounds like something we'd do well to avoid," Yakov Katzenelenbogen agreed with a nod. The Israeli's metal suitcase hung from the hooks of the trident prosthesis at the end of his artificial arm, and he carried an attache case in his other hand. "What's the fastest way out of here?"

"Follow us," Brackman urged. The CIA agent gestured with a wave of a hand as he led the way.

The nine men hurried through the corridors of the terminal. It was more crowded than one would expect in a country lodged between two warring nations. But Kuwait was a wealthy country with great reserves of petroleum and natural gas. Business executives from various nations teemed through the corridors. Most appeared to be Europeans, with some Americans and Japanese mixed among the crowd. Many corporations and industries were willing to risk the hazards of the gulf conflicts in order to continue doing business with rich oil nations like Kuwait.

Not all the foreigners represented petroleum companies. Manufacturing and construction were also major industries in Kuwait, requiring technicians, business managers, computer operators and others with valuable expertise. Engineers were needed to help build new buildings, for the desalinization of seawater and chemical processing. Teachers were necessary personnel in the ongoing educational effort in virtually every field. Kuwait was a modern Arab nation, and it intended to continue making new advances in the future. Kuwait's high standard of living, good salaries and relatively inexpensive goods and services helped to attract plenty of new faces every year.

Ahmed and Mohammad led the way to a narrow hall by the security office. Phoenix Force, Hillerman and Brackman followed, hauling the heavy luggage as they walked quickly through the terminal. They moved to a door labeled Employees Only in Arabic and English. Mohammad unlocked the door and they filed through it to step outside.

The Kuwaiti pair had led them to a restricted parking lot, used by aircraft service vehicles such as cargo and fuel trucks, and catering vehicles. Two airport security officers stood by a patrol car. They eyed the nine men and exchanged nods with Ahmed. Obviously the Kuwaiti intelligence personnel had already cleared their business with airport security, and with good reason. Kuwait took the protection of airports and commercial aircraft very seriously after the hijacking of Kuwait Airways Flight 422 in April of 1988.

Ahmed and Mohammad had two large black limousines parked near the front gate to the lot. A security officer in a guard shack waited for the nine VIPs to climb inside the limos. When Mohammad started the first vehicle's engine, the guard turned on the electrically powered gate. It rolled open and the limousines drove across the threshold, then headed up a short driveway to another security gate.

"These limos might attract some unwanted attention," Katz remarked. The Israeli sat in the back seat of the first limo with McCarter, Ahmed and Colonel Hillerman.

"There are many large limousines in Kuwait city," Ahmed assured him. "There is no need to worry, my friend. May I ask what name to call you?"

"I'm Anderson on this trip," Katz answered. "Do you mind if I ask what organization you work for, Ahmed? This mission was put together rather quickly. I know the colonel here works for British intelligence and Mr. Brackman is CIA, but we weren't sure which Arab security networks would be involved with this mission."

"I am with SIS," Ahmed explained. "Kuwait State Intelligence Service, not British SIS. Mohammad is actually with military intelligence, a special branch created to combat terrorism. Unfortunately it is a problem that never seems to go away."

"I know," Katz assured him with a nod.

The second security gate opened. Mohammad drove the first limo through the opening to the street beyond. Brackman drove the second vehicle with the rest of Phoenix Force inside and followed the lead limo.

There was a rising roar of angry voices from a crowd assembled in front of the airport. The men in the limousines heard the sound of the furious multitude before they rolled into view of the mob of demonstrators and an even larger group of equally upset Kuwaiti citizens aggrieved by the sign-bearing protesters. Two dozen uniformed police tried to maintain order between the two factions. Seriously outnumbered, the officers had their hands full simply trying to keep both sides at bay.

The demonstrators waved signs and chanted slogans in Arabic, English and French. Yakov Katzenelenbogen was a superb linguist, but some of the signs were written in a language less familiar to him. The writing resembled the ornate and graceful characters of Arabic script, yet it was a different tongue. Farsi, Katz realized. Modern Persian. The language of Iran.

The messages on the signs seemed pretty much the same regardless of the language used. Slogans protested Kuwait's "support of Iraq" and criticized the royal family for "oppressing the people" and "conspiring with imperialistic infidels of the West." A few signs urged an "end to Shiite genocide," and others condemned "American meddling" in Kuwaiti affairs.

The crowd of Kuwaitis offended by the demonstration shouted insults at the protesters and accused them of being traitors, idiots, communists or all the above. The demonstrators responded with similar insults and repeated slogans which matched their signs. Fistfights erupted between the more short-tempered members on both sides. When the law tried to break up the battles, they only found themselves assaulted from both directions.

Protesters used their placards to hammer the opponents across the head and shoulder and some began to throw rocks. Police batons lashed out, while other officers used their nightsticks to push back aggressors from either side of the conflict. There was an approaching wailing of sirens that indicated the arrival of more police reinforcements.

"A bleedin' mess," David McCarter observed. His voice sounded calm, almost disinterested, but the British ace was opening his briefcase as he spoke. "How long has this sort of thing been going on?"

"The Shiite population has been sympathetic to the Ayatollah's regime from the start," Colonel Hillerman answered. "At least the more radical elements. Nearly thirty percent of Kuwaiti nationals are Shiite Muslims."

McCarter reached inside his case and removed a Bianchi shoulder holster rig. A 9 mm Browning Hi-Power autoloading pistol was sheathed in the leather. McCarter drew the Browning and worked the slide to chamber the first round. He put on the safety and stuck the pistol in his belt.

"You won't need that, Mr. Stark," Ahmed told him.

"I'd rather have it ready and end up not needing it than be unprepared at a crucial moment," McCarter replied as he started to remove his jacket to slip into the shoulder holster rig.

"Words to live by," Hillerman commented. "Or should I say to *stay alive* by?"

"It's worked so far," McCarter stated.

Suddenly more than a dozen demonstrators noticed the two limousines. They pointed at the big black automobiles and shouted words which jumbled into a confused, multi-voiced snarl. The demonstrators charged toward the limos as if responding to a prearranged signal. An empty cola bottle streaked from the mob and struck the thick, tinted window near Katz's head. The Israeli instinctively raised the prosthesis of his abbreviated right arm to shield his face, but the shatter-resistant glass held.

"Oh, Christ!" Hillerman exclaimed and reached inside his jacket for a holstered pistol.

"We don't want any shooting," Ahmed said urgently. He called to Mohammad to drive faster and get them out of the area.

Mohammad was unable to oblige. The demonstrators blocked the path of the limousines. The other group swarmed after the sign-swinging zealots who attacked the cars. Shoving, punching and name-calling broke out amid the hostile cluster of enraged humanity. The police were too busy with other members of the crowd to try to assist the limos.

Protesters slammed their signs across the hood and roof of the first vehicle. The wooden stalks snapped from the impact. Boots smashed into the body and doors of the car. A flurry of fists hammered on the bullet-proof windows. A couple of people battered the thick glass with rocks. The second limo was attacked with equally unreasoning fury.

"The windows won't break..." Ahmed declared, but the tone of his voice suggested he was less than certain this was true.

"Any glass will break if they work on it hard enough and long enough," McCarter informed him.

One demonstrator began ramming his splintered placard against the windshield. A few men banded together to try to tip the car over.

In the interior of the limousine, McCarter snorted with disgust. Katz sighed and shrugged. The Israeli realized they had to take action before the mob turned over the limo. Upside down the vehicle and its passengers would be too vulnerable. The protesters might even puncture the gas tank and set the car ablaze if the frenzy continued to escalate.

"Let's try not to hurt any of them too badly," Katz instructed as he unlocked the door nearest to him.

"Ay!" Ahmed exclaimed, startled by the Israeli's actions. "What are you doing?"

"Edification concerning the unacceptable behavior of bad manners in an enlightened society," Katz answered.

He turned the handle and slammed a hard kick into the door. It swung open and struck one of the protesters with ample force to knock the youth to the ground. McCarter immediately bolted through the open door and literally dived into the mob. The Briton's hard skull and left forearm smashed into the stomach of one Shiite demonstrator and his right fist caught another young extremist in the lower abdomen. Both demonstrators groaned breathlessly and began to double up from the unexpected body blows.

McCarter shoved hard and pushed both opponents into other protesters. He glimpsed the faces of the pair. Dark, young features with the odd glow of fanaticism in their brown eyes. The glow was not as strong as it had been before the unexpected assault. McCarter was surprised to see one opponent had been a teenage girl, her pretty face contorted by pain. The other was a young man with a few strands of black hair on his chin, the beginning of a beard. McCarter swung a fist into the face with whiskers.

The youth toppled into the path of two of his comrades. They staggered awkwardly and tried to maintain their balance. Another protester swung the handle of his placard at McCarter's head. The Briton dodged the attack and the wooden shaft cracked against the roof of the car. McCarter swiftly grabbed the man's wrist with one hand to prevent him from using the pole again. With his free hand he seized the demonstrator's hair and shoved the youth's face closer. McCarter snapped his head forward and delivered a hard butt between the Arab's eyes.

The youth fell backward, eyes closed, a bruise already formed at the bridge of his nose and a droplet of blood oozing from a nostril like a crimson snot. Another half-crazed protester opened the blade to his folding knife and prepared to attack McCarter from the rear. The Shiite had just raised his knife overhead when a powerful grip of three steel talons snapped around his wrist. The knife man gasped with surprise and fear as he was yanked back by the metal claw.

"That's not sporting," Katz remarked, the hooks of his prosthesis clamped around the demonstrators wrist.

The Israeli twisted the captive wrist forcibly. Bone crunched, and the knife fell from the youth's fingers. The demonstrator screamed and staggered away from Katz, clutching his broken wrist close to his body. The Phoenix Force commander shoved a boot into the cowed man's backside to send him hurtling into the disoriented band of protesters who had been taken off guard by the reprisal of the men in the limo.

The girl McCarter had pushed aside, jabbed her placard at Katz's stomach, but the Israeli sidestepped and the wood lance rammed into a car door. Katz snapped his prosthesis hooks around the shaft and gripped the pole before she could attempt another attack. He almost threw a punch with his left hand but relented when he saw the girl's startled young face and instead shoved her hard enough to hurl her back against her comrades.

Another protester swung at Katz in an overhead stroke. The Israeli raised the confiscated stick like a quarterstaff and blocked the attack. Wood cracked on wood. Katz swiftly lashed a kick to his opponent's groin. The young Arab gasped in agony, his mouth opening into a black oval. He started to fold up from the pain, and Katz swung the stick in a butt-stroke swipe and clipped him on the side of the skull.

The demonstrator tumbled into a trio of his companions. They collapsed to the ground in a furious, shrieking heap. Another rioter snarled a curse that claimed Katz was a "wrinkled old infidel son of a pagan pig." Katz understood the insult and glimpsed an arm that rose above the heads of the crowd to hurl a rock at the Phoenix commander.

Katz gripped the stick in his left hand and raised it suddenly to bat the rock in midair. The projectile sailed back into the mob and bounced off the head of another demonstrator. The man dropped to the ground, a string of curses flooding from his mouth. Somebody with a short-bladed knife lunged at Katz. The Israeli veteran commando had a greater reach with the confiscated pole and used it to deliver a fast jab at his attacker's face. The youth recoiled and struck out at the shaft with both arms, but Katz's thrust was only a feint, and he quickly delivered a low backhand stroke that chopped across the knife artist's shins.

The young Arab cried out and fell to the ground. Katz whirled the pole overhead like a helicopter rotor blade to keep other attackers at bay. The rioters withdrew, amazed by the speed and fury of somebody who a short while ago had been a potential victim. A one-armed, middle-aged victim at that. The fallen protester abandoned any notions of using his blade and scrambled on all fours to escape.

"You're not in this bleedin' country for a full hour—" Colonel Hillerman began as he emerged from the opposite side of the car and slashed his walnut cane at the crowd "—but you already managed to get in a fight, Sergeant!"

McCarter realized Hillerman was speaking to him, but the British member of Phoenix Force was too busy to reply. A heavyset young demonstrator lunged at him, both hands aimed at the Briton's throat. McCarter quickly clasped his hands together and thrust them between the attacker's outstretched arms. His fists thrust into the air, and his elbows caught the Arab's wrists to knock his arms aside.

Then the Phoenix fighter's arms rose in tent position and suddenly snapped forward. His doubled fist chopped the assailant at the bridge of the nose. Cartilage crunched, and the man howled as blood poured from his broken nose. McCarter followed the first blow with a solid right cross to the jaw to drive the opponent back into the crowd. He turned sharply to confront another young zealot who swung a savate kick at McCarter's midsection.

The Briton's hands flashed and adroitly seized the attacker's ankle before the boot could connect with its intended target. The rioter hopped awkwardly on one foot, startled and frightened as he stared at McCarter. The Phoenix pro slid his hands to the man's foot and turned it hard as simultaneously he stepped forward and pushed. Shoved off balance, the youth hurtled backward and crashed into several of his comrades.

Hillerman parried an attack, then slashed his walking stick like a *katana* samurai sword. The hardwood smashed into the crown of the attacker's head and drove the young aggressor to the ground in an unconscious lump.

Another frenzied rioter, armed with a short club, prepared to jump Hillerman. Just then the front door by the driver's side burst open and Mohammad charged from the limo. The youth turned toward the big Kuwaiti agent, but the side of Mohammad's hand chopped the punk across the wrist and struck the club from his grasp. With his other hand Mohammad followed by a karate blow to the collarbone. The youth doubled over and received Mohammad's bent knee squarely in the face.

The blow broke three teeth and rendered the rioter unconscious. Mohammad grabbed the demonstrator before he could slump to the ground and hauled him into the crowd, where he knocked down two more opponents. An enraged rioter charged from the mob, a rusty blade in his fist. Hillerman stepped forward with an awkward limp and slashed his walnut cane across the side of the attacker's face. The youth dropped abruptly to his knees, a crimson-and-purple bruise on his cheek. Mohammad promptly kicked him in the face and knocked him out cold.

"*Alf shook,*" Mohammad remarked with a nod of thanks.

"*El-afu,*" Hillerman replied, accustomed to speaking Arabic almost as often as English. "Anytime, good chap."

Demonstrators had also attacked the second limousine, and the other three members of Phoenix Force had charged from the vehicle in an effort to deal with the situation rather than become helpless victims of mob violence. The rioters immediately discovered that harassing the wrong people could be a painful experience.

Gary Manning thrust open a door and lobbed an object which resembled a fountain pen from the limo. The Canadian demolitions expert took care to toss it at the feet of the protesters to avoid accidentally hurling it into an open shirt or loose hood attached to a jacket or sweat suit. Manning emerged from the car and slammed a forearm under the chin of a Shiite who tried to grab his neck.

The first opponent bounced backward just as the magnesium flare exploded near the feet of the demonstrators. The rioters cried out in alarm and astonishment as the white light burst from the "fountain pen." The flare was actually harmless unless it happened to ignite flammable material or came into direct contact with skin. Many covered their eyes and wailed that they had been blinded by the flash. The "flash blindness" lasted for a few minutes only and was similar to the effect of a powerful camera flashbulb, except the magnesium blast was far more brilliant and painful to behold.

Manning took advantage of the confusion and fear. He ignored those temporarily blinded, as they did not present an immediate threat. The others were distracted and disoriented, but still potentially dangerous. Manning struck swiftly before they could regain their wits.

His first move was to clip one opponent behind the ear with a big, rock-hard fist. Then the Canadian warmed into the job, and with a variety of blows, kicks and flying leaps, started to quell the crowd as though all he wanted was a little clearing around himself.

Calvin James had also emerged from the limo and squared off with two Shiite protesters who seemed prepared to take civil disobedience to homicidal extremes. One opponent was a small wiry man with a shaggy black beard and small bright eyes. The curved blade of the knife in his fist was also bright, as light glinted along the honed edge. His companion was taller, more muscular and grinned at James with an arrogant smile plastered across his broad face. The larger opponent held a bottle filled with sand in one fist, and a crudely made wooden knuckle-duster adorned his other hand. His fingers fitted into the holes like rings, with the wood knuckles extended across his fist.

"Couldn't you dudes just write a letter to the editor or somethin'?" James muttered, trying to keep calm enough to think clearly in the dangerous and stressful situation.

Anytime a man is confronted by armed opponents he is afraid...unless he is a fool. James was no stranger to fear and felt no shame in the emotion. He appreciated the additional speed and strength of adrenaline. Thanks to his medical background, he knew fear could actually be an advantage in combat. Experience had also taught him that harnessing the energy and using it to his advantage would prevent him from being frozen in place by terror. He had to act quickly, and relied on his years of training and battle-honed reflexes as he made his move.

James raised his arms in a fast, deceptive motion to draw the attention of his opponents. Their eyes followed his hands and James launched his real attack. The black commando swung a tae kwon do kick into the side of the knife-fighter. The toe of his boot caught the Arab under the ribs. The man groaned as the kick drove the breath from his lungs. James's foot seemed to recoil from the first opponent's body as he shifted his body to thrust his leg in a powerful side kick aimed at the second opponent's abdomen.

The larger Arab gasped as James's boot found its mark. He swung wildly with the bottle, but James had already stepped forward to slash a karate chop across the man's forearm. The side of his hand struck the ulnar nerve and the bottle dropped from inert fingers. James swung a left hook to the Arab's jaw and bent his right elbow to snap a frontal stroke to his opponent's mouth.

The big man went down hard as his knife-wielding comrade lunged at James's back. The Phoenix warrior caught the motion from the corner of his eye and suddenly whirled like a top. A leg shot out and James lashed a high wheel-kick at his attacker's head. The back of his heel crashed into the man's skull near his temple. As the Arab slumped unconscious to the ground, he opened a momentary line of vision that allowed James a glimpse of Encizo diving into the crowd.

A rock whistled past Rafael Encizo, followed by another projectile that barely missed his head and banged loudly against the roof of the limousine. A young Shiite protester charged forward and raised his short cudgel overhead threateningly.

"¡Cabrón!" Encizo exclaimed as he weaved away from the descending club.

The Arab's cudgel missed, and Encizo hooked a kick to his attacker's stomach. The man folded with a grunt, giving Encizo an opportunity to quickly snare his arm with both hands. He gripped the wrist and locked the demonstrator's elbow with his other hand. The Cuban turned and swung his opponent about so that his head slammed into a shatterproof car window. The fellow whimpered faintly before he folded into a crumpled heap.

A man who displayed a short-bladed dagger approached the Cuban in a crouched position. The Shiite zealot flashed a tight grin at Encizo and continued to slowly close in.

"Take it easy," Encizo urged as he turned slightly to present the left side of his body, palm held up as if ready to push back the knife artist. "Somebody could get hurt here, you know..."

The Cuban blocked his opponent's view of his right hand as he reached back to the handle of the weapon in a belt sheath by his hip. The demonstrator continued to grin and suddenly lunged, dagger pointed at Encizo's belly.

Encizo turned swiftly, his body angled away from the knife thrust. He swung the Cold Steel Tanto forward to meet the attack. The heavy six-inch steel blade struck the dagger hard. Metal grated against metal, and the Arab's knife dropped from his hand.

The Phoenix fighter executed a fast backhand sweep with the Tanto. The razor-sharp blade slashed the Shiite's black T-shirt and sliced a shallow cut in the man's flesh. The demonstrator jumped back and clasped both hands to his chest. He felt the warm blood oozing up. His eyes grew rounded in astonishment and fear as he stared at Encizo.

"You're out of your league, kid," Encizo hissed. "Quit while you're still breathing."

The youth may not have understood English, but he followed the advice, anyway. He retreated, and found that he was not alone. All the remaining Shiite demonstrators drew back from the two limousines. The protest was running out of steam, and more police reinforcements were arriving to help subdue the violence. Three television network vehicles also arrived, two American and one British. Reporters popped out of the rigs. Camera personnel emerged with video cams and Minoltas held ready.

"We don't need to be on the six o'clock news, fellas!" James shouted to his teammates as he retreated inside the limousine.

"Right!" Katz called back in agreement. "This is our cue to get out of here."

"Well," Ahmed remarked with a sigh, "the demonstrators are certainly out of the way now. Mohammad?"

"Yes, Ahmed," Mohammad replied and slid behind the wheel. Katz, McCarter and Hillerman climbed into the back with Ahmed. The Israeli glanced out the back window. The other three members of Phoenix Force had also entered the second vehicle. Mohammad started the engine, and the two car caravan resumed its progress from the airport. Hillerman folded his hands on the handle of his walking stick and leaned his chin on top. He looked at McCarter with a weary smile.

"So tell me," Hillerman began. "How do you like Kuwait so far?"

"Oh, pretty well so far," the other Briton replied. "It isn't dull."

"I should have known you'd say something like that," Hillerman muttered with disgust.

5

The limousines raced away from the international airport. The occupants noticed more police cars heading for the airport to help deal with the unruly demonstration. Then they were passing by the huge water towers at the edge of the city. Holding thousands of gallons of clean water in their globe-shaped containers, the towers were vital to the survival of Kuwaiti citizens. A unique and very expensive restaurant with a reputation for excellent food was located atop one of the towers, which stood more than four hundred feet high.

Kuwait city was impressive. It was a modern city by any standards, East or West. Hotels, office buildings and other structures towered above the well-maintained paved streets. Traffic was heavier than that found in most Middle East cities, as many Kuwaiti citizens owned private vehicles. Cars, buses, taxicabs and trucks filled the busy streets.

Among the most interesting structures were the parliament, and the palaces owned by members of the royal family. The former was an oddly compelling building because it looked like a concrete version of a giant Bedouin tent. The residences of royalty were lavish and exotic. Most notable was Seif Palace, the headquarters of the Sheikh. The white marble palace was surrounded by palm trees and a long, tranquil pool. A graceful clock tower stood by one wall. It vaguely resembled an Islamic version of Big Ben, with a tear-shaped crowning pavilion above the four faces of the clock.

"That looks like a storybook version of an oasis in a tale from *The Arabian Nights*," Gary Manning remarked as he gazed out at the palace.

"Kuwait city is one of the biggest and best oasis spots you'll ever hope to see," Brackman replied, glancing over his shoulder from behind the wheel of the second limo. "Would you believe they've got *two* ice rinks here? One is big enough for Olympic competition."

"Ice skating in the Middle East," Rafael Encizo said. The Cuban grinned at the unlikely prospect of such an activity. "Kuwait seems to have something for every one."

"Pretty close," Brackman confirmed. He kept his eyes on the road as he conversed with the three Phoenix Force pros in the back seat. "This isn't the easiest place in the world to find 'fun' female companionship, to get drunk or find a good rack of pork ribs. Of course, that's true about most Islamic countries. Still, about sixty percent of the population in Kuwait are immigrants. Iranians, Pakistanis, Indians and people from a number of other Arab countries live in Kuwait. That's not including all the Europeans, Japanese and the scattering of Americans who are currently stationed here on business. Not all of these folks are Muslims. The Kuwaitis are practical people, and they're pretty tolerant of others being different and having different beliefs. They're already catering to Western tastes quite a bit."

"Those guys at the airport didn't seem too tolerant," Calvin James commented. However, the people he saw on the streets of Kuwait city seemed contented and peaceful enough. He also noticed several women who did not cover their faces in public.

"The demonstration today is a rare incident in Kuwait," Brackman assured him. "Most Kuwaitis are Sunni Muslims. About twenty-five percent are Shiites, and most of them are perfectly happy with how this country operates. Of course, there are some that feel a sense of loyalty toward the Ayatollah, and Kuwait isn't on very good terms with Iran these days."

"I heard something about that," James said dryly. "Are those women among the non-Muslims you mentioned?"

"Not necessarily," the CIA agent answered. "Though the Koran is not insistent on it, women covering their faces in public *is* an Islamic teaching. However, it is also an Arab tradition. Kuwaiti fashions vary from traditional Arab garments to Levi's and sneakers. These people are living in the twentieth century and they're getting ready for the twenty-first."

"You sound like you like it here," Manning observed. "How long have you been stationed in the Middle East?"

"Five years," Brackman replied. "Mostly in Saudi Arabia. It's not bad duty. Less dangerous than Lebanon and not as frustrating as Egypt. Ever since Sadat was assassinated, Uncle Sam hasn't been too sure what the hell Egypt is going to decide to do in the future. Now, Egypt was good duty for me because there are a lot of black Egyptians, so I fit in better with the population. Some Arab countries aren't much fun if you happen to be black."

"Yeah," James said with a nod. "I seem to recall there's an old Arab proverb that Allah made the black man to serve the Arab."

"And there are some who still believe that's how things should be run," Brackman confirmed. "The worst place is probably Mauritania, a country about twice the size of Texas in northwest Africa. I was previously stationed in Morocco at a listening post for the Company. We were spying on both Mauritania and Algeria at the time. Anyway, Mauritania is a military dictatorship with Berbers pretty much in control, although the majority of the population is black. I'm not sure what it's like now, but back in 1980 and '81 they still had slave markets in Mauritania. Blacks being sold into slavery to Muslims of Moorish descent."

"Slave markets in the twentieth century?" Manning asked in astonishment. "That's hard to believe."

"You don't have to take my word for it," Brackman told him. "The London Antislavery Society estimated that nearly a hundred thousand black Mauritanians were still in slavery in 1981. Makes South Africa's apartheid look rather mild by comparison. But that sort of thing doesn't go on in Saudi Arabia or Kuwait or any of the other Arab oil countries along the Persian Gulf. By the way, the Saudis generally call it the 'Arabian Gulf.'"

"Whatever you call it," Encizo commented, "it's becoming the most volatile international powder keg in the world."

"I guess that's why we're here," the CIA man agreed, turning the steering wheel to follow Mohammad's limo onto Talata Street.

The limousines pulled into the underground garage of a handsome modern building of concrete and glass. Other limos and an assortment of expensive luxury automobiles including two Rolls-Royces were already parked there. A thick steel-and-cast-aluminum door rolled shut behind the limos as Mohammad and Brackman parked their vehicles.

"Wow," James commented and whistled softly at a big white Rolls that probably cost more than most people would make in a lifetime. "What is this place? A hangout for the rich and flashy?"

"It's a hotel with a very exclusive clientele," Brackman explained with a sly grin. "You ever been to a safe house on assignment? You know, a temporary headquarters disguised as something else for the sake of security?"

"We've been to so many safe houses over the years I doubt if any of us remember what our real homes look like anymore," Encizo replied.

"Well, I bet you've never seen a safe house like this one," Brackman declared.

"I can hardly wait," James commented, curious about what covert Kuwaiti hospitality would be.

The three Phoenix commandos and Brackman emerged from their limo as Katz and McCarter stepped from the other vehicle. The British and Israeli commandos seemed surprisingly grim. Ahmed and Hillerman joined them, followed by Mohammad.

"What's up?" Manning inquired. "Oil prices going on the rise again?"

"Colonel Hillerman informed us of some disturbing news from Oman," Katz answered. "We'll talk about it upstairs."

"This sure doesn't sound like good news," James remarked.

"Bad news can be like the tests of Job," Ahmed declared with a philosophical shrug. "Perhaps you are not familiar with the Torah or the Koran, but I believe Job is also mentioned in the Old Testament of the Christian Bible. Job endured his hardships and still called upon Allah as all-merciful. So God removed his afflictions and granted mercy to Job and his people. Allah is merciful, my friends. And He is just."

"That sounds nice," Encizo remarked. "We can use any help from any source we can get."

Encizo had been raised a Catholic, and though he didn't agree with the Church on many issues, he still regarded himself a good Catholic...more or less. However, he still respected others' religions and had no real prejudice toward Islam. What worried him was the tendency among many Islamic governments to promote individuals based on their proof of devotion to religion rather than on the basis of ability and experience in their profession. In some Islamic nations a soldier must make the hajj pilgrimage to Mecca before he can become an officer in the armed forces. In Encizo's view, a religious tradition should have little to do with one's ability in the military, and even less in the shadowy and uncertain world of espionage.

The Cuban didn't know how such things were handled in Kuwait. He hoped Ahmed's qualifications consisted of more than being a devout Muslim. Encizo mentally warned himself not to jump to any conclusions as Phoenix Force followed the Kuwaiti officers, Hillerman and Brackman to the elevator at the end of the garage.

"I don't suppose we could use the stairs instead?" Gary Manning asked. The Phoenix Force demolition expert did not like elevators. He knew how easily elevators could be sabotaged. There was no way to protect oneself from an explosion in an elevator shaft.

"Well, it's ten stories," Ahmed answered. "That would take rather a lot of time to walk up the stairs, and Mr. Anderson is right. We do need to talk privately and as soon as possible."

The elevator was large enough to accommodate twenty passengers. The nine men had ample room in the car. It was an ornate and attractive elevator with red felt walls, polished metal doors and a white cordless phone in a compartment near the control panel. They managed to ride to the tenth floor without incident, much to the relief of the Canadian demolitions pro.

The doors opened and the men stepped into a hallway with green walls, a white ceiling and a lush red carpet. Relief-style columns were designed in the walls every three meters. The wooden fluting was painted black. The color combination was patriotic rather than artistic—the Kuwaiti flag is green, white and red with a black trapezoid at the flagstaff.

Ahmed led the group past several doors until they reached a room with a thick mahogany door with two brass figures which resembled a large upside-down *V* with a letter *V* beside it. These were, in fact, Arabic numerals, to mark the room as Number 87. Ahmed turned the handle and pulled the door open.

They stepped into the spacious room of a luxury penthouse suite. Chairs and two sofas were grouped around a large color television set and entertainment center which included a stereo system, videotape recorder and shelves of VHS tapes and recorders. A massive brass bookcase, filled with leather-bound volumes stood at one wall. By the east wall, a lectern held a single book in a place of honor. It was the Koran. A small handwoven rug was rolled up by the wall near the stand. It was a prayer rug, positioned at the east, the direction a devout Muslim faces during prayer.

There was a kitchen, equipped with modern devices, including a microwave, large refrigerator and contraptions for making juice and coffee. Other rooms extended beyond an archway. The quarters were lavish, very comfortable and no doubt expensive. Ahmed gestured toward the leather furniture invitingly.

"Please make yourselves comfortable," he suggested. "Regard everything here as your own."

"Brackman said this place is a safe house," James commented. "He didn't mean the whole building, right?"

"Most of it, yes," Ahmed answered. "This building is used for a front...as you Americans say. All the floors above the fourth story are used by SIS. Those below are business offices. The entire fourth floor is actually a pretend office section, maintained simply to keep a division between the genuine business operations and our confidential affairs. This is a security measure, of course. There are scrambling devices to distort frequencies and prevent electronic spying by anyone in the offices below. The elevator will only go to the fourth floor unless one has been cleared by our security monitors. Don't worry. The place is quite secure."

"It's certainly the most comfortable safe house I've ever seen," Manning admitted as he sat on a leather sofa. "We usually wind up in a hole in the wall in a slum area."

"Hole in the wall?" Ahmed asked with a frown. He was unfamiliar with the expression. "Sounds dreadful. Would you care for some coffee? Juice? Soft drinks or perhaps some goat milk?"

"Coffee will be fine," James assured him. "I'm trying to cut down on the goat milk."

"Soft drinks include Coca-Cola?" McCarter asked.

"Absolutely," Hillerman answered. "You never broke the habit, eh?"

"Never really tried, to be honest," McCarter admitted.

"Mohammad, please see to refreshments for our guests," Ahmed told the other Kuwaiti officer. "I've always wondered how one became so fond of Coca-Cola."

"It can happen when you spend a fair amount of time in places where you can't trust the water," McCarter explained.

"The damn Communists during the Omani Dhofar War had a nasty habit of poisoning our water supply in the hills," Hillerman added. "That was a brutish little war. South Yemen was backing the guerrillas."

"*Jumhuriyah al-Yemen al-Dimuqratiyah al-Sha'abiyah!*" Mohammad spat out angrily.

"What's that?" James wondered aloud. He guessed there must have been some sort of obscenity in Arabic in there somewhere, from the vehemence in Mohammad's tone.

"I simply said the People's Democratic Republic of Yemen by its official name in Arabic," Mohammad explained. "That's what those stinking, dung-eating Communists call that accursed country. May Allah see fit to spit venom in the mouths of that atheist trash."

"Come now, Mohammad," Ahmed said with a sigh. "You have the name of the prophet, yet you seem to forget the Koran tells us of the fate in store for the Communist leaders in South Yemen in the chapter concerning 'the House of Imran.' A verse refers specifically to those who believe and now disbelieve. Allah shall not guide them and they shall face chastisement forever. Yet it also states that if they repent and make up for their errors, Allah will forgive them for God is all-merciful."

"I believe we were going to hear some details about an incident in Oman?" Gary Manning reminded the others.

"Oh, yes," Hillerman said with a nod as he lowered himself into an armchair and propped his stiff right leg across a footstool. "Another nasty incident by the terrorists, I'm afraid. They attacked a U.S. frigate in port near Muscat. Report I received on the incident said nine American naval personnel were killed. It would have been far worse if most of the crew hadn't been off the ship on liberty. Apparently, only two terrorists attacked the vessel from the pier. They used Soviet RPG rocket launchers with cyanide gas canisters in the warheads.''

James looked grim. "Do they have a definite ID on the attackers?''

"They were Omani nationals," Hillerman confirmed. "I've got the report copy on file with Ahmed's files on the Kuwaiti oil tanker incident. A bit sketchy still, but more details will come in when SIS . . . that is, British SIS in my station in Oman, has more information. The terrorists were both killed within about a minute after they launched the attack.''

"I'm not all that familiar with Muslim sects throughout the world," James admitted. "Are the majority of people in Oman Sunni or Shiite?''

"About seventy-five percent are Ibadhi Muslims," Hillerman answered. "Of course, there are both Sunni and Shiite Muslims in Oman.''

"Although I am Sunni, I ask that you do not be too quick to judge all Shiites on the actions of those zealots connected with the Ayatollah," Ahmed added quickly. "There are many Shiite Muslims in the Arab countries along the gulf, and most are fine men and women who disapprove of Iran's jihad. Bahrain, a small island nation off the coast of Saudi Arabia near Qatar, is seventy percent Shiite Muslim, yet Bahrain certainly has more in common with my country than Iran.''

"Yeah," Brackman agreed. Mohammad handed him a cup of black coffee and the CIA man nodded his thanks. "I've been to Bahrain a few times in the past. Very high standard of living, just like all the other nations in this region. Average national income for citizens of Bahrain is about ten thousand dollars. Since the government under the emir gives the people free medical care and education, and subsidizes housing and food costs, that's not bad at all. Especially since they don't pay taxes."

"True," Ahmed added with a smile. "Of course, here in Kuwait we have all that, as well. Telephone services and utilities are also subsidized, and the free education in Kuwait includes *university* level—up to and including travel abroad for one's education. The average income in my country is eleven and a half thousand."

"I appreciate you're proud of your country, and you have every right to be," Brackman said tactfully, "but I also wanted to mention that Bahrain has had trouble from terrorists. There was an effort by radicals to overthrow the royal government back in December of 1981. The evidence suggested the terrorists were connected with Iran. You know, the Ayatollah's regime claims Bahrain is part of its territory. Bahrain doesn't agree."

"As I recall," Katz began, then paused to accept a cup of coffee from Mohammad. He held the handle with the trident hooks of his prosthesis while he stirred the coffee with a spoon in his left hand. "Bahrain has remained on good terms with the West in general, and the United States in particular. The emir visited Washington, D.C. to discuss possible plans for peace in the Middle East. One has to admire a man who is willing to strive for a goal most believe to be impossible. Especially after what happened to President Sadat."

"All the other nations of the Gulf Cooperation Council have had no complaints about Bahrain's loyalty and efforts to help us remain economically strong and build up security," Ahmed declared. "Of course, it may seem this has been less than successful, or you wouldn't be here, but the Council has really helped us a great deal."

"I've no doubt about that," Katz assured him. "However, the Cooperative Council was created due to concerns of foreign problems connected with the Iran-Iraq War. What you're currently faced with is terrorists organized not only within one gulf country, but apparently spread across both Kuwait and Oman. Probably in some of the countries in between.''

"Well," McCarter began, sipping a chilled glass of Coca-Cola. "We don't know much about the terrorists except they use cyanide gas, the same as both sides in the Iran-Iraq conflict, and they don't seem very concerned if they happen to get killed during an attack. In fact, I'd say both the incident on the supertanker and the attack in Oman sound like suicide missions.''

"And that suggests they are Shiite terrorists," Ahmed stated. "Shiite beliefs are quite different from that of Sunni Muslims. The difference could be compared to the division between Christians among Catholics and Protestants.''

"Catholics and Protestants both believe suicide is a sin," Encizo remarked. He blew gently on his coffee to cool it and added, "A mortal sin. Perhaps even more serious than murder.''

"But haven't there been many Christian martyrs?" Ahmed replied. "Dying for a cause isn't the same as suicide. The Shiites believe that whoever dies fighting infidels in a holy war, he becomes a martyr and his soul goes directly to paradise. The soul of a martyr doesn't have to wait for the final day of judgment.''

"This is all very interesting," Manning stated with a sigh. "But we have to decide where to start. That Shiite demonstration at the airport proves there are some militant sect members in Kuwait. Now, the more radical organized groups sympathetic to the Ayatollah might be a place to start. Even if they're not connected directly with the terrorists, it seems highly probably that the enemy is recruiting from these sources.''

"Maybe we should check out Oman," James suggested. "The trail might be a lot warmer there.''

"We're already in Kuwait, gentlemen," Katz stated. "Let's see what we can do here before we make any plans for Oman. The best place to begin might be at the beginning.

Let's see if we can learn anything from the crew of the supertanker.''

"SIS already talked to the captain and the cooperation chief of the company he works for," Ahmed stated.

"CIA talked to them, too," Brackman confirmed. "Background checks were run on everybody on board that tanker, including the terrorists. Got biographies on all of them if you want to read them.''

"We'll look into it anyway," Katz said. "We'll also check any other possible leads. That means we'll have to split into teams. The terrorists aren't wasting much time between hits, so we can't afford to waste any either. A lot of lives are at stake. Washington thinks the attacks are acts of state-sponsored terrorism by Iran. We have to make damn sure we know whether it is or isn't before we report to the President."

"What if Iran is directly responsible?" Brackman asked.

"Then the President of the United States will have to make a very important decision," Katz replied. "He'll have to decide whether or not to declare war.''

6

Although Kuwait is roughly the size of the state of New Jersey, it's topography and climate have little in common with that state. Most of the country is barren, desert land with little soil. Yet, as a gulf country, fishing and shipping are also major industries in Kuwait. The harbors along the coast of Kuwait Bay are always filled with activity.

David McCarter, Rafael Encizo and Mohammad arrived at a tanker port at the north coast of the bay. Petroleum from the oil fields was transported to the port to be shipped out in the tankers. The enormous vessels waited in dock, each capable of carrying thousands of gallons of the valuable cargo. The three men wandered the piers, searching for Captain Nizar.

"I thought this bloke was supposed to meet us," McCarter commented. Patience was never one of the Briton's strong points. "Hell of a lot easier for him to spot two foreigners walking about the harbor than for us to find an Arab sailor among hundreds of other Arab sailors."

"Sixty percent of the population in Kuwait are foreigners," Mohammed replied. "You fellows don't stand out here as much as you might think."

"We'll find Captain Nizar," Encizo assured his partner as he glanced at the sea gulls that circled above the massive decks of the tankers. "There are only five supertankers in port. You couldn't get more than that in this harbor."

"True," Mohammed agreed. "I'm curious, Mr. Stark. You served with Colonel Hillerman in Oman?"

"That's right," McCarter replied, nearly failing to respond to his cover name. "He's a good man . . . for an officer."

"Did he injure his leg in Oman?" the Kuwaiti agent asked.

"Yes, he did," the Briton confirmed. "Why?"

"Just curious," Mohammed explained. "I admire you British for helping the sultan protect his country from the Communists. Just as I admire the Americans for assisting my country in transporting oil through the gulf. These are the actions that build strong friendships and mutual respect between nations. East and West are different in many ways, yet the higher qualities of man—honor, courage, sacrifice for others—these things can be recognized and appreciated by all. Colonel Hillerman sacrificed a limb in the service of his country, and also for the sake of Oman."

McCarter remembered the night they had to amputate Hillerman's leg. The SAS was pinned down in the mountains and low on supplies. They did not have enough morphine to keep Hillerman sedated throughout the rather crude and desperate surgery. Hillerman's screams of agony and repulsion, when he awoke to discover his men had pinned him to the ground and were sawing through the bone above his right knee, were sounds that still haunted McCarter in his dreams.

The British commando lived for adventure and thrived on action. He was a man of war and felt most alive and valuable on a battlefield. But McCarter, too, hated the terrible waste of human lives and dreadful agonies of the maimed and mutilated that was an unavoidable part of combat. That was why he felt a special commitment to the missions with Phoenix Force. Terrorists and gangsters didn't care how many innocent people they destroyed. They had to be stopped, and McCarter was very good at pulling the plug on them.

"There's Nizar," Mohammad announced, tilting his head toward a beefy figure dressed in navy blue slacks and matching turtleneck shirt.

Nizar stood near a tanker truck with a hose and pump attached. Another hose extended to the hold of a supertanker in port. The big Arab captain turned from the pumps and tilted back his cap to stare at the approaching trio. They did not look like what he had expected. The captain had been interrogated by CIA and Kuwaiti SIS before. The man in white robe and *keffiyeh* was no surprise, but his companions lacked the neat, polished appearance of the CIA personnel he had met before. Encizo wore a tan leather jacket, black T-shirt and Levi's with boots. McCarter's wrinkled sports jacket and baggy trousers appeared to have been slept in, and the cloth cap pulled low on his forehead was better suited for an English country gentleman than an American espionage agent associated with the U.S. embassy.

"Good afternoon, Captain," Mohammad greeted, speaking English, a common second language for Kuwaitis. "I believe you are expecting us?"

"I was told to expect three men with your general descriptions," Nizar replied. "Perhaps we should talk inside."

He led the trio past a group of laboring workmen who struggled with hoses, tubes and pumps to transport oil from tanker trucks to the supertanker. Nizar walked to a building that rather looked like an airplane hangar. Several dockworkers had gathered around a table in a bay area inside the hangar. They were drinking tea or coffee and munching on dates, melons and grapes from a large bowl in the center of the table.

Nizar escorted McCarter, Encizo and Mohammad to a room at the opposite side of the bay section. They entered a small, sparsely furnished office. The captain leaned against the edge of the desk and looked at the three visitors with a weary expression, already bored with the coming conversation.

"I take it your friends don't speak Arabic?" Nizar inquired.

"Not very well," McCarter answered. "We'll probably understand each other better if we stick to English. If you figure you can explain something better in Arabic, that's fine. Our mate here will translate for us."

The Briton nodded toward Mohammad. He almost gestured with a thumb to indicate the Kuwaiti agent, but had stopped himself in time because he remembered that the "thumbs-up" motion was regarded as an obscene gesture in many Arab cultures.

"I've already answered dozens of questions for the SIS and the Americans," Nizar said with a sigh. "I've answered them in both Arabic and English. I fail to see what I can add to my previous statements."

"We've read your previous statements, Captain," Encizo told him as he leaned against a wall and folded his arms on his chest. "No one is trying to cast any blame on you or your crew. There was no reason for you to suspect any of your men might be terrorists. I just have a couple of questions I'd like to ask. Okay?"

"Very well," Nizar agreed with a weary nod.

"Now, in your statements you said that there was nothing unusual about the three crew members who turned out to be terrorists," the Cuban began. "After the incident, you broke the locks to the wall lockers assigned to those characters, right?"

"Yes," Nizar confirmed, "but there was nothing in any of those lockers except clothing. SIS, CIA or some police agency confiscated it."

"No personal items?" Encizo wanted to know. "That's a bit unusual. How did they get along with the crew? Did they pretty much stick with the Shiite members?"

"A man's religion is his own business, sir," Nizar said stiffly. "Many of my crew members are Shiite Muslims and

I trust them with my life. Those three were all fairly new to my crew and, frankly, I can't tell you for certain if they were Shiite, Sunni or even Christian. I don't think they made any friends among the crew, but they weren't troublemakers or fanatics. At least they didn't seem to be."

"Are any of the men who were on board the tanker during the terrorist attack around the dock today?" McCarter asked.

"Yes," Nizar answered. "Several of them are on the tanker now. I don't know how many of them are Shiite or Sunni. Some others are helping with the hoses and pumps. Four of the fellows taking a break in the bay section are members of my crew."

"Good," Encizo said with an eager nod. "May we talk to them?"

"They are good men," Nizar said defensively.

"No one is questioning that," Mohammad assured the captain. "We just want to ask them some questions."

"All right," Captain Nizar agreed, obviously irritated but willing to cooperate. "I'll bring them in."

He called the four sailors into the office. They seemed slightly nervous, but a certain amount of apprehension was understandable under the circumstances. Nizar and Mohammad acted as translators while Encizo directed the questions in English.

"All of you knew the three terrorists who infiltrated your crew," Encizo began. "We need to know any details you can tell us about them."

The sailors exchanged words with Mohammad and Nizar in rapid Arabic. The Kuwaiti agent turned to Encizo and spoke.

"They insist they hardly knew those treacherous dogs," Mohammad explained. "They all agree that the scum were less than friendly, especially toward the Shiite members of the crew. One of them even remarked that the Shiite were heretics."

"That's a term you don't hear much these days," McCarter remarked as he stuck a Player's cigarette in his mouth.

The Briton mentally reviewed his sketchy knowledge of the Shiite Muslems. He recalled that the Shiites had been regarded as heretics and blasphemers by the Sunnites when the division between the two sects of Islam occurred in 632 A.D. after the death of the prophet Mohammad. The separation was due more to the disagreement about Mohammad's successor than actual doctrine.

The Sunni acknowledged Omar, trusted aide to the prophet as the successor of Mohammad, while the Shiite believed Ali, Mohammad's son-in-law was the rightful new leader of Islam. That created a growing gap between the sects. Bitter feuding, heated debates and violence had erupted between the two major philosophies of Islam. The division still existed, yet the gulf nations of Kuwait and its progressive neighbors had seemed to put the religious bickering aside.

"Perhaps the terrorists were not devotees of the Ayatollah after all," Mohammad, the Kuwaiti agent, commented.

"All this proves is that the terrorists didn't mind if others *thought* they were anti-Shiite," Encizo stated. "That doesn't mean they weren't Shiites. After all, if they were followers of the Ayatollah, I doubt they would have admitted it to your crew."

"A fanatic loyal to the Ayatollah would probably reckon a jihad-happy non-Shiite was a traitor to true Islam anyway," McCarter said with a shrug. "Ask these fellas if they recall seeing any of the terrorists hangin' about with any of the blokes who work at the docks here. Especially anyone with the crews for other tankers."

"Now there's a different question," Nizar remarked.

"An important one," Encizo told the captain. "It's pretty unlikely any large terrorist organization would only send three men on a mission to infiltrate the crews on board these tankers, and that all three would just happen to wind up on your ship, Captain. They'd probably have a number of 'sleeper agents' either working on the docks or among the other crews, either to serve as a source of intelligence for the enemy or to infiltrate other crews in the hopes they can carry out similar missions to the first terrorist hit.''

The sailors recalled that the terrorists—their former shipmates—had seemed to discuss personal matters with a fellow at Building Three. The description they provided was of a muscular dockworker with a black beard, drooping mustache and a black eye-patch. The sailors from Nizar's crew were not certain if the terrorists associated with other personnel at the dock, but the man at Building Three was well remembered due to his eye-patch.

''I know the man they speak of,'' Nizar declared. ''Not by name, but I have seen him in Building Three. He drives a forklift and also performs some manual labor. Would you desire me to lead you to him?''

''I think we can find Building Three,'' Encizo answered. ''We'd rather keep you out of the possible line of fire in case the man is armed. Thank you for your assistance, Captain.''

''Let's go find this one-eyed chap,'' McCarter declared. ''Maybe he's just a passing acquaintance who didn't know any more about the terrorists than we do, but we've got some questions for him.''

''I just hope he has some useful answers,'' Mohammad remarked.

The two Phoenix pros and their Kuwaiti companion left the hangar and headed toward Building Three. A cold wind blew in from the bay and forced McCarter and Encizo to grip the left lapels of their jackets to prevent the wind from pushing back the garments to reveal the holstered 9 mm pistols both men carried under their shoulders. They approached the wide entrance to the building. Mohammad unbuttoned his white *abayah* robe as they reached the threshold.

"You know this fella might be innocent," Encizo whispered. "Let's not jump to conclusions, but it's best to be prepared for trouble just in case."

"I am aware you gentlemen can take care of yourselves," Mohammad replied. "You certainly proved you're good with your hands and feet during that riot at the airport. I hope you're as skilled with those pistols."

"Don't worry about that," McCarter assured him. The Briton was, in fact, a former Olympic Pistol Team contender for Great Britain. "If anything goes wrong, we'll be ready."

They stepped inside the building. It was similar to the hangarlike structure where they had previously met with Captain Nizar and his men. Columns of crates and large metal drums lined the walls of the bay area. Several men dressed in work clothes were busy in the building. Some checked inventory. Others hauled heavy wooden boxes onto dolly carts or rolled drums across the concrete floor. One man sat in the control seat of a forklift. He was a musclebound fellow with a beard, mustache and a black eye-patch on the right side of his face.

Mohammad approached the man on the forklift, while Encizo and McCarter followed behind the Kuwaiti agent. The Phoenix pair scanned the bay area, keeping an eye on the others. Several workmen noticed the three strangers. More than one seemed alarmed by their presence. The one-eyed man on the forklift started to turn the steering wheel to his machine and saw the trio via his single orb.

"Al-salumu Alaykum," Mohammad called out with the standard Arabic greeting of "peace be with you."

The one-eyed man switched off the engine to his forklift and slowly climbed down from the machine. He was slightly shorter than Mohammad, but probably outweighed the Kuwaiti agent by at least twenty-five pounds. He glared at Mohammad like a miniature cyclops challenging a titan.

Encizo did not understand any Arabic, and McCarter's small vocabulary was only adequate to catch words and phrases as Mohammad and One-Eye exchanged a rapid-fire conversation. The two Phoenix Force commandos continued to watch the others inside the hangar while the discussion between the two Arabs began to turn into a heated exchange.

A small, thin man with a blue construction helmet was determinedly marching toward Mohammad and One-Eye. He carried a clipboard under his arm and seemed to have an air of authority. He glanced at McCarter and Encizo, then demanded, "You speak English? I'm the foreman here. Will someone tell me what this is about?"

Encizo and McCarter barely acknowledged the presence of the man and were not quite sure what he'd said. They were still trying to divide their attention between One-Eye and the other men in the bay section. A grinning young Arab with a thick, unkempt mane of shaggy black hair seemed particularly suspicious because he flashed insolent looks at the Phoenix pros.

Most of the other workers were either mildly curious or barely paid any attention to the visitors. Two exchanged whispers and moved into a corridor at the back of the bay area. Another laborer watched his companions walk away from the dolly cart and simply shrugged, leaned on a crate and waited for them to return.

"Oh, shit," McCarter rasped under his breath.

"It's gonna hit the fan," Encizo added.

As if to confirm their suspicions, One-Eye suddenly grabbed his foreman's shirtfront and swung the startled man into Mohammad. He slammed the foreman into the Kuwaiti agent with such force it knocked Mohammad off balance. The agent fell to the floor with the foreman sprawled across his chest.

Encizo was closer to the cyclops than McCarter. His hand streaked from his jacket, a Heckler & Koch P9S autoloader in his hand. However, One-Eye was not intimidated by the pistol and charged straight for Encizo. The Cuban did not want to kill, and there wasn't enough time to attempt to shoot to wound. He held his fire a moment too long. One-Eye swung a big fist like a hammer and chopped it across Encizo's forearm.

The blow struck the H&K pistol from the commando's grasp. He heard the gun clatter on concrete as the hefty Arab descended upon him. The man was bigger than Encizo, heavier, possibly stronger, and certainly at least a decade younger. The Cuban warrior realized he could not hope to win a shoving match with the one-eyed man. Instead Encizo seized the larger man's sleeve and shirtfront and moved with his opponent's motion.

As Encizo pulled One-Eye toward him, he dropped backward to the floor on his left rump and thigh. His right foot rose to the Arab's abdomen as he rolled back and straightened his knee. One-Eye hurtled headfirst above Encizo in a judo circle-throw. He crashed to the floor hard, the wind driven from his lungs. Encizo rolled onto all fours and reached for the fallen H&K pistol.

David McCarter had also drawn his weapon when One-Eye made his move, but the Briton had other matters to occupy him while Encizo struggled with the big Arab opponent. The two men who had disappeared for a conference into a corridor now burst on the scene with firearms at the ready. One man carried a short-barreled submachine gun and the other held a pistol in both hands.

The dockworkers in the bay had been surprised by the sudden outburst of violence, and when they saw the unexpected bristling of guns around them, they scrambled in all directions. Shouting with alarm, they tried to flee the building or find cover. One man darted between McCarter and the two gunmen at the corridor. The Briton was forced to hold his fire for fear of hitting the innocent passerby.

The enemy gunman did not share McCarter's concern. The man with the subgun triggered his weapon. McCarter had dropped to one knee, his Browning Hi-Power in a two-hand Weaver's grip, as he tried to get a true aim at the enemy. The salvo of full-auto rounds snarled within the bay area like thunder in a tunnel. McCarter felt the heat of high-velocity projectiles slice air above his head.

A fleeing dockworker screamed and collapsed to the concrete floor, a trio of bullet holes in his back. Blood soaked his shirt as he twitched a few times on the hard surface. The killer with the chattergun tried to adjust the aim of his weapon to spray the British commando with a burst of 7.62 mm slugs.

McCarter's Browning pistol spit flame. He triggered two rounds and blasted both 9 mm parabellum into the chest of the opponent with the subgun. The bullets struck left of the sternum and punched into the gunman's heart. He fell backward and triggered his weapon to blast a harmless volley into the ceiling before his lifeless body hit the floor.

The pistol man swung his weapon toward McCarter as Rafael Encizo aimed his H&K P9S and opened fire. A 9 mm slug tore into the enemy gunman's torso, then, as Encizo fired another round, the man was spun about in a final morbid dance.

McCarter saw the second gunman fall and quickly raised his Browning to point it at the ceiling as he scanned the bay for other potential opponents. The Briton was particularly interested in the shaggy-headed youth he had noticed earlier, because something about the man gave the impression of a mad dog that had learned to walk upright. Fortunately the innocent bystanders had managed to escape or find cover behind crates in the bay. However, one person appeared to have ducked behind a row of drums for a different reason.

The unkempt mane of black hair and glimpse of wide, glassy eyes identified the man adequately for McCarter. McCarter also noticed the labels on the drums that served as cover for his opponent. Warning: Flammable was printed in both English and Arabic in large red letters, with a symbol of jagged flames in the center of the label just to make sure anyone who saw the warning would realize the potential danger of the contents.

"Bleedin' hell," McCarter rasped, aware that to fire a shot near the drums might ignite the contents if a bullet hit one of the barrels.

Encizo also saw the figure behind the drums and started to move toward the column of metal barrels. He hoped to get into a better position to either shoot the man or force him to surrender. Suddenly a hard blow between the shoulder blades sent the Cuban hurtling forward. He grunted in pain and landed on his knees, breaking his fall with his left hand while the right held on to his H&K pistol.

A boot lashed out and kicked the gun from his hand. Encizo quickly turned and grabbed the attacker's ankle. He glanced up and saw the one-eyed Arab towering over him. Encizo twisted the ankle forcibly to prevent his opponent from putting all his weight into a vicious stomp. The Phoenix fighter was angry—not because he had been attacked by the cyclops, but because he had forgotten about the man. He had been careless, and this made him furious with himself. Encizo knew better than to turn his back on an opponent who was not definitely out of commission. He realized he had been fortunate One-Eye had only hit him between the shoulder blades with a fist instead of a knife blade or a bullet.

Encizo dropped on his left side and swung his right leg in a sweep against his opponent's leg, then felt the limb buckle from the stroke and heard the man cry out in surprise. The man hurtled to the floor and landed hard. Encizo still held his opponent's ankle and pulled as he thrust a boot along the length of the Arab's leg, using it for a guide to drive his heel into the other man's most vulnerable parts.

The opponent howled in agony and his body jackknifed on the floor while his mouth hung open in wheezing gasps. Encizo quickly scrambled atop the man and hammered a fist into the side of the neck. The brute sprawled senseless on the floor, but Encizo hit him again to be certain he would not be a threat for a while.

Mohammad had started to rise from the floor, but quickly changed his mind as a few bullets zinged by. He pushed the foreman flat and urged him to stay put. The Kuwaiti agent had drawn a large stainless steel pistol with an eight-inch barrel from his robe. The big .357 Auto-Mag was an impressive weapon, but he did not have a ready target to contend with. McCarter and Encizo had already taken care of the enemy except for the deranged character behind the drums.

The grinning face of the fanatic appeared above the top of a drum. He raised his hand to reveal the small metal object he held. The man flipped open the lid to the cigarette lighter, laughed and uttered something unintelligible as spittle formed a silver spray from his mouth. His thumb sat on the wheel to the lighter, prepared to strike up the flame.

McCarter made an instant judgment call. To take any action was risky, but to take none at all would allow the martyrdom-obsessed fanatic to blow them up in a fiery blaze of demented glory. The Briton snap-aimed and triggered his Browning. He fired a single shot and pumped a 9 mm Silvertip hollowpoint bullet squarely between the eyes of the fanatic. The man's head was jarred by the impact, and the back of his skull exploded to splash blood and brain matter on the wall behind him. The man slumped behind the drums, the lighter still clenched in his lifeless fist. He was dead before he could fire up the lighter.

"I got a live one," Encizo announced as he moved to the unconscious One Eye and drew a strip of unbreakable plastic from his belt. Riot cuffs which can only be removed by cutting through the plastic.

"That's good," McCarter replied. He knelt beside the workman who had been shot by the machine gunner during the battle, checked for a pulse, but found none. "The others are dead, including this poor bloke."

"Praise Allah," Mohammad said with a sigh of relief and helped the foreman get to his feet. "I am glad that's over."

The sudden roar of an engine drew their attention to the entrance of the building. A forklift appeared at the opening, a large crate braced across the forks and load backrest. The driver peered out from the operator's seat and looked around the crate as he drove the machine forward. Two figures followed the forklift, one armed with a cut-down double-barrel shotgun and the other holding a black pistol that resembled a German Luger.

The forklift charged toward McCarter, Mohammad and the unlucky foreman. Mohammad fired his Auto-Mag at the vehicle. The powerful .357 projectile struck the crate on the forklift. It splintered wood and pierced the heavy wooden box, but failed to pass through the crate to threaten the forklift driver. The crate was obviously filled with something that deflected even Magnum bullets, probably machinery parts.

"Cheeky bastards," McCarter hissed as he threw himself to the floor and shoulder-rolled clear of the path of the advancing forklift.

The crate served as a shield for the lift operator, and the forklift itself offered cover and protection for the two gunmen behind the rig. The British ace realized that it would be a waste of ammunition and precious time to fire directly at the new trio of attackers. He had to get into position to hit the enemy from an unguarded angle.

He rolled across the floor and landed on one knee, the Browning pistol clenched in both hands and pointed at the side of the forklift. The startled driver stared back at the Phoenix commando and grabbed a chrome-plated pistol from his lap. McCarter fired his weapon before the enemy could aim his piece. A well-placed 9 mm round caught the forklift driver at the bridge of the nose and plowed into his brain.

The attacker with the shotgun swung his weapon around the rear of the forklift and pointed the twin barrels at McCarter. Mohammad spotted the threat and fired his Auto-Mag twice. Sparks erupted at the barrels of the shotgun as the .357 rounds slammed into the weapon and sent it hurtling from the gunman's hands.

McCarter jumped onto the frame of the forklift, grabbed the overhead guard with one hand and swung into the cab section. A boot propelled the dead driver from the operator's seat and dumped the body onto the concrete. McCarter climbed into the seat and quickly put on the brake before the forklift could roll into the wall near the flammable contents of the drums marked with the warning labels.

The gunman with the Luger look-alike tried to aim his pistol at McCarter's back, but the metal grillwork of the cab to the forklift blocked the killer's view of the Briton. The pistol man just started to advance to get a better position to attack McCarter when Rafael blocked his path.

The Cuban warrior did not have time to search for his Heckler & Koch pistol so he drew the Cold Steel Tanto from the belt sheath. The enemy gunman was roughly seven feet away, too far to try to rush a pistol-packing opponent while armed only with a knife. Encizo had to try a desperate tactic, and quickly. His arm shot forward and hurled the Tanto. The weapon was not designed for throwing, but Encizo was an expert at knife fighting of every kind. The Tanto struck the gunman in the chest. The sharp point pierced the solar plexus, and two and a half inches of steel sank into the man's chest.

The killer staggered backward, startled by the unexpected wound. He fired his pistol, but his aim was off because of the terrible pain in his solar plexus. The bullet hissed inches from Encizo's shoulder as the Cuban charged for the showdown. The Tanto jutted from the gunman's chest, and blood spread across his shirt. He tried to point the pistol at Encizo with one hand and grip the handle of the knife with the other, to attempt to yank the blade from his flesh.

Encizo closed in swiftly and swung a roundhouse kick to boot the Luger from his opponent's hand. The pistol flew across the bay section, and Encizo snapped a back fist to the man's face. The attacker staggered from the blow, and Encizo raised a boot and thrust a hard kick at the chest. His heel struck the butt of the knife handle and drove the Tanto deeper. Five inches of sharp steel plunged deeply into the aggressor's chest. The man opened his mouth to howl in agony, but a stream of bright crimson poured from his mouth instead. The would-be killer crumbled to the floor, twitched weakly and died, the knife still lodged firmly in his torso.

The last opponent reached for a sheath knife at the small of his back. Mohammed had shot the double-barrel shotgun out of his grasp and the fellow's blade was his only backup weapon. Mohammad advanced and pointed his Auto-Mag at the man's chest as he barked an order in Arabic. "Surrender or die!"

The guy's face contorted with animal fury, but he did not become still in surrender. Mohammad could not see what his opponent was trying to grasp, but he realized the man was going for a weapon of some sort. He stepped closer, less than two yards from the would-be assassin, and raised the Auto-Mag to fire a well-aimed round at extreme close range.

The .357 bullet crashed into the man's right shoulder. The violent impact shattered the joint and splintered the collarbone. The terrorist spun about from the force of the Magnum slug. His arm hung useless from the crushed shoulder, and the short-bladed knife fell from trembling fingers. The man staggered forward and his knees folded under him. He fell to all fours in front of Mohammad. The Kuwaiti agent promptly slugged the opponent to knock him unconscious.

"I think that's the last one," Encizo remarked as he retrieved his H&K pistol.

"That's what we thought before," Mohammad commented. "I wonder where they came from."

"Must be other terrorist sleeper agents," McCarter stated, stepping down from the cab of the forklift. "Things went pretty well, except for the poor chap who got killed in the line of enemy fire."

"You think it went well?" Mohammad asked with astonishment. Nearly getting killed was not his idea of a cheerful encounter.

"We're still alive," Encizo told him, and McCarter's crooked grin was in perfect agreement.

7

Rafael Encizo spread the scarf out on the glass-top coffee table. The other men in Ahmed's first-class safe house gazed down at the purple cloth. A symbol in the center represented an anchor, and it was flanked on both sides by slender crescents. The characters were bright red. Gary Manning stared down at the cloth and raised an eyebrow.

"You found this in the pocket of one of the terrorists?" he inquired.

"That's right," Encizo confirmed. "The one-eyed fella had this in a shirt pocket, next to his heart. I don't know what it is or if it's important, but I figured it might be. Anybody recognize it?"

"The symbol in the center is the Persian word for Allah, or God if you like," Ahmed explained. "However, this is not the Iranian flag. The flag of the so-called Islamic Republic of Iran is green, white and red, with this symbol in the center of the white bar in the middle. I don't recall seeing this symbol in Persian or Farsi on a purple cloth before."

"Neither do I, Ahmed," Colonel Hillerman added as he lowered himself into an armchair and propped his walnut cane alongside the armrest. He placed a briefcase in his lap and opened the lid. "Nonetheless, I have some more information concerning the terrorist incident at the harbor in Oman. A point of particular interest is the list of items found on the person of one of the terrorists."

"A purple banner like this one?" Manning inquired, almost afraid to hope for such a clear connection.

"*Exactly* like it," the British SIS officer confirmed as he handed the Canadian member of Phoenix Force a printout sheet with a color dot-matrix reproduction of a photograph.

Manning examined the latter. It depicted a purple cloth with a red Farsi symbol in the center. The size of the scarf or banner was given as eight inches by four inches, the same as the cloth Encizo had found on the one-eyed terrorist. Manning passed the data to his Cuban partner.

"I think we found a pattern," Encizo said with a sly smile. "A clue to the people responsible for the terrorism."

"Well, you said you took two of those villains at the docks alive," Hillerman remarked. "Maybe we can get them to talk."

"Mr. Anderson and Mr. Washington are with Mohammad and Mr. Stark," Ahmed explained. "They will all join our personnel in interrogation of the two prisoners."

"Who?" Encizo asked. For a moment, he forgot the cover names being used by Katz, James and McCarter. "Oh, yeah. Those guys."

"Using aliases is a bit tiresome, isn't it?" Ahmed asked, with a sympathetic smile. Encizo wondered what the Kuwaiti officer's real name was. Of course, that was hardly important.

"I know you guys bend the rules a lot," Brackman began as he carried a cup of coffee from the kitchen, "but I hope you realize that there are certain forms of interrogation that aren't acceptable for us to use. I mean, we are supposed to be the good guys, and Uncle Sam doesn't need any bad press about American agents or mercenaries or whatever you guys call yourselves. Torture is the sort of thing that can give us a real bad image."

"The CIA has a lot of room to talk about anyone giving the U.S. a bad reputation," Encizo snorted. The veteran of the Bay of Pigs fiasco was not apt to forget the CIA's role in that abortive mission.

"I assure you, Brackman," Gary Manning said quickly, eager to cut off any confrontations, "we don't resort to torture. Not only is it immoral, it's unreliable as well. People will certainly talk to get the pain to stop, but that doesn't mean they'll tell the truth. They'll say whatever they think the torturer wants to hear to get him to stop."

"Besides," Ahmed added, "the terrorists are fanatics. Religious and political fanatics. Shiite extremists are well-known for their high tolerance of pain and willingness to sacrifice their lives for their jihad."

"They didn't seem too worried about getting killed when they attacked us at the harbor this afternoon," Encizo confirmed. "And of course, we're here because the terrorists have been using suicide tactics with their attacks on American personnel."

"Yeah," Brackman said with a sigh. He sat on the sofa and placed his coffee cup near the purple scarf. "I don't know that any sort of questioning will do any good with fanatics like those guys. What method do you usually employ with people like that?"

"Scopolamine," Manning answered. "It's the only reliable truth serum, you know."

"It's also dangerous," Brackman stated. "You can kill a man using that stuff."

"Mr. Washington has used it many times in the past and no one has died from it so far," the Canadian assured him. "He always checks a subject's blood pressure and heart before he uses the drug. If Washington suspects the scopolamine might kill a subject, he won't use it."

"That's not a major concern in this case," Ahmed stated as he walked to the kitchen and opened the oven door. "We execute terrorists in Kuwait."

"Your government can do whatever it wants with the terrorists after we've interrogated them," Manning assured him. "Washington isn't going to kill the prisoners to try to get information from them, but none of us are going to criticize how Kuwait has dealt with terrorism...either in the courtroom or with your country's policy of refusing to negotiate with terrorists."

The pleasant and prosperous nation of Kuwait had certainly suffered from terrorism in the past. In 1985, a suicide attack by a fanatic in a car bomb killed five people when the vehicle exploded at the Sheikh's motorcade. The Sheikh himself was injured, but the assassination attempt did not frighten Kuwait's royal leader into surrendering to the demands of terrorists.

Kuwait had stubbornly held to its convictions when Shiite extremists hijacked Flight 422 in April of 1988. Although two members of the royal family were among the hostages, Kuwait refused to negotiate with the terrorists or bend to their demands that seventeen convicted terrorists be released from Kuwaiti prisons. The hijackers murdered two hostages, but the Sheikh and his government still refused to give in. After fourteen days, the terrorists released the hostages at Oran International Airport in Algiers.

The hijackers managed to escape, but they failed to accomplish their goals by kidnapping and murder. As the Kuwait Ambassador to the United States said in an interview after the incident, "Our position will remain steadfast against any form of terrorism." Kuwait was proving the nation was as good as the word of its leaders.

"Our dinner is ready, gentlemen," Ahmed declared as he began to remove the racks from the oven. "I hope you like *hamam*."

"I never had it before," Manning replied as he joined Ahmed in the kitchen. He glanced down at the racks and saw several roasted birds that looked much like small chickens. Each was roughly the size of a cornish hen. "Need some help with anything?"

"The table is already set, but you might be good enough to take the crock with rice to the table," Ahmed declared cheerfully. He obviously enjoyed cooking and did not feel anything demeaning about a chore many Arabs regard as "women's work."

The men assembled at the dining room table and sat at the places already prepared for them. Ahmed turned to the east and uttered thanks to Allah for the meal, bowing several times as he spoke his grace in whispered Arabic. The others waited at the table for their host. Ahmed invited his companions to help themselves to the food. Besides *hamam* and rice, there were cucumbers, boiled potatoes, green beans, salmon and Edam cheese on the table.

"Bil-hana!" Ahmed declared, the traditional Arab wish for a good appetite.

The sound of someone at the door drew their attention. Ahmed gestured for the others to remain seated and went to the door to see who was there. He opened it and greeted Katz, McCarter, James and Mohammad. All four men looked like they had spent the last five hours struggling with a tax audit.

"I prepared enough food for all of us," Ahmed assured them. "Please, help yourselves to the food in the kitchen. There are hot *hamam* in the oven."

"Haven't had that since I was in Oman with the colonel," McCarter remarked as he headed for the kitchen.

"I seem to recall you could always be counted on to finish off anyone else's bird if they didn't eat all of their meal," Hillerman commented.

"Considering some of the things we wound up eating in those hills, anybody who left any pigeon was a bloody fool," McCarter replied.

"Pigeon?" Manning asked, staring down at the small bird on his plate. "This *hamam* is a pigeon?"

"Hamama," Katz corrected, accustomed to to Middle East food. *"Hamam* is plural. Thank you, Ahmed. This is very considerate."

"You are very welcome," Ahmed replied. "Please, let us sit and have dinner—a rather late dinner, true—and exchange information."

"I really don't have much news for you," Mohammad confessed as he placed a *hamama* on a plate and carried it to the table. "Stark and I spent our time with the local authorities and immigration offices. They wanted some explanations for why five men without any criminal record were killed at the docks today. Six, including the poor fellow killed by the terrorists. May Allah grant him peace and mercy."

"How was immigration involved?" Manning asked.

"Because three of the blokes we killed turned out to be immigrants who had moved to Kuwait nearly ten years ago," McCarter answered as he sat at the table with a plate in one hand and a can of Coca-Cola in the other. "Surprise, surprise, they all came from the same country and arrived in Kuwait only a few days apart. Anyone care to guess what country was their place of origin?"

"Iran?" Encizo asked, his tone suggesting he had little doubt that he would be right.

"Got it at the first try," McCarter confirmed. "After we finished convincing the local police that we weren't a band of homicidal lunatics on a murder spree, we managed to get them to help us search the homes of the terrorists. Not that we found much of interest. Just a bit of literature that suggested they were all Shiites. That wasn't too hard to guess. We also found some evidence we expected. Weapons, cleaning equipment, odd-looking stains in the toilets which suggested papers had been burned and dumped into the commode. Probably maps and such."

"Don't forget the scarf," Mohammad reminded him.

"I was saving that last for dramatic effect," McCarter said with a grin. "We found two more of those scarfs or banner-type cloths like the one over there on the coffee table. Mohammad said he thinks it might be Farsi."

"Iranian symbol for Allah," Ahmed confirmed. "Same as on their flag. We also know that the terrorists at the harbor in Oman had a purple cloth with the same red letter in the center."

"Sounds like we're putting together some sound connections that seem to point to Iran," Encizo commented. "What did you learn during interrogation?"

"Well," Calvin James began with a sigh, "I could only use scopolamine on one of the prisoners. The big one-eyed dude. The other guy was heavily sedated, pumped full of pain killers 'cause a .357 Magnum round damn near took his arm off at the shoulder."

"Sorry," Mohammad said with an insincere shrug. "It seemed like a logical action at the time."

"Yeah," James replied. "You can't handle life-and-death, kill-or-be-killed situations with kid gloves. Still, I couldn't use scopolamine on the guy. Probably would have killed him, with all the other drugs he'd already been given. So, I had to settle for hypnosis."

"Really?" Hillerman asked with surprise. "Does that stuff really work? I always figured that was sort of like astrology and such."

"There is a sound basis for hypnosis," James answered. "And it's more than a parlor trick. Sometimes it works and sometimes it doesn't. The best results are with an intelligent, responsive subject who concentrates and cooperates, but it can also work when you have a subject whose natural resistance has already been broken down. This guy was doped up, so he wasn't able to fight suggestion too much, but he wasn't able to concentrate, either. That means about fifty-fifty odds for success...at best. Didn't make it any easier that English isn't his native language."

"I translated Mr. Washington's instructions into Arabic," Katz explained. "We've done this before with other subjects under similar conditions, and it's worked in the past."

"Did it work this time?" Brackman inquired.

"Hell, no," James said with disgust. "The son of bitch had already put *himself* in a sort of hypnotic state. The guy was in a goddamn trance, and I couldn't get through to him.

Just sat on his bed chanting and bobbing his head up and down. Never saw anything like it.''

"He was repeating passages from the Koran and anti-infidel slogans," Katz added. "A real religious fanatic."

"What about my one-eyed sparring partner?" Encizo asked.

"We had better luck with that guy," James answered. "He told us a few things of interest under the influence of scopolamine. Among others, he stated that the purple banner is sort of a badge of authority within the Purple Warriors of Righteousness."

"What the hell is that?" Hillerman inquired. "A splinter group of the Sufi or the Yezidis?"

"Those are both mystical sects," Ahmed stated. "I have never known Sufi or Yezidis to get involved in political movements, let alone terrorism."

"Aren't the Yezidis found in Yemen?" Brackman asked. "They're some sort of Islamic devil worshipers aren't they?"

"Actually that's a misconception," Katz answered. "The Yezidis believe the devil has been reformed by God, and the evil that remains on earth is man's own doing. They have such faith in the mercy and forgiveness of Allah that there's no need to worry about Satan. Anyway, neither the Sufi nor the Yezidis have anything to do with the Purple Warriors. It seems to be a cult led by a man who calls himself Qabda. These extremist Shiite cult members are spread across the gulf nations, carrying out 'righteous warfare' on the forces of the infidels. Apparently anyone who isn't a Shiite fanatic is regarded as an infidel."

"With Americans at the head of the list," Encizo remarked.

"The list includes just about everybody," James stated. "Christians, Jews, Sunni Muslims and Shiites who aren't part of the jihad holy war. These loonies believe the Ayatollah is a modern-day prophet of Allah and this Qabda dude is sort of God's enforcement arm on earth."

"Sacrilegious scum," Mohammad hissed with contempt.

"I know, my friend," Ahmed said with a sigh. "It is a pity these Shiite fanatics haven't paid more attention to the lessons taught in the Koran. I recall a passage that tells us that true piety is to help those in need—orphans, travelers and beggars. To believe in God and happily be God-fearing."

"It is sad that all too often religion is twisted to serve less than noble causes," Katz declared. "Islam isn't the only religion that's been used as an excuse for bloodshed. There are examples in Christianity: one can look at the actions of the Inquisition, the Reverend Jim Jones and his suicide commune, et cetera. There are also some Jewish extremists who'd like to annihilate all the Arabs in the Middle East. Personally I doubt that God approves of murder in His name regardless of what religion is involved."

"I agree, Mr. Anderson," Ahmed said with a sly smile. "Or whatever your name really is. I suspect it isn't as Anglo-Saxon as 'Anderson,' but no matter. Please, continue."

Katz nodded. He realized Ahmed was hinting that he recognized what nationality Katz was and also that he felt no animosity. Katz made a mental note to discuss the matter with Ahmed at a more appropriate time. He was curious as to how the Kuwaiti agent had come to this conclusion.

"The prisoner also told us about a base here in Kuwait," Katz continued. "He gave us the location and approximate number of his terrorist brethren who will probably be there."

"Is this Qabda gonna be at the base?" Brackman inquired eagerly.

"No," Katz replied. "The prisoner isn't sure where Qabda's main base is set up, but it isn't in Kuwait. The top-ranking member of the Purple Warriors here is a fellow named Ali Kamel. Qabda apparently travels from country to country, recruiting young Shiite zealots and planning missions. If we can capture Kamel alive, he may be able to give us more details about Qabda."

"So we still don't know if this terrorist 'prophet' is running the cult himself or if he's an agent for Iran," McCarter said with a grunt of disgust.

"Hell, man," James replied. "We haven't been in Kuwait for a full twenty-four hours. All things considered, we've made pretty good progress."

"Bloody remarkable progress," Hillerman added. "Better than all the rest of us put together. I guess that's what happens when you spend too much time with bureaucratic outfits like CIA and SIS. You don't even think of chatting with the sailors about the men on that supertanker. All of us thought the damn captain would be in the know more than anybody else about the first three terrorist attackers. I feel like a ruddy fool for not having those blokes interrogated at the docks before."

"No offense, Colonel," Encizo began, "but you think like an officer, not an enlisted man or a regular seaman. Officers tend to think other officers know their men. They don't. There's always a division between the guys in authority and the men under them. For future reference, question someone who worked with a person if you want to learn any details about him."

"Thanks," Brackman muttered. "Now that the Colonel and I are suitably embarrassed, maybe you can tell us what we do next."

"I can't believe it's a pigeon," Manning whispered, staring at the bird on his plate.

"We try to find out as much as possible about the terrorist base here in Kuwait and raid the rats' nest before they scatter," Katz answered Brackman, hoping the Kuwaitis had not noticed Manning's dismay about the meal. "We'll have to do it soon, and we'll have to be careful how we carry it out. It will be very dangerous, not just for us but for anyone within at least a kilometer of the site."

"The terrorists have cyanide gas canisters stored there," James added. "Since these guys are suicide-happy and want to die as martyrs, that presents a real problem. If they figure they're gonna get busted, they'll pop open those canisters just to take some of us with 'em."

"My God," Brackman said, shaking his head. "How the hell are we going to handle a situation like that?"

"We'll come up with something," McCarter said cheerfully. "Things are just getting a bit interesting now."

"Sergeant," Hillerman said with a sigh. "You are such a crazy bastard that I wonder how you've stayed alive so long."

"It does boggle the imagination," the other Briton grinned. "Doesn't it?"

"Maybe the Company can start looking for Qabda in Oman and Qatar or wherever he might be hiding out," Brackman suggested. "Don't you have any information on the leader of the Purple Warriors?"

"The prisoner only met Qabda once," Katz answered. "He said the 'warrior prophet' was tall and stately with 'the proud features and cunning eyes of hunting falcon,' and he always wears a purple turban with a blood-red *keffiyeh* and a white robe. Symbolic colors of royalty, martyrdom and purity."

"A purple turban?" Manning asked with an astonished expression suddenly splattered across his features.

"Sounds like a fashion that might be popular in some parts of San Francisco," James commented, "but these guys are serious. They consider themselves to be the 'royal martyrs of God,' which is the reason they call themselves the Purple Warriors."

"The turban," Manning continued, disturbed by this information. "It's probably just a coincidence and I . . . never mind."

"Bullshit," Brackman told him. "Let's hear it."

"Well," Manning began reluctantly. "Are any of you familiar with the prophesy of Nostradamus?"

"Michel de Notredame," Katz said with a nod. "A sixteenth century French astrologer who is regarded by some people as a great seer and mystic who allegedly predicted the rise and fall of Napolean, Hitler and Franco hundreds of years in advance. As I recall, Nostradamus made more than a thousand predictions. Many people believe a lot of them have already proven to be true."

"Oh, man," James scoffed, "I can't believe we're even talking about this crap. Nostradamus supposedly predicted the big earthquake for May 10th, 1988, which was gonna bust up California and make it sink into the ocean. Well, 1988 came and went and California is still around."

"That belief was based on some people's interpretations of the works of Nostradamus," Manning insisted. "He wrote about events in places that didn't even exist in his day. When he referred to 'new cities' and 'mountains to the west' it's hard to say if he meant America let alone California."

"I never thought you'd go in for any of this mumbo jumbo nonsense," McCarter muttered, shaking his head. "Nostradamus predicted wars to be about twenty years apart, and you don't have to be a mystic to realize men could never manage to live in peace for more than two decades. The Iran-Iraq war certainly qualifies as a major conflict right now, and there are at least three smaller wars currently in progress that might escalate as well."

"Maybe," Encizo spoke with a slight shrug, "but I seem to recall reading that Nostradamus actually referred to Franco *by name* in his predictions and mentioned a German tyrant called Hisler. Maybe that's more than coincidence."

"And maybe it means whoever wrote those 'interpretations' did it *after* World War Two," James said with a cynical chuckle. "After all, if you want somebody to buy a book about Nostradamus and his great predictions, you wouldn't admit he predicted a Spanish dictator named Pedro would rise to power, or Germany would plunge the world into war under the leadership of Kaiser Seymour."

"I can't say I put much stock in this sort of thing, either," Hillerman declared, "but what's this rot about purple turbans?"

"Nostradamus predicted the rise of three great tyrants who would plunge the world into war," Manning began, feeling a bit foolish even as he spoke. "Each more terrible than the one before him. Three anti-Christs. The first is believed to be Napoleon. The second is supposedly Hitler and the third is said to be a warlord from the east. A man who would rise from the Mohammadan nations. A man with a purple turban. Some sources say a blue turban . . ."

"Yeah, yeah," James grunted. "So what's this anti-Christ supposed to do? Raise the postal rates? I think somebody already beat him to it."

"He's supposed to form a mighty army, equipped with weapons that can set entire cities aflame and reduce them to poisoned rubble," Manning answered.

"Nuclear weapons," Ahmed said softly.

"And in 1999," Manning continued, "World War Three will begin."

The room was silent for a long, surprisingly tense moment. Ahmed placed his fingertips together and stared at his hands as he spoke.

"The Koran states that there will be signs, and warns that these should not be mocked," he said in a serious tone.

"And I recall a verse from the Book of Matthew," Encizo added. "'There shall arise false Christs, and false prophets.'"

"When did we slip into the twilight zone?" McCarter asked with disgust.

"Well, gentlemen," Katz began. "I've learned over the years that it's best to keep an open mind and not dismiss the possibility that there are things that happen that we don't fully understand. However, I've also learned there's little to be gained by fretting about things when you've got a job to do. Let's just concentrate on that. If the world comes to an end, at least it won't be because we sat on our hands when we should have taken action.''

"And we got a pretty good idea where to start," James declared. "Bet Nostra-know-it-all-damas didn't predict that."

"I wish I'd kept my mouth shut," Manning muttered.

"Finally something I can agree with," McCarter said with grin. "So you want to check your horoscope before we get on with the mission?"

"Ah, shut up," the Canadian replied sourly.

8

Qabda barely remembered his real name. He fought the memories of the past whenever they began to slip into his mind. Occasionally past scenes broke through his resistance when he slept. The dreams would startle him from his slumber, and he spent the night sitting alone. He would face east and wait for the dawn when he would say the first prayer of the new day. Often he read the Koran to himself aloud, repeating those passages that seemed to support his actions.

A favorite verse for Qabda concerned Allah's instructions to Moses and the people of Israel. Moses was regarded as a great prophet by Muslims, although the Koran's version of events in the life of Moses was different from that of the Bible. In fact, many characters found in the Bible—Adam, Noah, Moses, David, Solomon and Jesus among them—were also written about in the Koran.

Qabda's favorite verse concerning Moses told how Allah had instructed the children of Israel to be ready to fight in God's name. Yet, when the time came, most turned away and refused to fight. Allah knows all and knew those who refused his commands and those who truly followed His path.

To Qabda this passage explained why so many Muslims, even Shiite Muslims, refused to heed the call to fight the infidels. They justified their cowardice by claiming the Ayatollah was not a true prophet and accusing his followers of being fanatics, but Qabda believed these were only weaklings' excuses for lack of faith and courage. The Arab nations in the gulf had become fat and greedy, corrupted by the wealth created by oil trade with the Christian nations of the west. They were not true Muslims, Qabda believed. They had betrayed Islam for the sake of profit.

The Koran also stated that God would not support people who were believers but then turned against Islam and became disbelievers. Qabda felt certain that particular verse had been written about nations like Iraq, Kuwait, Oman and all the rest. Only Iran and the Ayatollah's regime dared to heed "Allah's call to fight." Only they and those few Shiite believers who followed them would find paradise on the day of judgment.

Qabda thought of these things while he sat on his knees on his prayer rug, his face turned toward Mecca as he waited for the sun to rise above the mountain peaks that surrounded his secret base. He did not doubt that he was right. The Koran stated that a true believer's battle would be backed by five thousand angels. This, he believed, was why the Ayatollah had successfully seized control of Iran after the fall of the Shah, and why he had already come so far with the Purple Warriors of Resistance.

Qabda had once been Honsi Najaf, son of a wealthy Shiite scholar who had been an adviser to King Faisal of Iraq and later to his son and successor, King Ghazi. However, after Ghazi died in a car accident, Honsi's father lost his position with the royal family in Iraq when Ghazi's three-year-old son inherited the throne. Sunni Muslim overseers did not want a Shiite feeding "misinformation" about Islam to the impressionable boy-king.

However, Honsi's father was still respected and prosperous, an educated and honorable man in the Baghdad community. Honsi had the advantages of an upper-class education and might have followed in his father's footsteps if fate had been less cruel. In 1958, the young king and his uncle were assassinated. The military junta led by Abdul Karem Kassim suddenly took over Iraq. Honsi's father was arrested and sent to prison because he had formerly been an adviser to the king. The fact he had been removed from his office nearly twenty years earlier meant little to the soldiers. None of them intended to listen to the "heretic bleating of a Shiite goat."

Honsi was only eleven years old when his father was taken away. His family was forced to leave Baghdad due to the persecution that followed. He saw his mother grow weaker and lose any desire to live. He saw his older sister stoned to death because some Sunni merchant accused her of being a prostitute. Honsi remembered the night his younger brother was dying of an infection and was unable to get medical assistance from the local Sunni population or the American Christian missionaries who had erected a church near Mosul.

"You must come to accept Jesus Christ as your savior, my son," the American clergyman insisted. "If you do not denounce the false teachings of Mohammad and the hated book of the Koran, there is little point in administering to the ills of your brother. You cannot be physically sound when you are spiritually crippled, my son."

To denounce Islam was against everything his father had taught him. Honsi could not betray his beloved parents to satisfy the foreigner and his Christian mission. As a Shiite Muslim, Honsi had been taught that Jesus was not the Son of God but an honored prophet of Allah. The Koran taught that Jesus was not of divine birth, had not been crucified and did not die to be Honsi's savior or anyone else's. Why should he denounce his father's religion for these Christians? What made their Bible more valid than his Koran?

Perhaps if the missionaries had shown some "Christian charity," they would not have taught young Honsi Najaf to hate Christians and Americans with the same passion he already felt toward the Sunni Muslims. Instead the overzealous clergy at the missionary church had attempted to blackmail Honsi into accepting Christianity in order to save his brother's life. Since the Najaf family had little left except their faith, Honsi refused and sat up with his brother until dawn and buried him the following morning.

Heartbroken and defeated, his mother no longer cared about living from one day to the next. She did not want to see her only remaining child, Honsi, the older of her sons, die before her. She seldom ate or slept in the last days. Weak and welcoming death, she contracted a serious case of pneumonia and died less than a month after Honsi had placed his brother into the ground.

Alone, armed with nothing but his intelligence and fierce religious dedication, Honsi swore that he would one day make the infidels—Christian and Muslim alike—pay for what they had done to his family. If Allah saw fit for him to survive, he would take it as a sign that his desire for vengeance was in fact a righteous cause, approved of by the only true God. The bitter youth began to travel on foot to the southern portion of Iraq and eventually crossed the border to Kuwait.

He learned to fight with his hands, feet and knives. Afraid to use his family name because of past persecution, he called himself "Qabda"—the Fist. Many a battered opponent could testify that this chosen name suited the tough young man. Qabda found work where he could and lived on scraps of others' garbage when he could not. He took pride in the fact that he never begged or stole, regardless of how his belly ached with hunger.

Eventually he established a small group of followers, outcasts like himself who all felt persecuted because of their Shiite creed. Many of them were suffering from delusions, and some were opium addicts or petty criminals who resorted to self-pity rather than to face their own shortcomings. Qabda would not allow his friends to touch drugs, and he either reformed the addicts and criminals or drove them away with his fiery zeal. Those who stayed came to regard him as their guide and spiritual protector. To them, he was a great holy man and a prophet in his own right.

For nearly three decades, Qabda's cult grew very slowly. However, the Islamic jihad—first by the Palestinian groups and then by the Ayatollah in Iran—steadily increased the number of new radical Shiite fanatics who entered his fold. Finally Qabda was prepared to take action against the infidels. He had waited until Allah showed him how. First he needed weapons. A contact within Iran supplied him with part of what he needed, and others inside Iraq's army supplied most of the rest. Weapons reported lost on the battlefield of the Iran-Iraq conflict found their way to Qabda's terrorist cult. He also acquired weapons through black market arms dealers. Weapons were not difficult to get in the Middle East if one knew the right people and had enough money to purchase them.

When the Ayatollah's forces tried to attack American vessels with small, swift "suicide boats," Qabda saw the flaw in the tactic and realized how his private army of zealots could effectively join the holy war. The small boats were useless against the infidels from the United States. Their ships were too well armed, too thickly armored and equipped with modern devices to detect such attacks. The attacks had to come from a source the Americans would not expect and could not be certain of guarding against. From the ranks of the Arabs the United States regarded as allies.

Qabda had planned his missions with care. For the past three years he had been assigning his followers to jobs that would allow them to be in position to launch the attacks against the American devils. If the plan worked to its ultimate degree, the United States would turn against Kuwait, Oman, the United Arab Emirates and all the rest. Qabda assumed somewhat naively that the other Western nations would refuse to back the predominantly Sunni Muslim gulf countries if the United States withdrew support.

Without the help of America or Europe, Qabda felt certain Iran would defeat not only Iraq, but eventually all the countries of the Middle East. In the end, Islam would be the only religion in the entire world, or every single true Shiite

Muslim would die a martyr to God. It would be a victory either way, Qabda thought and looked up in surprise. The night had flown by while he was consumed by his plans.

The man stationed at the minaret to the covert mosque began calling the faithful to morning prayer as the sun announced the new day. Qabda placed his head to the prayer rug and chanted his praise to Allah, then he emerged from his small tent. The men stationed at the base stood in formation, righteous soldiers all eager to fight and sacrifice for their divine cause.

"No sight can better stir the heart of a Shiite commander than to stand before the flower of Islamic manhood," Qabda declared as he addressed his troops. "I have no wife or sons, yet I know the pride of a father when I look out at you."

Qabda watched their faces beam with pride and their chests expand like columns of peacocks. His praise may have sounded insincere, yet whatever his flaws might be, Qabda was a sincere man and his followers knew this. Their commander never said anything that he did not honestly believe to be the truth.

"If I had any doubts that any of you are less than true believers," Qabda continued, pacing before his men, "I would grieve that any of my sons might face the terrible harsh judgment of those who walk with Satan. The Koran tells us Satan promises and deceives. All who follow the Evil One will inherit Gehenna, the fiery pit of eternity.

Qabda raised his arms and stared up at the morning sky with a broad smile on his face. The others began to grin in response to their leader. They did not know what pleased him, but simply seeing Qabda smile made them feel good. It was as if he controlled their emotions and thoughts with his every action.

"But the death of a Shiite martyr is a reason to rejoice," Qabda declared cheerfully. "When the angel of death comes for you, it shall be to deliver you to Allah in paradise. We shall all be together in the next world."

Qabda lowered his arms. His Purple Warriors stared at their leader's gaunt, severe-looking features beneath the familiar purple turban.

"More of our brothers will soon give up their lives to martyrdom for Allah and the jihad," Qabda said in a solemn voice. "Let us pray that their mission will be successful and they will pass from this world to the next with a minimum of pain and suffering. May Allah give them strength to endure whatever ordeals necessary to accomplish their goals."

The congregation bowed their heads in unison.

"And may God grant us strength and courage as well," Qabda added. "The time is coming when all of us will have to make our final sacrifice for the jihad. We may feel fear, but we must overcome it with faith. We need not fear death unless we fail to believe in Allah and the Koran. Unless we fail as good Shiites to do His bidding and assist the prophet in Iran in his war against the infidels. The Koran tells us to fight for our religion, and the Ayatollah has struck at the true enemies of our faith. He has condemned the Communists of the Soviet Union. Those godless atheist Russians have meddled in the governments of Iraq, South Yemen, Syria and Libya. They are not Muslims and they do not fight for Islam. Know that they are infidels and our enemies."

Qabda waved an arm in a massive gesture as he continued, "The Ayatollah has condemned the Jews in Israel. Those Zionist butchers who stole Palestine from our Arab brothers. They are of a false creed and are also our enemies. The Christians, too, are Satan's spawn. They have twisted the teachings of Jesus, ignored the teachings of Mohammad and followed a false faith instead of Islam. They have chosen their Bible stories of distortions instead of the true word of God in the Koran. They have sealed their fate and go blindly into the gates of hell.

"Perhaps worst of all," Qabda said, shaking his head, "are the Sunni Muslims, who still claim to believe in Islam, yet they fight against us in Iraq, Kuwait, Saudi Arabia and elsewhere. They have become like the Christians of the West. Like the Americans who supported the Shah of Iran and his oppression of the Muslim faith. They have no religion except the worship of wealth. They are all capitalist versions of the Communists who at least admit they have no god!''

Qabda pointed at his men and said in a loud, firm voice, ''When the people of Moses bowed before the calf of gold, the Koran tells us Allah said it would be better for them to turn to Him and slay one another than to live with such blasphemy on their souls. The Christians are already misled, but for a Muslim this is truly outrageous that any who still considers himself a true follower would worship a golden calf—an oil well or an American dollar bill.''

The congregation seemed to grow angry at the thought of Muslims betraying their religion due to greed. None of them considered the fact that Iran also sold oil to West European countries. None of them thought for a moment and wondered why the holy Ayatollah lived in a palace in Tehran while many Shiites in that country slept in the streets. None appreciated the great social programs for the people of the Arab countries Qabda condemned, or the high standard of living and efforts to educate their population. Iranian achievements in this regard were practically nil, and more than half the people of Iran were unable to read the Koran, which Qabda claimed all Muslims should live by.

The Purple Warriors of Righteousness did not think of such matters because their minds were fixed on the goals of martyrdom and destruction. They had found a god that was not in the Koran, yet they worshipped it with a zeal as powerful as any prophet or saint. They had become followers of a nameless god of death and hatred. Their leader, for all his claims of purity and condemnation of the weakness of others, had become a prophet of a terrible religion of violence. For terror and fear can mean power, and power, not wealth, is the most intoxicating corruption of all.

"All the enemies of God shall feel our fury," Qabda vowed, talking more to himself than his men. He looked at their faces, yet he saw heartless Sunni Muslims and Christian missionaries of his youth in Iraq. "We know our cause is just, and the infidels will suffer the pains of Allah's sword of final judgment. Before this month ends, the Persian Gulf will be bathed in fires of righteousness and revenge!"

9

Ali Kamel was a senior employee at the Shakush Chemical Plant, located near the Manaqish oil fields in the southwest region of Kuwait. A trusted veteran, praised for his years of loyalty and devotion to work, Kamel had been promoted to supervisor of an entire section of the plant. The Shakush Chemical Company considered the forty-three-year-old native-born Kuwaiti citizen to be one of its best people.

Kamel had been assigned many duties at the plant and entrusted with numerous responsibilities. He supervised the processing of certain petroleum-based chemical products, organized schedules for personnel in his section and assigned work to a number of truck drivers for transporting tankers of chemicals throughout Kuwait. No one suspected that Kamel had chosen members of the Purple Warriors of Righteousness to drive these trucks in order to transport weapons, money and assorted equipment to other members of the terrorist cult. Nor did anyone suspect that one vehicle contained four canisters of cyanide gas.

Since Ali Kamel had supposedly renounced the Shiite faith of his deceased parents and became a Sunni Muslim, he seemed an extremely unlikely suspect for involvement in terrorist activity in Kuwait. In fact, Kamel was well-known for his vocal criticism of Shiites and had been warned by his employers to curb his outspokenness to prevent offending any co-workers who did not share his beliefs.

However, Phoenix Force had learned the truth about Ali Kamel after questioning their captive terrorist under the in-

fluence of scopolamine. Kamel was the section leader of the
Purple Warriors of Righteousness terrorists in Kuwait, personally selected and appointed to his duties by the mysterious Qabda. The commando unit also knew that Kamel
sometimes arranged covert meetings for the men under his
command. They congregated at the Shakush Plant, in the
section the company had assigned to his supervision.
Shakush knew that Kamel and several of his co-workers
occasionally spent Friday afternoons at the plant, which was
very unusual because Friday was the Islamic day of worship, but the employers praised Kamel's devotion to his
work. Little did they know that Kamel was using their
property for a conspiracy against Kuwait and numerous
other nations in the name of the jihad.

Such a meeting was scheduled to take place that morning
even as the five men of Phoenix Force approached the site
beneath the pale dawn sky. Ahmed, Mohammad and half a
dozen Kuwaiti paratroopers accompanied the group of ul-
traprofessional foreigners. The troopers had been trained in
antiterrorist commando tactics, tutored by instructors from
the British SAS and the American Special Forces or Rang-
ers. Two of the men had actually completed training courses
with the Green Berets in the United States, and one was a
veteran of Special Air Service instruction in Great Britain.
All six Arab commandos spoke English in addition to their
skills in weapons and tactics.

They approached the Shakush Plant in two small one-ton
trailor-style trucks, bright yellow with the company logo on
the side of each vehicle. The trucks were highly visible as
they traveled the desert road toward the plant. Any attempt
to approach the site in broad daylight in a stealthful manner would have been very difficult and time-consuming.
Time was not in the favor of Phoenix Force and their Kuwaiti allies.

If Kamel had assembled the other Purple Warrior terrorists in his section of the plant, he would soon learn several
members of the group were absent. More likely than not,

other less impetuous sleeper agents had been present at the docks when their comrades unsuccessfully attacked Mc-Carter, Encizo and Mohammad. Even if no one had first-hand information about the fate of the missing terrorists, Kamel would quickly suspect something had happened to them, because all the absentees had jobs at the same port. When the terrorists realized they were in jeopardy, they would certainly scatter and seek new havens elsewhere.

"I wish we could have come up with a less risky plan of action," Ahmed confessed as he rode in the back of the lead vehicle with Katz, Encizo and James. "We can't even be certain how many opponents we'll have to face, or how well armed they might be."

"They'll outnumber us," Calvin James said with a fatal-istic shrug, "but that's not the main concern, Ahmed. Those bastards may be sitting on enough cyanide gas to kill hundreds of people. If they let that stuff loose, we're all as good as dead, and so is anyone with at least five kilometers of this area, depending on how strong the wind happens to be when they release the gas."

"And you say gas masks wouldn't do any good?" Ah-med inquired.

"Against cyanide?" James replied, shaking his head. "It'll seep through the skin. It's a very fast and deadly poi-son. Doesn't take much to kill ya. Need something like the protective suits worn by people who work around radia-tion. You know, the rubber gloves, boots, plastic fish tank on your head? We wouldn't be able to do our job dressed up in those getups. Besides, there's all those innocent civilians to consider. No way we could get adequate protection for all of them in time."

"We've been over this before," Katz commented as he slipped the strap to an Uzi submachine gun over his left shoulder. "This is the only way to handle the situation that gives us a chance to protect the surrounding occupants and capture the terrorists. I should say 'hopefully' capture some of the terrorists. Since these fellows are suicidal, that might not be easy."

"*They're* suicidal?" Ahmed said with a nervous smile. "I wonder if we aren't inviting Allah to claim our souls by charging into this lions' den without knowing the odds. There are only thirteen of us. That terrorist you interrogated said sometimes there are more than fifty Shiite fanatics at these meetings. Five to one isn't good odds."

"Thirteen to fifty?" Encizo chuckled softly. "That's only three-point-nine to one. We've had far worse odds than that."

"That's not much comfort, my friend," Ahmed confessed with a frown. "I wish we could have gotten more men for this action."

"The time factor was against that," Katz replied. "Besides, a large force would attract too much attention. These trucks aren't big enough to carry more men than what we've got. I agree this isn't an ideal situation, but under the circumstances, it's the best we can do."

"Well," James began as he peered out a vent at the plant. "I guess we'll know soon how well theory holds up in reality and whether or not this scheme will work. We're almost there."

The Shakush Plant was a huge complex that covered an area of more than one square kilometer. Enormous globular storage tanks and cylinder-shaped towers stood above the blocklike buildings within the high steel wire fence. Two uniformed security guards were posted by the front gate. They waited for the trucks to draw closer and come to a halt.

The vehicles stopped, and a guard emerged from his shack and walked to the first truck. The gate remained closed, and the second security man stayed behind the barrier. James noticed the guards seemed very serious about their job. Dressed in short-sleeve khaki shirts and light blue trousers, the sentries presented a professional paramilitary appearance with a glossy shine on their low-quarter footgear and the black brims of their service caps. Each guard carried a holstered pistol, handcuffs, walkie-talkie radio and batons on their belts.

The driver spoke briefly to the guard and sent him to the rear of the vehicle. He opened the back of the rig to stare inside with astonishment at the three Phoenix commandos and Ahmed. The four men were dressed in tan desert fatigue uniforms, sand-colored berets and paratrooper boots. They carried submachine guns, except for James who held a M-16 assault rifle. Each man wore a pistol in shoulder leather and plenty of ammo pouches on their web belts.

The guard started to reach for his side arm. Ahmed said something low in Arabic and held out a hand with SIS credentials. The guard left his pistol in leather and climbed into the back of the truck. Encizo and James listened to Ahmed and Katz explain the situation to the security man. The Cuban warrior and the black badass from Chicago did not understand Arabic, but they noticed the guard nodded his head as a sign of cooperation.

The guard climbed from the truck and headed back to the shack. He spoke briefly with the other security man. James watched them from the vent peephole. He tensed as he saw one guard pick up a telephone receiver.

"One of them is calling somebody," James said tersely to the others.

"He's expected to," Katz assured his partner. "We instructed him to call the president of the Shakush Corporation to confirm this 'special delivery of chemical compounds' complete with order number. That's to let the security personnel know we're here on legitimate business with authorization from the Kuwaiti state in cooperation with the Shakush Company."

"The guard is to ask about the false delivery of chemicals as a cover, just in case the terrorists have a phone tap on the guard's line," Ahmed explained. He realized as soon as he said it that professionals like his mysterious companions would already understand the reason for the charade.

"Sure you can trust these guards?" Encizo asked. "One or more of them could be in league with the terrorists."

"Not among the men stationed here today," Ahmed assured him. "All the guards who work on Fridays are Christians. They've been with the firm for years, and their supervisor vouches for everyone of them."

"There are eight guards posted here," Katz stated as he pulled a watch from his shirt pocket and checked the time. They were running two minutes behind schedule, but the plan did not depend on precision timing until they got inside the plant. "As soon as they clear out, we start."

Encizo and James nodded in unison. They were ready for action. The Cuban carried a Heckler & Koch MP5 submachine gun in addition to his H&K P9S and Cold Steel Tanto. The subgun was chambered for 9 mm parabellum, same as the pistol. James's M-16 was loaded with an extended 40-round banana-shaped magazine with an M-203 grenade launcher on the underside of the barrel. He carried a Beretta 92-F 9 mm pistol in shoulder leather under his left arm and a Jet Aer G-96 fighting dagger sheathed under the right.

Katzenelenbogen was armed with his Uzi submachine gun and a SIG-Sauer 9 mm pistol in a shoulder holster under his right arm. The three-prong prosthesis jutted from the right sleeve like the steel talons of a mechanical eagle. All three men also carried spare magazines for their weapons and several tear gas and concussion grenades. Each wore a canvas case on his belt, which contained an M-17 protective mask. As James had stated earlier, gas masks would not protect them if the terrorists released cyanide gas, but the M-17s would shield them from the effects of tear gas.

Ahmed was armed with a British Sterling submachine gun and a 9 mm Browning pistol. The Kuwaiti SIS agent was trained in the use of weapons, but lacked the extensive experience and exceptional skill of the Phoenix Force commandos. Ahmed did not lie to himself about his ability. He realized he was basically a desk jockey, not a combat expert. Nonetheless, he was not without training and experience, and he wanted to participate even if it meant he would be low man on the figurative totem pole. Ahmed had agreed to follow orders from the Phoenix pros.

Brackman, the CIA agent, had also volunteered to join in the raid, but he had been forced to admit he had never fired a weapon except at a firing range and had practically no real combat training or experience beyond fistfights as a kid. Brackman had gone into the Company directly from college and did not even have the Basic Combat Training that an army PFC had. It was a popular misconception that "spies and secret agents" were all experts with every conceivable weapon and half a dozen martial arts. In reality, most intelligence personnel were intellectuals, more adept with decoding machines and computer terminals than firearms and close-quarters combat.

Phoenix Force had convinced Brackman that he could better assist their mission by staying away from the battlefield. They had reservations about Ahmed, but had reluctantly agreed to let him participate because the Kuwaiti agent helped them get the cooperation of the Arab paratroopers who would have been less eager to follow orders from foreigners than a fellow countryman. Ahmed had also helped them put the plan of action together...not that it was a complicated or elaborate strategy.

They waited for the gate to roll open. The trucks drove across the threshold while the eight security guards hurried from the plant premises. The two vehicles with Phoenix Force and their allies had entered the Shakush Plant. The showdown with the terrorists was about to begin.

ALI KAMEL LISTENED GRIMLY as fellow members of the Purple Warriors of Righteousness reported the news about the gun battle at the port, which occurred less than twelve hours before the terrorists assembled at the plant leader's section at the plant. Kamel struggled to conceal his anger and keep his features calm while two comrades related how several of the sleeper agents had overreacted when the authorities approached them for questioning. The result had been that the idiots were either killed or captured. The informers were not certain if any of their friends at the pier had been taken alive.

"We'll have to assume the worst," Kamel announced through clenched teeth. "It is possible one or more of our brothers has been captured and forced to tell the Sunni traitors and the CIA infidels about us."

"Never!" a zealous young fanatic shouted. "We are all true Shiite crusaders! Everyone of us would sooner be torn apart by red-hot pliers than tell the infidels anything! The worse tortures of this earth are nothing compared to the eternal agonies of the damned in hell. No brother would betray the cause and condemn himself to such harsh judgment by Allah Himself!"

The crowd erupted into cheers and chanting. Forty-two voices sang out the glories of their cause and repeated the slogans of their dogma. Several waved weapons in their fists. Most held pistols, a few brandished rifles and some waved knife blades. Two extremists produced flails with chains to lash themselves.

Kamel looked on grimly and wished he could cut out the tongues of every man in the storage room. For the first time, he saw that the great weakness of the Purple Warriors of Righteousness was the same fiery philosophy and blind devotion that gave it strength. They all believed they were fighting God's holy war, and that meant God would personally protect them and give them strength to endure any hardship. Kamel waved his hands to urge for silence and quickly considered how to best address the fanatics under his command.

"My brothers," Kamel began. "I do not doubt the strength or the faith of any Shiite warrior, but the enemy will not employ crude tactics of physical torture to extract information. They have drugs which can make them talk..."

"No drug can withstand the power of God!" a zealot called out. "Allah will give them the strength of thousands of angels to endure whatever ordeal those swine put them through. They shall hold out until death and die as great Shiite martyrs!''

The remark triggered another wave of cheers and chanting. More fanatics began flogging themselves with chains. Kamel suddenly felt as if he were the keeper of a lunatic asylum. The eagerness of the cult members to become martyrs for Shiitism and the jihad had probably prompted those morons to attack the authorities at the harbor. They must have seen an opportunity to die fighting in the holy war against infidels. So they jumped at a chance to hop aboard the escalator to paradise, even if it jeopardized the entire Purple Warrior operation.

Kamel had never expected to find himself faced with such a problem. Damn Qabda and his unbending creed! Damn the Ayatollah and the never-ending praise of martyrdom for the jihad! Kamel could not tell them that God would not stop the infidels from using truth serum any more than divine action would prevent their enemies from blasting Iranian aircraft out of the sky or blowing their boats to bits. Allah had not given the hijackers any special powers to win against the Kuwaiti royal family so the Sheikh would give in and release Shiite prisoners previously convicted of terrorism. Allah had not steered American missiles off course to prevent them from blowing up Iranian oil derricks or stopped Iraqi tanks from driving back the Ayatollah's army to recapture Iraqi territory.

Yet if Kamel tried to explain any of this, his followers— Qabda's followers—would certainly question his courage and faith. As Kamel watched more of them whip themselves with chains and roll their heads in a dazed, mindless trance, he realized his own men might turn on him like starved jackals on a wounded goat if he said the wrong thing to the congregation.

A terrible thought struck Kamel like a thunderbolt from the sky. What if the jihad was a farce? What if the Ayatollah was not a modern-day Islamic prophet and Qabda was just a raving fanatic who had helped dupe them into a conflict that was not the will of Allah? What if all those Shiite martyrs had died for nothing or, worse yet, for a false crusade conceived by liars and extremists? The sudden doubts twisted inside Kamel's stomach like a vicious knife blade.

"We must not jeopardize our mission, my brothers," Kamel announced, choosing his words with care. "While we serve Allah's will on earth and fight His sacred battles, we are still men, and none of us is perfect. The enemy may indeed be able to get information from our captured comrades, and we must prepare for this circumstance if we are to remain at large in order to carry out the jihad."

"Qabda told us to wait until our time came to strike against the infidels," a bearded youth declared as he gestured with a Russian pistol held overhead. "He told us to wait for our orders and act only when the time was right in order to serve the will of Allah to the best of our ability!"

The crowd uttered confused remarks as if uncertain what would now be the proper choice of action. Kamel saw his opportunity to try to get control of the congregation.

"Martyrdom in the name of God is righteous," Kamel stated, gazing at the shining faces of his followers. They were desperate for an answer that accorded with their extremist Shiite creed, and Kamel hoped to give it to them. "But martyrdom for the sake of personal glory is meaningless. Let us leave now, scatter to places of safety and wait for the time to resume the fight."

"Ali Kamel!" an aide interrupted the speech and waved one arm urgently to get the commander's attention. He held a two-way radio in his other hand. "I have just received word that two vehicles have entered the plant. Company trucks, small, painted yellow and bearing the Shakush markings. The vehicles are headed toward this section of the plant even as we speak."

"There should be no deliveries or pickups of chemicals today," Kamel said with a frown. "Not on Friday, and not from my section. It is very strange and disturbing: I would have been informed of anything unusual, at any rate."

"Stranger still," the aide continued, "Abdul says he also saw the security guards file out of the front gate as the trucks entered. Something is definitely wrong, I fear."

"Only two trucks?" Kamel asked thoughtfully. "Those small company trucks aren't large enough to transport a large attack force. Abdul did not see any other vehicles beyond the fence?"

"No," the aide confirmed. "Perhaps there is only a small strike team inside the trucks because the enemy has underestimated our number. Or they may be perfectly innocent company vehicles."

"Perhaps," Kamel replied, uncertain how to handle the unexpected situation. It certainly did not sound like a genuine attack, yet the coincidence was too great to ignore. "We'd better prepare for trouble. Get your weapons ready, my brothers."

The crowd responded with enthusiasm. They raised their weapons and chanted their devotion to God and their willingness to fight to the last man for the jihad. Kamel felt less thrilled about the possible confrontation than his congregation as he headed for his small office cubicle and marched behind the desk. He opened a drawer and removed a 9 mm Spanish Star automatic pistol. Kamel stuck the gun into his belt at the small of his back and rejoined the others.

"I want some of you men on the catwalk stationed by the windows," Kamel instructed. "Others get behind the drum at the west wing. That will provide cover if we have a fight. Those of you who work here in my section help people get into position. We'll also need a few men in the motor pool. The trucks will offer cover in a firefight and, if there's no other option, we can detonate the warheads to the canisters in the tanker rig."

"The cyanide?" a zealot inquired with a lunatic smile on his sweat-sheened features.

"We'll release the gas if we must," Kamel confirmed with a grim nod. He wondered if these eager young extremists really believed dying was so wonderful. It did not have much appeal to Kamel at that moment. "Hurry, my brothers. We must be ready by the time those trucks arrive."

10

One yellow truck headed across the paved interior of the plant and weaved between buildings and silos. Abdul and another lookout, posted at the top of a cylinder-shaped storage tower, watched the vehicle through binoculars. The two Purple Warrior sentries were puzzled by the truck. It seemed to be wandering aimlessly around the compound. The other vehicle had apparently parked in a different section of the plant, somewhere out of view of the lookouts.

Neither man glanced down at the ladder which extended from the ground to the summit of the tower. David Mc-Carter had silently climbed halfway up the ladder. The British commando wore desert fatigues and paratrooper boots, like the other members of the raiding party. His left hand was empty to grab the rungs, but the right fist held a Barnett Commando crossbow. A modern version of an ancient weapon, the Barnett's skeletal frame was sturdy and lightweight, with a cocking lever to allow the crossbow to be rapidly ready to fire. It was ready at that moment, bowstring cocked and a bolt set in the groove. A telescopic sight was mounted on the Barnett, but McCarter wanted to get as close as possible before he used the weapon. There was too much at stake, too many lives in danger, to take any chance of missing the target.

McCarter also carried a 9 mm KG-99 machine pistol, which hung from a sling over his right shoulder, and the Browning Hi-Power in shoulder leather under his left arm. In addition he carried an assortment of grenades, ammo pouches, and a quiver for the crossbow bolts hung on one hip and an M-17 case on the other. He did not like carrying so much gear into combat, but it was all necessary for the moment.

Moving quickly and quietly while burdened with so much equipment was no small feat. Probably the Briton would have been spotted by the terrorist lookouts if it were not for the wandering truck drawing their attention. McCarter, Gary Manning, Mohammad and three Kuwaiti paratroopers had parked the other vehicle out of sight and crept toward Kamel's work section while the first truck continued to roll all over the plant like a confused rat in an unfamiliar maze.

They had located the sentries on the tower. McCarter elected to take the tower, while the others backed him up and scanned the area for any more opponents who might be stationed in the immediate area. McCarter had managed to reach the tower and scale most of the ladder toward the top without being noticed by the enemy, but the closer he got the more likely that one of the terrorists would glimpse movement below.

Abdul lowered his binoculars and frowned. He sensed something was wrong, but he could not comprehend what it was. The truck did not seem to be getting closer. The driver's behavior did not seem to make any sense. Even if the man behind the wheel could not find the section he wanted, the security guards must have told him there were people working in Kamel's portion of the plant. If nothing else, the driver ought to have enough sense to turn around and find the other vehicle which had parked somewhere in the Shakush Plant.

Suddenly Abdul noticed something move along the ladder. He gathered up his AK-47 assault rifle and leaned over the handrail for a better look. The terrorist stared down at McCarter as the Briton leaned back, his left fist clenching a rung and both feet firmly planted on another step. The Barnett Commando rose in a single, swift motion. The butt stock found McCarter's shoulder, and the Briton snap-aimed and triggered the weapon before Abdul could even try to point his rifle at the Phoenix fighter.

The bolt hissed from the Barnett. The twang of the bowstring was no louder than Abdul's startled gasp of pain and fear. The steel tip of the crossbow projectile struck the terrorist in the chest, just under the sternum. It sank deep into Abdul's flesh and pierced his heart as the split fiberglass shaft leaked its contents on impact. Liquid cyanide oozed into Abdul's punctured organ and spread rapidly through his blood and nervous system.

Abdul fumbled with the Kalashnikov rifle, but already his hands refused to respond. His brain began to die even as he tried to concentrate on making his limbs move. His heart had already stopped, and his upper torso froze as if clenched in the iron fist of an invisible giant. Abdul fell backward against the dome of the tower. His corpse slid down the curved surface and sprawled across the platform. The unfired AK-47 was still in his fists as his body quivered in a weak convulsion.

The other lookout spun about and stared down at Abdul. As though he couldn't quite comprehend what had happened, he looked long at Abdul's open, lifeless eyes and the short black shaft of the crossbow bolt stuck in the dead man's chest like a feathered banner. Then, as understanding dawned, he quickly reached for the walkie-talkie and unslung his rifle, uncertain whether to report in to Kamel immediately or prepare to defend himself.

Suddenly none of that mattered to the terrorist lookout. The front of his skull caved in as a small, incredibly fast object crashed between his eyes. It sizzled into his brain, obliterated his thoughts and created a burst of terrible pain. The agony was mind-shattering, but it lasted only a fragment of a second. Then the sentry toppled over the handrail and plunged fifty feet to the pavement below. Bones cracked and splintered on impact, but the man had already been dead before he'd taken the swan dive from the tower.

"Remarkable shooting," Mohammad whispered, impressed by Gary Manning's marksmanship.

The Canadian Phoenix Force pro was crouched behind a scrap metal vat with the Kuwaiti officer. Manning held his FAL assault rifle in his fists. Smoke curled from the foot-long silencer attached to the barrel. A Bushnell telescopic sight was mounted to Manning's weapon of choice. He was a superb rifleman and sniper. Manning's skill with a rifle was rooted in his childhood as a hunter in his native Canada. His ability as a sniper was first developed during a tour of duty as a "special observer" in Vietnam, attached to the Special Forces. Manning's years with Phoenix Force had perfected his skills.

"I've never seen anyone fire a silenced weapon with such accuracy," Mohammad added, staring at Manning as if he had just finished turning water into wine. "I've never been able to hit anything with a silencer blocking the front sight."

"That's why we brought personal weapons from the States instead of picking up equipment after we arrived in Kuwait," Manning explained as he slid the rifle sling onto his shoulder. "We're familiar with how each particular weapon handles recoil, pulls right, left, up or down, and how a silencer changes the trajectory of bullets—either semi- or full-auto. The scope on this FAL is for use with the silencer. It compensates for the change in the pattern of the projectiles."

"It seems to work well enough," Mohammad remarked and gripped his Heckler & Koch submachine gun. Like Encizo, the Kuwaiti officer favored the MP5. "I hope the others are in position."

"If they aren't, we may find ourselves in the middle of a giant economy-size gas chamber," the Canadian replied.

"What a cheerful thought," Mohammad muttered.

"We're not given cheerful assignments," Manning commented as he watched McCarter wave from the tower to signal that all the terrorist lookouts there had been taken out and that he had not spotted any more from the elevated vantage point.

YAKOV KATZENELENBOGEN had also seen the Briton's gesture and knew it meant that everything was going fairly well so far. Katz gestured with his steel hooks to signal Rafael Encizo and Calvin James to go forward. The Cuban took the point, MP5 subgun held ready. James and Katz followed, with Ahmed at the rear. They moved along a narrow pathway between the storage silos and the fence. They headed toward Kamel's section, alert to sentries or surveillance devices. Even booby traps were a possible hazard when dealing with fanatics like the Purple Warriors.

They heard voices as they drew closer. The jumbled combination of curt orders, excited shouts and methodical chanting revealed the general confusion among Kamel's group. Encizo silently approached the corner of the storage building. He raised the H&K chopper in one fist and placed his back against the wall as he slowly moved closer. The Cuban tensed when he saw shadows flicker on the pavement.

A man suddenly stepped around the corner—a young Arab with a clipped beard and hawk-bill nose. The terrorist carried a pistol in his fist, barrel pointed upward. Although his dark eyes had a wild look, he obviously had not expected to run into trouble. Encizo's left hand immediately struck out and slashed the hard edge into the youth's gut. The man doubled up with a startled groan, and Encizo quickly grabbed the terrorist's gun hand. The enemy's pistol was an American 1911A1 Colt, standard military issue, government .45 auto. Encizo jammed his thumb between the trigger and firing pin to prevent the terrorist from firing his weapon.

Encizo swung the MP5 in his other fist and slammed the barrel across his opponent's skull. The Arab moaned softly and squeezed the trigger of his Colt pistol, but the Colt did not fire. The Cuban responded by ramming a knee between his opponent's legs and whipped the H&K blaster across the youth's hard skull twice more. The terrorist's knees buckled and his body sagged. Encizo dragged the man along the wall and lowered him to the ground.

James shuffled past Encizo while the Cuban hastily bound the unconscious terrorist's hands behind his back. The black commando carefully peeked around the corner of the building, using only one eye to prevent exposing any more of his head and face than absolutely necessary. He saw men moving among the tanker trucks in the motor pool and a few headed toward stacks of barrels along the wall of the storage building near the entrance. Others probably lurked inside the bay area of another building across from the storage section. The wide metal sliding doors were closed, but a smaller door shut as a man with a rifle hurried away from it.

The black warrior turned to Encizo and Katz and pointed in the general direction of the motor pool. He pantomimed holding a steering wheel and turning it to let the others know about the vehicles. James indicated the direction of the barrels and gestured with his hands to cut a vertical oval-shape in the air. Finally he cocked his head toward the main building and moved his hands in a wide, rectangle pattern to suggest a large structure. Encizo and Katz nodded to confirm they understood.

Ahmed was not sure what was going on, but he waited for the Phoenix Force pros to tell him what to do. They exchanged understated gestures, communicating with their eyes and head movements more than hands. Ahmed was fascinated by this subtle, swift and silent understanding between the three commandos. It was almost a form of telepathy. The men of Phoenix Force had developed such an understanding of each other, knew one another so well, that they could communicate with little more than a look.

Katz cradled his Uzi in his right arm and held out his left hand to shove down air with the palm in a signal for Ahmed to stay put. The Arab nodded in reply. James and Encizo were ready to make their move. Katz nodded and used the hooks of his prosthesis to yank open the canvas case to the M-17 at his right hip. He removed the protective mask and slipped it onto his head. The others followed his example and donned their masks.

James leaned around the corner of the building with his M-16 braced on a hip. He triggered the M-203 attachment under the barrel. The grenade launcher belched harshly and the recoil rode back against James's hip with considerable force. The 40 mm grenade hurtled from the stubby barrel of the M-203 and rocketed into the motor pool. The projectile smashed into the side of the cab section of a tanker truck. It exploded on impact and a dense cloud of noxious tear gas spewed across the motor pool as dazed and coughing terrorists stumbled about half-blind in the green fog.

Encizo pulled the pin from a tear gas canister and hurled it a heartbeat after James triggered his M-203. The Cuban threw the explosive egg at the barrels where several terrorists were hidden. A second cloud of punishing gas erupted, and more of the fanatics staggered among their places of shelter, choking and spitting in the chemical mists.

''Rock 'n' roll!'' James exclaimed as he dashed forward, his M-16 pointing the way.

He charged in the direction of the motor pool, but he glanced about as he ran. A figure appeared at the door, a short-barreled submachine gun in his fists. James had just a brief look at the snarling young face of the Shiite zealot, at eyes ablaze with hatred. The gunman swung his weapon toward the black commando. James instinctively aimed his M 16 and triggered the automatic rifle as he ran.

Three 5.56 mm slugs ripped into the Arab's torso. The man's subgun blasted a wild burst of 9 mm rounds at James, but the Phoenix pro was a rapid and elusive target. The force of high velocity projectiles in his flesh also disturbed the gunman's aim, and the subgun bullets missed James by more than a foot. The terrorist shrieked, anger and frustration mixing with mortal agony in an unearthly sound. He toppled against the open door and slid to the pavement, blood seeping from the trio of bullet wounds in his chest. The heart beat weakly and erratically for the last time, and with a final shiver the eternal chill of death swept across the fallen fanatic.

James continued to race for the tanker trucks. A shape stumbled toward him, an unsteady figure among the green fog of tear gas. The terrorist pawed at his eyes with one hand and tried to aim a pistol with the other. James fired from the hip. The gunman's head snapped back from the impact of two bullets through the frontal bone of the skull. The terrorist tumbled to the ground as James scrambled for cover along the side of the nearest truck cab.

A salvo of submachine gun bullets raked and the grill-work on the front of the cab. Projectiles sparked, and James heard the whines of ricochets. He ducked low, his guts twisted with fear, yet already grateful that the shots had come from opponents who were not in position to get a clear claim at him. He heard more automatic fire and a scream. The voice did not sound like Encizo or Katz, but James had never heard either man scream. He hoped the voice belonged to one of the terrorists.

James resisted the urge to peer around the edge of the cab to see what had happened. There was nothing he could do to help his teammates at the moment, and he might stop an enemy bullet with his head if he stuck it out into plain view. James had to concentrate on the trucks. The cyanide canisters were supposedly inside one of the rigs. The poison gas was the most serious immediate threat and had to be dealt with before the Shiite extremists released the lethal cargo.

Moving cautiously, James searched for the source of the coughing, sputtering and puking at the rear of the trucks. He heard some wheezing and remarks in Arabic and wished he knew what the enemy had said. If nothing else, it may have been some sort of colorful profanity he could have filed away for future reference. Sometimes he exhausted all the profanity he knew in English and found himself using

French and Spanish expressions. One never knows when one might need a larger vocabulary for particularly frustrating events.

A choked-up young man appeared in view. Both hands over his eyes, the man had allowed his Skorpion machine-pistol to dangle from a shoulder strap. Virtually blinded by tear gas, he did not present an immediate threat. James did not intend to kill under such circumstances. He stepped forward and jabbed the muzzle of his M-16 into the young Arab's stomach. The terrorist's hands dropped from his face as he doubled up, mouth open in a throaty groan. James next swung a butt stroke to the face, then followed up with the barrel of the M-16 swooping in a fast arc for a hard chop across the side of the neck. He fell senseless to the pavement. James stepped around the unconscious youth and moved to the rear of the nearest truck. A hand suddenly reached around the corner of the tanker and seized the barrel of his rifle. A strong tug pulled James forward toward the knife in the opponent's hand. The long, curved blade of the *jambiya*—a traditional Arab fighting knife—slashed for James's throat.

The American released the front stock of his M-16, and he whipped his arm high in a karate block. His forearm caught the attacker under the wrist and drove the fist with the *jambiya* above his head. The knife blade cut a harmless stroke in the air, and James quickly seized the man's wrist. The knife man's face was less than an inch from the lenses of James's M-17 mask. The terrorist's eyes were watery, and mucous flowed from his nostrils, yet he managed to hold on to James's rifle barrel with one fist while he tried to make use of his knife.

As the black warrior struggled with the knife-wielding opponent, he noticed somebody else behind the blade man. The second terrorist had drawn a medium-sized pistol and tried to get a bead on James. Thanks to the effects of the tear gas, the pistol man's vision was blurred, and he was reluctant to open fire for fear of hitting his comrade. As if his situation was not bad enough, James also heard another terrorist being sick somewhere behind him in the billows of noxious fumes.

James suddenly stamped a boot heel into the knife artist's shin and followed with a hard stomp to the instep. The man groaned from the unexpected pain. James shoved the M-16 against his opponent to keep him off balance and swung the barrel at the one with the pistol. James triggered his assault rifle. A 3-round burst blasted a lethal salvo of searing metal into the torso of the pistol man. The terrorist cried out and fell to the ground, but the knife-wielder still held on to James's M-16, and he was bringing his *jambiya* closer to the left lens of James's protective mask.

Desperate situations require desperate actions. James released the frame of his M-16 and suddenly drove a heel-of-the-palm uppercut to the knife man's jaw. The terrorist's head snapped back from the impact. Still holding the wrist above the *jambiya* with his left hand, James seized his opponent's shirtfront. Movement just to his right warned James of another threat. The third terrorist had recovered somewhat and was about to hammer the stock of an AK-47 into the American warrior's skull.

James lashed out with a tae kwon do side kick and drove his boot into the new opponent's stomach. That move incapacitated the man, and the Phoenix pro turned sharply and hauled the knife man against his sickly comrade. James shoved hard to send both of them tumbling to the pavement. However, the knife artist still had the *jambiya* in one fist and the barrel of James's M-16 in the other. The other opponent was also armed with the AK-47, and he was already groping for the trigger.

James grabbed the butt of the Beretta pistol under his left arm and swiftly drew the piece. His thumb hit the safety catch as he pointed the pistol at the terrorist pair. It was very difficult to aim and fire accurately while wearing a protective mask with fogged lens, but James had done it during many a training operation with Phoenix Force between assignments. He did not hesitate and opened fire.

The first 9 mm parabellum plowed into the face of the man with the Russian assault rifle. The high-velocity slug smashed the terrorist's jawbone and shattered several teeth. James fired the Beretta again and pumped a second 115-grain bullet into the side of the other's neck. The parabellum severed the carotid artery and drilled into neck vertebrae. Bone splinters ripped into the man's windpipe, and he was dead within a quarter of a second.

James triggered two shots, rapid-fire, as the knife artist began to rise. Both rounds slammed into the terrorist's chest, and his heart burst apart. He folded up and joined his lifeless comrade. Alerted by a sixth sense, James spun about to face yet another terrorist who stood at the metal door at the rear of a tanker truck.

The fanatic swung a blue-black revolver at James, but the Phoenix pro was faster and wasn't suffering from the effects of tear gas fumes. He fired his Beretta twice and blasted one round through the attacker's rib cage and another upward through the solar plexus. The terrorist triggered his .38, and the bullet hissed inches from James's left shoulder. The heat and high-pitched shriek of the projectile slicing air near his ear made James's stomach knot, and a cold chill bolted up his spine. He fired a third parabellum into the gunman and punched a scarlet hole in the terrorist's forehead. The man fell lifeless from the truck and hit the ground like a slab of beef.

"I'm gonna tell Brognola I want a raise," James rasped inside the sweat-heated M-17 mask.

He rushed to the truck door and peered inside the tanker, his Beretta pistol at the ready. The great cylinder frame of the tanker was empty. James climbed down from the truck and headed for the next vehicle. The door of the second tanker stood open, but no enemy gunman was poised at the threshold. James approached cautiously, eased the barrel of his pistol around the edge of the metal doorway and peered inside.

Two terrorists knelt by a compartment at the nose of the interior of the tanker. They had opened a trapdoor to the compartment and removed four canisters, each roughly the size of a small fire extinguisher. One of the men held a canister in his hands while the other knotted a thick black cord and prepared to insert it into a block of pale yellow putty-like substance. The block, slightly smaller than a house brick, had been cut in half, and the guy began to press the black knotted rope into one section.

James realized what the man was doing. He had a block of C-3 plastic explosive and a length of prima-cord. The terrorist was about to detonate the explosives. The blast would be great enough to blow the tanker truck to pieces. The two Purple Warriors would then gain their longed-for martyrdom with a bang and not only release the cyanide from the canisters but spew it from the truck with the force of the powerful explosion.

"Screw you," James growled as he held the Beretta in both hands and aimed.

He squeezed the trigger. A 9 mm parabellum smashed into the side of the head of the terrorist demolitions man. The bullet struck under the temple, streaked through the brain and split open a gory exit wound. The explosives technician collapsed lifeless across the block of C-3 while his startled companion turned and glared at James.

He shouted something in angry Arabic and suddenly hurtled the canister he had been holding. James instinctively dropped his pistol and reached for the flying canister with both hands. His fingers touched the metal cylinder and his palms slapped around it firmly. He was not sure whether to sigh with relief or kick himself in the behind. The canister was loaded with cyanide gas, but it was unlikely the sturdy metal container would have ruptured if James had not caught it. He had acted on instinct and was left unarmed. Now he saw the remaining terrorist draw a Walther P-38 pistol from a hip holster.

James quickly lowered the canister to the floor of the tanker with his right hand while his left hand reached for the handle of the G-96 dagger in a sheath under his right arm. The knife cleared leather, and the canister safely touched the floor. The terrorist pointed his German autoloader at James and started to thumb off the safety catch. James gripped the tip of the Jet Aer, and simultaneously he let go of the handle. James's arm snapped forward and he released the knife blade. The dagger hurled toward the terrorist, somersaulted once in midair and struck the enemy gunman in the chest. James threw himself to the floor the instant the knife left his fingers. He heard the Walther pistol erupt, the report of the shot like a cannon in a tunnel within the confines of the tanker truck.

The whistle and whine of the 9 mm bullet ricocheting within the metal walls sounded like an angry hornet trapped in a tin can. James hugged the floor, afraid the slug might still crash into his flesh. The sound stopped, although James was not certain exactly when the noise ceased because the ringing in his ears was nearly deafening. His head throbbed painfully as he glanced up and stared at the terrorist gunman.

The man had fallen to his knees. The P-38 pistol lay on the floor next to him, apparently forgotten. Both his hands clutched the handle of the dagger. Three and a half inches of the double-edged steel blade was buried in the man's chest. James climbed to his feet. His head still ached and his legs were unsteady. The lenses of his M-17 mask were foggy from hard breathing and perspiration. James realized his hands were shaking slightly. It was the aftermath of the fear involved in such close encounters with death. He had been too busy concentrating on the task of survival, and acting or reacting to danger, for his body to respond in the normal manner to sheer terror. Now it had caught up with him.

"Son of a bitch," James rasped as he approached the wounded terrorist.

The man yanked on the knife handle with both hands. The blade came free from his flesh with a sickly, sucking sound. Blood flowed across the terrorist's shirtfront and he screamed in mortal agony as he dropped to all fours. James punched the dying man in the side of the head and knocked him unconscious. Under the circumstances, this crude sedative was the most humane thing he could do. James could not afford to take the time to administer first aid to a wounded enemy. Not when his fellow Phoenix Force commandos and their Kuwaiti allies were still in danger.

RAFAEL ENCIZO HOSED the barrels with 9 mm rounds from his MP5 and watched another Purple Warrior terrorist convulse from a trio of bullets to the chest. The others ducked behind the barrels for cover, too confused and physically weakened by tear gas to put up a decent fight.

"Ahmed!" Encizo shouted, H&K chopper braced against his hip with one hand, while with his other hand he reached for a grenade on his belt. "Keep them pinned down!"

The Kuwaiti SIS agent fired his subgun at the barrels. Sparks appeared on the metal kegs, and slugs whined off the barrels without striking the terrorists hidden behind them. Ahmed thought his efforts were a waste of ammunition, but he obeyed Encizo's instructions. While the Arab officer kept the enemy busy, Encizo yanked the pin from the concussion grenade and lobbed it behind the barrels.

The explosion bowled over half a dozen kegs and sent four terrorists hurtling into the open. Others lay sprawled on the ground, battered and bloodied by the blast. The men who crash-landed on the pavement were dazed or unconscious. Encizo figured Ahmed could cover them on his own and told the Kuwaiti agent to stay there while he dashed toward the main section of the building to help Katz.

The Phoenix Force commander had headed for the door next to the bay entrance. A terrorist had made the mistake of poking his head outside, and Katz had nearly decapitated him with a burst of Uzi rounds. The door was sprayed with blood, and the corpse was draped across the threshold as Katz jogged to the side of the building. The Israeli inserted a hook in the pin to a concussion grenade and yanked it free from the casing. He tossed it through the open doorway, stepped back and seized the Uzi's pistol grip and waited.

The concussion blast roared within the building. Encizo rushed to Katz's side. The Cuban quickly pulled the pin to a tear gas canister and lobbed it through the doorway as well. They allowed the fumes of noxious gas to pour into the interior of the building and tried to determine how to best assault the structure.

Three figures appeared at the edge of the building. Katz and Encizo pointed their weapons at the new arrivals, but held their fire when they saw the figures were dressed in desert fatigues and M-17 protective masks. The Phoenix pair recognized Gary Manning's build and the usual FAL assault rifle the Canadian carried. The size of one of his companions suggested it was probably Mohammad behind the mask. The third man was one of the Kuwaiti paratroopers.

"What have we got here?" Manning asked through the muffling rubber and plastic filters of the M-17.

"Washington is handling the enemy by the trucks," Katz replied, using James's cover name. "He may need help."

"Right," Encizo agreed with a nod. He pointed at the paratrooper. "Come with me, fella."

The soldier nodded and followed Encizo to the trucks in the motor pool. Encizo had volunteered for the job because he realized Manning's skills would be better used to help the others get inside the building.

"Okay," Katz continued. "We seem to have most of the enemy boxed inside here. Is the other side of the building covered?"

"Stark and four paratroopers have it taken care of," Manning replied. He reached for his small backpack as he spoke. "They've already lobbed some tear gas and concussion grenades through windows, but there isn't a door on that side and none of the windows are big enough to get through. This is the only way in or out."

"They'll be waiting for us," Mohammad said grimly.

"Let's not disappoint them," Gary Manning remarked as he slipped off his pack and opened the canvas flap.

The Canadian removed two small packets of white doughlike material, wrapped by electrical tape. He walked to the large sliding metal doors and pulled loose the ends of some of the tape around one packet. Manning placed it against the corrugated metal and pressed the tape so it would stick to the surface. He repeated the process with the second packet on the next door.

Katz led Mohammad away from the doors to find cover by the corner of the building. Manning finished preparing the charges and calmly stepped back. The Canadian demolitions expert had supreme confidence in his skills. He gathered up his FAL and jogged to the corner, certain that the explosives would not go off until he reached cover. His timing was indeed accurate.

The C-4 plastic explosives erupted with twin blasts that echoed into a single mighty roar. The doors burst loose and fell back inside the bay area within the building. The brick archways were barely scratched by the explosions. Manning was that precise in his use of demolitions and the exact amount needed for the job.

Manning and Katz dashed to the big gaps where the doors had been. The Canadian hurled a concussion grenade into the bay area while Katz fired a short volley of Uzi rounds just to discourage anyone inside from raising his head and taking potshots at the Phoenix pair.

The concussion blast rumbled within the bay section. The concrete floor was already littered with unconscious and dead Purple Warrior terrorists. Katz dashed across the threshold and fired a salvo of Uzi rounds at two large steel vats, from behind which at least one terrorist was starting to poke out his head.

Manning followed, covering his partner with the FAL rifle. A burst of automatic fire erupted from the catwalk above the bay. Bullets raked the concrete floor between Katz and Manning. The Israeli dived for cover behind a large cart loaded with several large tanks. Katz questioned how reliable the shelter would prove to be. The tanks were labeled in both English and Arabic. Both languages declared the contents to be liquid oxygen, highly flammable and apt to explode under the right conditions. If a bullet struck a single tank and pierced the metal skin . . .

Gary Manning scrambled to cover by the edge of the truck ramp. He swung his FAL toward the muzzle-flash at the catwalk. The Canadian spotted the terrorist gunman. A stocky Arab, armed with a French MAT submachine gun, leaned over the handrail of the catwalk. The triggerman was not alone. Manning briefly caught sight of two more terrorists on the narrow walkway thirty feet overhead. The other two fanatics appeared to have suffered more from the effects of the concussion and tear gas grenades than their buddy with the MAT subgun. One terrorist held on to the handrail and shook his head to try to clear it, and his companion pressed his palms over his ears, probably in agony from a ruptured eardrum. But both men were still armed and potentially life-threatening.

The Canadian dealt with the most serious threat first. He aimed the FAL rifle and squeezed the trigger. A trio of 7.62 mm slugs tore into the chest of the terrorist with the French chopper. The Purple Warrior extremist jerked violently from the impact of the high-velocity bullets. The MAT slipped from his grasp and the French subgun dropped to the floor below with a metallic clatter. The enemy gunman's body wilted to the walkway in a final surrender.

One of the other terrorists on the catwalk managed to regain enough composure to retaliate after his comrade dropped dead. He swung a Beretta M-12 subgun over the rail and trained the weapon on Manning's position. Automatic rifle erupted before Manning could shift the aim of his FAL rifle toward the new opponent. The Canadian gazed up at the terrorist and saw a trio of bullet holes tear a diagonal line across the gunman's chest. The Purple Warrior fell backward against the rail, then toppled over the top bar with a scream as he plunged to the unyielding concrete below.

Manning glanced over his shoulder and saw Mohammad with his H&K subgun raised toward the catwalk. Wisps of smoke curled from the barrel of the Kuwaiti officer's MP5. The Canadian turned his attention once again to the catwalk where a single terrorist opponent remained. The lone enemy was armed with a Chinese T-50 submachine gun. He held one hand over his ear and used the other to point his chattergun at Mohammad.

The Canadian's FAL and the Kuwaiti's H&K roared in unison. The terrorist was hit by half a dozen 9 mm and 7.62 mm rounds. His torso spewed blood from the numerous bullet holes as the impact spun his body around like a top. The T-50 subgun hurtled from his hands and he fell across the top bar of the handrail, his arms and head dangling limply over the side.

Another volley of automatic fire exploded from the metal vats. Manning ducked low as bullets raked the truck ramp near his position. The Canadian sucked in air with a nervous gasp as he felt the rush of projectile-heated air near his left cheek. Manning stayed low and crept to a new position farther along the ramp as the roar of automatic weapons continued.

He glimpsed violent movement where Mohammad had stood and turned to see the Kuwaiti agent collapse to the concrete. Mohammad had dropped his MP5 and clasped both hands to his M-17 protective mask. One of the plastic filters had popped loose from the mask and lay dented and punctured next to Mohammad's head. Fragments of clear Plexiglas also littered the floor. An enemy bullet must have hit one of the lenses, Manning realized as he watched Mohammad thrash about on the concrete. A crimson pool formed around the Arab agent's head as he ceased to struggle and surrendered to the final judgment of death.

Yakov Katzenelenbogen did not see Mohammad fall, but he spotted the enemy gunman by the metal vats as the fanatic fired on the Kuwaiti officer. Katz returned fire with his Uzi submachine gun and nailed the killer with a trio of 9 mm rounds in the upper chest and throat. The gunman's AK-47 dropped from his fingers as he staggered forward from his cover, blood gushing across his shirtfront. The terrorist's eyes bulged as he pawed at his bullet-ruptured throat. The mortally wounded man fell to his knees but still tried to crawl to safety.

Manning cut off the man's path with a burst of 7.62 mm roadblocks. The Canadian marksman blasted the wounded terrorist in the side of the head and exploded the man's skull like an eggshell hit by a sledgehammer. The hit man was out of the fight for good.

Randomly aimed gunfire snarled from the small cubicle office and rest room within the building. The tear gas canisters, tossed through windows by McCarter and the paratroopers at the other side of the building as well as by the assault team at the bay section, spewed blankets of dense choking fumes. The clouds of noxious gas effectively reduced visibility for both sides as the green fogs grew steadily thicker. Phoenix Force and their Kuwaiti allies still had the advantage of the protective masks which spared them the sickening effects of the fumes.

However, at least two terrorists who were holed up in the rest room had fashioned makeshift protective masks by using damp cloths to cover their noses and mouths. Their vision was still blurred, their eyes watered from the effects of the tear gas and the crude face masks did not prevent the fumes from causing some illness. Nonetheless they were faring better than the others.

A bullet whined against an oxygen tank on the cart Katz used for cover. The Israeli tensed when he realized a tank had been hit, but sighed with relief because the container had not exploded. The projectile was probably from a small-caliber handgun and merely grazed the thick metal tank, Katz guessed. He realized though that he could not count on his luck holding much longer.

Shapes appeared at the bay door entrance. The bug-eyed lens and rubber snouts of the M-17 masks revealed they were friendly forces. Katz recognized Calvin James and Rafael Encizo, despite the masks. Two Kuwaiti paratroopers accompanied the pair. One soldier cried out, his voice muffled by the mask, and suddenly fell to one knee. His Sterling subgun scraped along concrete as he clapped a palm to his bullet-punctured chest. The paratrooper slumped on his side and moaned softly while a scarlet stain slowly spread across the front of his fatigue shirt.

"Washington!" Katz shouted to James. "Take care of the cubicle! The rest of you cover me and keep the enemy at the loo busy!"

James realized why Katz had chosen him to handle the terrorists at the cubicle office. The black commando was armed with the M-203 launcher attached to his assault rifle. Using concussion grenades in an enclosed area would be risky for their people as well as the terrorists. James's M-203 was loaded with another 40 mm shell filled with tear gas. He aimed the weapon at the cubicle and triggered the launcher. The big round sailed into the glass panels of the office and exploded. Windows shattered from the force.

The thick billows of concentrated tear gas was too much for the men inside the office to endure. Men staggered from the cubicle. Only two carried weapons, and neither attempted to fire at the Phoenix commandos. James covered the group with his M-16, prepared to stop any attempted aggressions.

Manning and Encizo fired at the rest room door to drive the terrorists back. Splinters spit from the door and framework. The enemy retreated into the room, and Katz rushed for the loo, knees bent and head down as he ran. The Israeli kept low while Encizo and Manning fired high to prevent hitting Katz. The Phoenix commander reached the rest room, the Uzi braced across his prosthesis as he kicked open the door.

Katz tossed a grenade inside. It hit the tile floor and rolled near the feet of one of the startled terrorists. Katz saw three figures before he jumped away from the door. He had noticed one man was armed with a compact machine pistol, another had a handgun, but Katz had not seen what the third man carried. The Israeli assumed the guy was also packing heat.

Experience and a fundamental understanding of human nature told Katz how the enemy would react. They would naturally try to grab the grenade and either attempt to throw it back out the door, out a window or perhaps into a toilet bowl. They might attempt to kick it across the threshold instead, but the important factor was that the enemy would be busy trying to get rid of the grenade. Katz hoped they would be too busy to notice the pin had not been pulled from the grenade or to pay attention to the door for a moment or two.

Katz took a deep breath and dropped to one knee. He shoved the door open with the barrel of his Uzi and pointed the subgun at the terrorists inside the room. They were still scrambling for the grenade on the floor. Two of them bumped into each other as they reached for the egg-shaped explosive at the same time. The other terrorist turned to face Katz, a Tokarev-style pistol in his fist. Katz triggered the Uzi. A three-round burst pitched the gunman backward against a wall.

The other two Purple Warriors spun about to stare at Katz. The Israeli fired a long burst and sprayed both opponents with 9 mm slugs. The pair collapsed to the tiles, but Katz could not afford to take any chances with the terrorists. He hosed the fallen foes with another volley of Uzi rounds to make certain they offered no further threat.

Manning approached Katz, his FAL rifle slung on his shoulder. The Israeli knew that meant the battle was over.

Otherwise Manning would still have his assault weapon ready for action. The Canadian nodded his head as his face was still concealed by the M-17 mask.

"Got any live ones in there?" Manning inquired.

"Sorry," Katz replied with a shrug. "I don't think any of them felt like surrendering today. Any luck elsewhere?"

"A few," Manning confirmed. "Cal has a couple herded into a corner, and I'm told there are more outside. And some of these sleeping beasties might be alive, too. I'm not sure, but I think we may have been lucky enough to get Ali Kamel himself among the prisoners."

"Well," Katz replied. "Let's hope they can tell us something of value. Such as where we can find Qabda and the main base of the Purple Warriors of Righteousness before they launch another attack."

11

The explosion at the oil platform near the refinery erupted without warning off the coast of the United Arab Emirates. Oil technicians and engineers were hurled from the ball of fire in the center of the derrick. Flaming figures plunged into the Persian Gulf. The blaze rose into the afternoon sky, and the platform burned fiercely, as if hell had suddenly thrust a giant finger through the floor of the ocean to attack the derrick.

The unexpected destruction horrified onlookers. Arab and American personnel witnessed the explosion, helpless to do anything but watch their coworkers burn to death. Coastguardsmen boats immediately headed for the derrick, their fire hoses jetting water across the rig. It would take hours to put the fire out. Bodies were fished out of the sea; charred, dismembered and drenched in salt water and blood. The more fortunate victims were already dead. The others would not survive long enough to reach the hospital in Abu Dhabi.

It was impossible to investigate the derrick explosion until the fire was put out. More bodies, and mangled ghastly parts of bodies, waited inside the wreckage. Television reporters and newspaper journalists congregated on the dock to cover the story. It was a grisly, terrible scene—the sort that was certain to be a major news feature throughout the world.

Engineer inspectors, criminal investigators, demolitions experts and medical examiners pored over the site. The possibility that the explosion had been an accident was quickly dismissed. The blast had occurred by the diesel engines of the pumps. It had ignited the fuel tanks and increased the force of the explosion. The scattered remains of human beings were found in this section, all but vaporized by the explosion.

Evidence was taken to crime labs and studied under microscopes and chemical tests of various sorts. Eventually they learned plastic explosive had been used. Tattered bits of leather revealed the blast had occurred within a thin casing of cowhide. Although no one would ever know for certain, the investigation's immediate conclusion was that the explosion was an act of sabotage, probably carried out by a suicidal fanatic who detonated plastic explosive concealed inside a belt. The saboteur had blown himself to bits and killed more than a dozen derrick workers in the process.

THE INCIDENT WAS KNOWN BY Phoenix Force, Ahmed and Colonel Hillerman before their plane arrived at the airport near Dubai. Twilight had fallen as the Kuwaiti Airways 707 touched down on the runway. A small reception committee waited by a pair of black limousines on the airfield.

"You intelligence guys in these gulf countries aren't hard to spot," Calvin James commented to Ahmed as they stepped off the ramp.

"Only because we know what to look for," the Kuwaiti agent assured him.

"Let's hope none of the Purple Warrior blokes have figured it out as well," David McCarter muttered, glancing about the airfield as if he expected terrorists to pop up from the ground like guntoting gophers.

The United Arab Emirates' reception indeed resembled the one Phoenix Force had encountered when they arrived in Kuwait. A small, slender Arab, dressed in garb identical to Ahmed's, stood next to the first limo. A large, muscular man stood beside him. The big man wore a gray chauffeur's uniform, complete with cap and highly shined boots.

A holstered pistol was plainly visible on the driver's hip, which was not unusual in Arab countries. Servants often doubled as bodyguards in the politically tense gulf nations. After numerous assassination attempts on Arab leaders, such defensive measures were not surprising.

As if to complete the image of déjà vu, Anton Brackman stood next to the two Arabs by the limousines. The CIA officer had arrived at the U.A.E. on an earlier flight. He nodded at Phoenix Force and their companions, but his grim expression revealed he was not the bearer of good news. The chauffeur opened a door to the limo and invited the visitors to enter.

"We have some rather special luggage," Yakov Katzenelenbogen told the U.A.E. man in white.

"Yes," the Arab replied with a thin smile. "We were informed of that, Mister Anderson. That is the name you're using?"

"That's right," Katz confirmed. "Our gear, sir?"

"My people in the other car will see to it," the U.A.E. agent assured him. "We've already taken care of customs. Your luggage will be brought along without anyone disturbing it."

"Not that we don't trust your people," Rafael Encizo began, "but we'd like to stay close to our equipment. We've needed it on more than one occasion already."

"Okay if a couple of us accompany your fellows in the other car?" Gary Manning inquired.

"Certainly," the Arab agreed. "My men speak English, of course, so please tell them to do whatever you wish. I'm certain they'll make you quite comfortable. Welcome to the United Arab Emirates, gentlemen."

"Thanks," James said. "I wish the circumstances were different."

"The circumstances of our meeting or those of the gulf?" the U.A.E. man inquired with a slight shrug. "Troubled times we live in."

"The times are always troubled," Katz replied. "We'll see if we can't do something about some of the current troubles."

"I sure as hell hope so," Brackman remarked with a sigh.

Katz, Ahmed and Hillerman entered the first limo. Brackman and the U.A.E. agent joined them while the driver assumed his place behind the wheel. The other four members of Phoenix Force collected their gear from the cargo hold of the 707 and carried it to the other limo. Both vehicles rolled forward.

"Introductions are obviously in order," the Arab announced. "You may call me Bassam. The man acting as our driver is Mohammad."

"Mohammad," Ahmed said softly with a trace of sorrow in his voice, his thoughts turned toward his slain Kuwaiti colleague.

"We lost a good man with the same name this morning," Hillerman explained. "A friend of Ahmed's."

"May Allah grant him mercy and the rewards of Paradise," Bassam said with a short bow. "Of course you gentlemen are aware that Mohammad is a very common name in virtually all Arab countries and those which are predominantly Islamic. It is the name of the great prophet of our religion."

"Mohammad is actually the most common name in the entire world," Katz stated. "Evidence of how far Islam has spread over the centuries."

"Something many in the West wish had never occurred," Bassam said with a sigh. He placed his fingertips together and formed a small tent with his hands.

Bassam was a small man, very thin with frail long fingers and a lean face with an exaggeratedly pointed black goatee. It certainly gave him a goatlike appearance. His brown eyes were gentle, almost sad. He spoke flawless English with a Cambridge accent, which suggested Bassam had been partially educated in England.

"Many people in the West don't understand Islam," Katz stated. "There are a lot of misconceptions about your religion. The first translations of the Koran in Latin in the twelfth century were inaccurate and purposely distorted by Christian scholars hostile toward Islam. The later translations in French and English weren't much better. In fact, I don't think there was a fair and objective translation of the Koran in English until 1955. Even then, much of the poetry and beauty of the suras are lost when it's written in any language other than Arabic."

"You've read the Koran?" Bassam asked, surprised and pleased by the stranger's knowledge of the Islamic holy book.

"In three languages," Katz confirmed, "including Arabic. Religion is a fascinating subject, but I feel we best discuss our mission instead."

"You heard about what happened at the oil derrick off the coast?" Brackman inquired. "Officially, they haven't declared the cause to be either an accident of an act of sabotage. Unofficially, we already know."

"Sabotage?" Ahmed asked, already certain of the answer.

"Suicide terrorist," the black CIA agent confirmed. "Had about a pound of plastic explosive around his waist and set it off. Fourteen killed, including Mr. Martyr. Among the remains—and there wasn't much—they found a tattered piece of purple cloth."

"Sounds like our Shiite maniacs again," Colonel Hillerman remarked. He turned to Bassam. "Sorry if you're a Shiite Muslim, mate. Nothing personal, you understand."

"I'm not a Shiite," Bassam explained. "Mohammad is, however, but don't worry that he'll be offended by comments about the terrorists. We've discussed the subject many times in the past, and Mohammad has no more sympathy for Shiite terrorists than any other sort. Perhaps he has less because they're giving his religion a bad name. He'd probably throttle the Ayatollah if he could get his hands on that ancient Iranian troublemaker.''

"That might be a waste of time," Brackman remarked. "Our intelligence sources say the Ayatollah is either dead or dying from cancer. Information about Iran is hard to come by and not always terribly reliable, but we're about eighty percent sure about this."

"Well, if the Iranians are like the Soviets when it comes to announcing the death of a leader," Hillerman began, "then the Ayatollah might be dead for six months before they'll publicly admit it."

"We're hoping there will be some major changes in Iran after the Ayatollah's gone," Ahmed commented. "Perhaps the country will change just as China changed after Mao's death. I doubt those changes will come about rapidly, but there have already been indications that Tehran would like to see the war come to an end and possibly establish better relations with other countries."

"The recent terrorist activity isn't going to encourage anyone to trust Iran," Bassam remarked.

"The Purple Warriors of Righteousness may not even be connected to Iran," Katz stated. "Qabda seems to be leading the terrorist cult, and there's no evidence he's working for Iran or any other government. This could very well be an offshoot of the jihad movement. When fanatical zeal gets started, it isn't easy to stop. The Ayatollah might be an inspiration to Qabda, but he appears to be acting independent of Tehran."

"Too bad we don't have some definite proof," Brackman said. "Even though today's incident hasn't been officially recognized as an act of terrorism, that's already the popular opinion among both U.A.E. Arab personnel and American diplomats. Both sides are ready to blame the Iranians. After all, the Iranians *have* attacked a lot of ships, tankers and oil rigs in the past. American, British, West German, Russian, Japanese and Arab vessels of at least three gulf countries have been victims of Iranian military attacks and Shiite terrorism—probably linked to Tehran. Uncle Sam and the emirates are ready to kick some Iranian ass over this incident.''

''It's happened before,'' Hillerman commented. The Briton tapped his walnut walking sticks against his artificial leg as he spoke. ''The Yanks fought a pretty-good-sized battle with the Iranians in the gulf in 1988. No question that the Iranians were the losers in the encounter. They're certainly no match for the military forces of the United States.''

''Another battle will mean more lives lost,'' Katz declared, ''American as well as Iranian. Probably U.A.E. citizens will be killed as well. Quite possibly, Kuwaitis, Saudis and others will be victims, not to mention the risk to foreign tankers and their crews. That's a lot of people to die because of a misunderstanding. The Purple Warriors of Righteousness are responsible, and they should be our target, not Iran.''

''Eventually we may have to crush Iran and its present regime anyway,'' Bassam remarked grimly. ''The Ayatollah or whoever is running that country has taken this jihad madness too far already. We've all tolerated it, and I'm not so certain we should have. If the United States and Britain would join forces against Iran, I assure you my country and all the other Arabian Gulf nations would support you. That includes Iraq. Perhaps even the Soviet Union would back us up. Together we could easily defeat Iran and take over the country.''

''I understand your frustration, Bassam,'' Brackman assured him, ''but such an action would make all of us pretty unpopular with the rest of the world. Especially the countries of the Third World. They'd regard such massive military action as excessive and abusive use of power.''

''Why should we care what they think?'' Bassam asked, his hands spread in a wide gesture of frustration. ''They already hate you Americans. They hate the British, too, and they resent the prosperous and progressive Arab gulf countries. What will they do? Refuse to accept your foreign aid money? Break off trade and diplomatic relations so they can cut their own throats economically and politically? Refuse to buy Arab oil? No, my friends, they'll whine and complain, but they won't do any more than that. It would also be a bloody good lesson for those dictators in Libya and Syria to back off as well. Might even put a scare in Israel so they'll stop invading their neighbors' territory.''

"Let's not get into a discussion about Israel," Ahmed urged. He cast a short, nervous glance at Katz. "We Arabs might have some complaints about Israeli policies, but this isn't associated with those grievances."

"Gentlemen," Katz began. "Whether or not the world would be a better place without the Ayatollah's regime isn't the matter that concerns me. The idea of hundreds of young men going off to kill one another because of today's incident is the immediate concern. Military personnel and civilians of a variety of nationalities could die. When men go off to war it's bad enough, but when they're not even fighting the right enemy, it's inexcusable."

"A noble thought," Bassam agreed. "However, I fail to see how we can convince your government or mine that the Iranians aren't at fault here. Indeed, you don't have any clear evidence to prove the terrorists are not state-sponsored fanatics from Iran."

"So far the terrorists we've encountered have been predominantly Arabs, not Iranians," Katz stated. "Apparently all the members of the Purple Warriors of Righteousness are Shiite Muslims, but Qabda seems to be their leader, not the Ayatollah. Now, we launched a successful raid on the terrorist base in Kuwait and managed to capture eleven Purple Warrior members. One bit off his own tongue and bled to death. Another died from wounds suffered in the battle, but we got the other nine to Ahmed's safe house where they were interrogated under the influence of scopolamine."

"Mr. Brackman told me the black man in your group is very skilled in administering truth serum," Bassam said with a nod. "Did you learn anything of value from the prisoners?"

"Enough to convince us to come to the United Arab Emirates," Katz answered. "We were already preparing for our flight to your country before we heard about the explosion at the oil rig. One of the terrorists we captured was Ali Kamel himself, the top-ranking member of the Purple Warriors in Kuwait."

"And he told you something that convinced you to come to my country?" Bassam asked with surprise.

"Yes, indeed," Ahmed stated. "He told us he met Qabda here in Dubai three years ago. The terrorists still have a base in the United Arab Emirates, according to Kamel."

"Are you sure that's reliable?" Brackman inquired. "I mean, one of those guys you fellas interrogated after that shoot-out at the docks was such a fanatic even scopolamine didn't work on him."

"Kamel seems to have had some doubts about the jihad in general and the Purple Warriors of Righteousness in particular," Katz explained. "He isn't a true believer anymore. In fact, he seems to resent Qabda after deciding the holy war is an experiment in lunacy. Kamel talked quite freely under the influence of the serum. I wouldn't be surprised if he agrees to testify against the other cult members when and if this matter comes to trial."

"Did he say that the Purple Warriors aren't connected to the Iranian government?" Bassam asked.

"He said that as far as he knew Qabda had started the movement on his own and was not directly connected with Iran or any other government," Katz answered. "I believe Kamel is correct. Iran may have carried out some absurd and extremist policies in the past, but Tehran must realize that multiple terrorist attacks on the Arab gulf countries can only serve to create more problems for them at this time. With the high possibility of a change of leaders in Tehran, the economic woes and the constant stalemate nature of the

Iran-Iraq war, they have nothing to gain by causing more friction and hostility among their neighbors."

"True," Bassam agreed. "However, Iran has a history of insane behavior. I don't know that we can rule out state-sponsored terrorism in this case."

"Well, if we can't prove this is state-sponsored terrorism," Hillerman began, folding his hands over his cane as he leaned forward, "then we'd better advise the politicians, military leaders and whoever else is involved to resist the urge to retaliate against Iran. Mr. Anderson has a good point, Bassam. I'm an old soldier myself. That's how I lost my bloody leg in a military campaign. I can't say I don't regret losing my leg, but at least it wasn't a senseless action. God knows, I'd hate to recall how I wound up with this metal limb and think I was maimed because some bleedin' politicians made a mistake. I'd hate to think I killed men who weren't really enemies because the blokes in parliament had decided to send in the military due to false information."

"We'll see what we can do about convincing the Emirate Council to be patient until all the facts are in," Bassam assured his guests. "Meantime, I trust you gentlemen have some idea of how we can hunt down the terrorists who are still at large. You say there's a terrorist base here in the U.A.E. Do you happen to know where it's located?"

"We know where it used to be and the names of some of the members of the Purple Warriors," Ahmed answered. "They've probably moved their base to a new site by now, but we may be able to find the individuals Kamel told us about."

Mohammad had remained silent and concentrated on driving the limo until the two-way radio on the dashboard crackled with static and a voice uttering something in quiet Arabic. The driver immediately stuck the jack of an earphone into an outlet of the radio and inserted the earpiece. Mohammad listened to a moment and spoke into the radio. The men in the limousine understood Arabic, but all the passengers heard was Mohammad affirming that he understood the message and signing off.

"Excuse me," Mohammad began in thickly accented English. His tone seemed urgent and his voice was loud and firm. "The driver of the other limousine informs me that a green van has been following us since we left the airport."

"Is CIA or SIS following us for some reason?" Bassam demanded, directing the question to his passengers.

"Brackman's CIA, Ahmed is Kuwaiti SIS and I'm British SIS," Hillerman replied. "Why would any of us have your cars tailed without telling you? We're right here so we're getting information firsthand. No need to have blokes tagging after you with rifle microphones trying to snatch bits of the conversation."

"You don't think it could be the terrorists?" Brackman asked, his tone suggesting he did not expect to hear the answer he was hoping for. "Hell. How could they have us pegged?"

"The most serious mistake one can make is to underestimate the enemy," Katz declared. The steel hooks of his prosthesis clicked in a nervous gesture of anxious anticipation. "Bassam, tell your driver to try to find a road that's not used much by civilian vehicles and get us as far away from populated areas as possible. Let's reduce the risk to bystanders as much as circumstances allow."

"Do you really think these are terrorists?" Ahmed asked, reaching inside the robe for his holstered pistol.

"Until we know otherwise," Katz replied, "we'd better assume that's who they are."

Mohammad drove the lead limo onto a little-used road at the outskirts of the city. Dubai is one of the largest and most prosperous sections of the United Arab Emirates, with the second largest population in the entire country. The busy port city resembled Miami at night. The streets were brilliantly lit pathways that snaked between the modern concrete-and-glass buildings. The Dubai Trade Center towers rose above the other buildings. Nearly forty stories, it was the tallest building anywhere in the Middle East.

But the men in the two limousines paid little attention to the city lights and majestic buildings. They were more concerned about the mysterious van that pursued them. Mohammad's choice of roads was sound. Although unpaved and seldom traveled, the bumpy dirt path suited their needs. It was clear of the busy main roads to the city and they encountered few vehicles. Most of these were dusty trucks, some with camels in penlike containers in the backs of the rigs. Despite the Arab Emirates' modern cities, great wealth and emphasis on education and improved technology, raising camels was still a major business in the U.A.E., and the traditional beasts of burden of the deserts were still widely used by citizens inland.

The van continued to follow the limos. Mohammad looked for a place to pull over to the shoulder of the road in case they needed to stop. Suddenly large shapes loomed before them in the harsh glare of the headlights. Two trucks blocked the path, parked end to end in order to prevent the limousines from driving around the barrier. It was apparent that men had taken cover behind the vehicles. Rifle barrels poked around the corners of the trucks. The big, gaping mouth of an RPG jutted above the hood of one vehicle.

"Son of a bitch!" Brackman exclaimed as he stared at the blockade. "The bastards suckered us right into an ambush!"

12

Calvin James was muttering with disgust as he drew his Beretta 92-F pistol from shoulder leather. "I put the rifle case with my M-16 in the trunk."

"Yeah," Gary Manning added, glancing out the rear window at the headlights of the approaching van. "My FAL is in there too."

"Nice thing about machine pistols is they're easier to carry," David McCarter commented as he opened a briefcase and removed his KG-99 subgun.

The compact 9 mm machine pistol easily fit in the valise. Even after McCarter snapped the folding stock into place, the KG-99 was still less than two feet in length. Yet the ammo clip in the magazine contained 30 rounds of parabellum. Rafael Encizo also carried his Heckler & Koch MP-5 in a similar case and took his weapon from the valise.

Omar, an U.A.E. agent in the second limo with the four Phoenix Force commandos, was surprised by the firepower carried by the foreigners, but under the circumstances he was also glad they were packing so many weapons. A handsome, thirty-three-year-old intelligence officer with a deceptively innocent face, highlighted by large soft brown eyes with long black lashes, Omar had little genuine combat experience. However, he had been well trained by British SAS instructors and had taken "spy courses" with MI6.

The Arab agent reached inside his jacket for the 9 mm Beretta holstered under his arm. Omar wondered if it would do any good. The first limo, driven by Mohammad, had come to a sudden halt. Rashid, the driver of the second car, also stepped on the brake. Omar heard him whisper a prayer for Allah's mercy and protection. The cynical Omar figured that was a waste of time and energy, but if it gave Rashid a little hope that they might survive, maybe it was not a total waste.

Unlike most of his countrymen, Omar was an agnostic who only gave lip service to Islam. The enemy positioned by the trucks that blocked the path of the limousines were armed with assault rifles and at least one rocket launcher. Unless Allah intended to strike down the terrorists with lightning bolts, Omar figured firearms were more valuable than prayers at the moment.

The doors to both limos opened the moment the vehicles stopped. Katz emerged from the first car, his SIG-Sauer pistol in his fist. The Israeli's trusted Uzi was also in the trunk of the second limo. Katz was slightly annoyed with himself for not keeping the submachine gun always ready during a mission. It seemed to be a minor error, but it was the sort of mistake that could cost him his life, as well as the lives of others.

However, Katz did not waste any time moping about the error. The Phoenix Force commander had never suffered from any illusions that he was perfect. The only weapon he had at the moment was the 9 mm autoloader, so he would use it the best he could. Orange flame streaked from the muzzle of the SIG-Sauer as Katz crouched behind the open car door and fired around the edge. He aimed for the figure armed with the RPG rocket launcher, the most serious immediate threat to the commando team and their allies.

Enemy bullets pelted the door Katz used for a shield. The U.A.E. government car was bullet-resistant, constructed of reinforced steel. Katz felt the limo door vibrate violently from the impact of rifle slugs. A loud crack erupted from the window and a spiderweb pattern appeared in the thick glass near the Israeli's head.

Katz drew in his breath, tense from the threat of being so close to death. Yet death was not a stranger to the veteran war-horse. He had felt the frosty presence of the Grim Reaper countless times before. Occasionally it had been even closer. The familiar old fears did not inhibit Katz's reflexes or disturb his aim as he triggered two more shots at the terrorist with the RPG.

The shadowy figure behind the Soviet-made launcher suddenly convulsed in a wild fit. The terrorist's head recoiled as a 9 mm slug punched a hole through it. The RPG belched flame as the owner fell backward. The rocket sailed overhead, white comet tail sizzling across the dark sky. The projectile crashed to earth and exploded against an embankment two hundred yards away. Clumps of dirt showered the combatants, but no shrapnel rained down on the group.

Mohammad emerged from the door by the driver's side and fired a .45 auto at the enemy. The Arab agent used the door for cover in the same manner as Katz. Colonel Hillerman also climbed from the car. He nearly stumbled without his cane, but the tough British SIS pro managed to balance himself in preparation for firing his pistol at the truck blockade.

Brackman's arm extended from the limo, a S&W .38 snub-nose revolver in his fist. The CIA agent squeezed off three shots at the ambushers, although the enemy were roughly sixty feet away and beyond accurate range of the short-barreled gun. Brackman did not know much about firearms, but he realized he had little chance of hitting a target with his snubby revolver. Nonetheless, the Company man hoped to assist his more able companions by pursuading the enemy to keep down for a moment of two.

Anton Brackman's efforts were more successful than he would have dared to hope. One of his haphazardly aimed bullets struck an enemy gunman. The terrorist groaned and staggered backward, AK-47 still clenched in his fists. Hillerman saw the figure straighten up and stumble away from cover. The British officer fired two rounds into the center of the man's chest. The terrorist collapsed, more dead than alive before he hit the ground.

The remaining terrorists returned fire. Bullets raked the limousine and ricocheted against reinforced steel and shatter-resistant glass. More enemy forces appeared from the green van, which had stopped fifty feet from the rear of the second limo. The other four members of Phoenix Force, Omar and Rashid had already climbed from the second car, weapons held ready.

McCarter's KG-99 spit fire as the door to the passenger's side at the front of the van swung open. An armed figure had begun to step from the vehicle. Parabellum rounds hammered the door and smashed the window. The glass was not shatter-resistant. A 9 mm round pierced the window and caught the terrorist in the side of the skull before he could duck behind the shelter of the open door. His corpse fell to the road, head split open by the 115-grain missile.

Encizo blasted a volley of MP-5 rounds at the windshield of the van. The driver was hit in the chest and face by bullets that shattered the glass barrier. More terrorists emerged from the rear of the van. The barrels of automatic rifles poked around the end of the vehicle and a hail of high-velocity projectiles sprayed the limo.

The Phoenix pros and their Arab allies took shelter along the big government car. The second limousine, like the first, was constructed of sturdy, bullet-resistant materials. Slugs whined against metal and glass. The defenders crouched low in the deadly hailstorm.

Gary Manning removed two objects disguised as fountain pens from a jacket pocket and tossed one to Calvin James. The black commando recognized the magnesium flare device. James was practised enough with the mini-explosive, and he understood why Manning had given one of the flares to him. James nodded in confirmation to the Canadian.

"Count of three?" Manning suggested, his voice loud enough to be heard above the roar of the automatic fire.

"Start counting," James replied and gripped his flare-pen in both hands.

"We'll cover you," Encizo declared, aware of what his companions planned. "Omar, you and Rashid help us keep the enemy pinned down while our amigos get into position."

"The blockade..." Omar began, but he swung his Beretta toward the van.

"Let's take care of these blokes first!" David McCarter said sharply and opened fire on the van with a chattering roar of 9 mm slugs.

Encizo also triggered his submachine gun and blasted another salvo of high-velocity parabellums across the frame of the enemy vehicle. Bullets sparked against the side of the van. One ricochet round caught a terrorist in the side of the face and split his cheekbone. The man cried out and clapped an open palm to his face, but he held on to his assault rifle.

"One! Two!" Manning called out as he rushed to the rear of the limo and snapped the pen to ignite the flare fuse. "Three!"

The Canadian hurled his flare-pen at the van. Calvin James was positioned at the opposite side of the limo and threw the other flare a split second after Manning released his magnesium explosive. The small objects whirled in the air and traveled roughly twenty feet, unnoticed by the preoccupied terrorists.

The flares exploded in twin blasts of brilliant white light. Omar shouted something in angry Arabic as he covered his eyes with one hand and pointed his pistol toward the sky to avoid threatening any allies. The glare temporarily blinded the U.A.E. agent, although he had expected an explosion of some sort. He realized the effects of the white flash would be far more effective against the enemy.

The four Phoenix Force commandos immediately rushed toward the van, weapons blazing as they ran. McCarter reached the vehicle first, closely followed by Calvin James. The British ace jogged to the rear of the van, his KG-99 pointed at the enemy position. James held his Beretta 92-F in both hands, barrel raised, but ready to snap-aim at any opponent who might appear.

Encizo and Manning ran to the side of the van and approached the rear of the enemy rig. The Cuban was in the lead, his H&K subgun pointing the way. Manning stayed close behind, Walther P-5 in his fists. The pair advanced slowly, aware that McCarter and James were already in position and closer to the rear of the van. The possibility of accidentally shooting one of their own men was a genuine concern.

A young Arab, dressed in black trousers and a pale blue shirt, stepped from the back of the vehicle with a Kalashnikov rifle in one hand as he pawed at his eyes with the other. The terrorist snarled something and suddenly grabbed his AK-47 with both hands and swung the barrel toward Encizo and Manning. Whatever effect the glare of the magnesium explosion had on the youth's eyes, the terrorist could still see enough to know the Phoenix pair was present.

Encizo triggered the MP-5, and a trio of 9 mm rounds ripped into the terrorist. The impact hurled the man backward to collide with another terrorist who was trying to point an RPG at the limos. The dying fanatic slammed into the rocket launcher and struck the weapon from the other man's grasp. The startled and suddenly unarmed terrorist jumped behind the van for cover as Encizo fired another burst of parabellums.

McCarter heard the chatter of a submachine gun, guessed it was probably Encizo's weapon because he had not noticed any of the enemy armed with a subgun. The British pro dashed to the rear of the van, dropped to one knee and pointed his KG-99 at the three enemy figures who stood there. The terrorists were disoriented, and their vision was still blurred from the effects of the flares. Their attention was on Encizo's position at the opposite side of the van, and they did not notice McCarter.

The Briton's submachine gun blasted the nearest opponent with a trio of 9 mm slugs. The terrorist crashed lifeless to the ground as McCarter fired into the upper torso of another enemy gunman. The would-be killer stumbled backward from the impact, his arms uselessly grasping the air for support. An assault rifle hurtled from his fingers as he fell against the van and slumped to the ground, shirtfront splattered with blood.

The third terrorist was the one who had dropped the RPG launcher. Though he was willing to die a martyr for the jihad, he had not expected to find the occasion so soon. The ambush was supposed to be simple. Box in the enemy and kill them, blast them to pieces. However, the quarry had fought back with astonishing speed, skill and ingenuity. The terrorist's training had not included how to respond to sudden blinding light, having one's weapon unexpectedly knocked from one's hands, or what to do when all one's comrades are slain and one must face the enemy alone. The young zealot had intended to give his life for the holy war, but he had imagined he would die in glorious battle and slay a hundred infidels in the process of making his sacrifice. He was not supposed to die alone and quivering with fear without claiming some sort of victory.

"Allahu akbar!" the terrorist cried out and reached for the pistol holstered on his hip.

McCarter triggered his KG-99. The weapon merely clicked in response. The Briton had exhausted the ammo from the magazine. The youth realized McCarter's weapon was empty and smiled with renewed confidence and satisfaction that God was indeed great and had heard his shouted prayer. The terrorist yanked the pistol from leather and snapped off the safety catch.

The British Phoenix fighter realized he could not hope to draw and fire his Browning automatic before the young fanatic could blow him away, so he lunged with the empty

KG-99 in his fists. McCarter closed in as the terrorist drew his pistol and prepared to fire. The barrel of the KG-99 machine pistol chopped the aggressor across the wrist and knocked the handgun from the terrorist's numb fingers.

McCarter quickly followed with a knee kick to his opponent's groin. The blow wasn't fully effective because it hit the terrorist in the inner thigh, but it still served to keep him off balance and give McCarter time to swing his left fist into his face. The punch spun the terrorist around to come face-to-face with Rafael Encizo.

The Cuban rammed the barrel of his MP-5 into the terrorist's stomach. The zealot gasped breathlessly and started to fold up. Encizo's fist caught him under the jaw hard and straightened him up again, but McCarter hit the unlucky fanatic from behind and stamped the butt of his KG-99 between his shoulder blades. The terrorist groaned and fell forward, dazed and winded, blood trickling from his open mouth.

Encizo mistook the youth's forward motion as an attack and quickly slammed the steel frame of his H&K chopper against the side of his opponent's head before he realized his error. The terrorist dropped heavily to the ground and landed facedown. He would not be in a hurry to fight in another jihad when he came to.

CALVIN JAMES HAD NOT followed McCarter around the rear of the van. He had problems of his own to deal with. A side door to the van had suddenly burst open and slammed into the black commando. The unexpected blow struck James's forearm and sent the Beretta autoloader spinning from his hand. A bearded terrorist sprang from the open door, an AK-47 in his fists.

The man's eyes opened wide with fury and hatred. He started to point the Kalashnikov at James, but the Chicago-bred survivor quickly swung a tae kwon do "sword foot" kick to the terrorist's rifle. The barrel was knocked away from James just as the terrorist squeezed the trigger.

A burst of 7.62 mm rounds tore into the ground as James closed in and whipped a back fist to the center of the fanatic's face.

Blood gushed from the nostrils of the man's broken nose, but he still attempted to swing the wooden stock of the AK-47 at James's head. The black warrior grabbed the frame of the rifle and shoved it against the terrorist's chest before the gunman could carry out this tactic. The shove drove the Purple Warrior killer backward into the side of the van. James held on to the Kalashnikov and tried to push the rifle under his opponent's chin.

The young terrorist was strong and driven by religious frenzy as well as desperation. He pushed the rifle back with considerable force. James did not intend to get into a shoving match with the guy. Instead he moved with the motion of the terrorist's thrust and pulled on the AK-47. The combined motions increased the terrorist's forward momentum. The American commando suddenly turned, dropped to one knee and twisted the rifle in a circular manner.

The terrorist was thrown off balance and tumbled head over heels to the ground. The fanatic landed hard, and James wrenched the Kalashnikov from his stunned opponent's grasp. The terrorist growled and started to climb to his feet. James lashed out a boot and kicked the man squarely in the face. The zealot collapsed with a groan and lay unconscious at James's feet, his black beard now streaked with crimson stains.

James glanced around the rear of the van and saw that the enemy had been defeated there. McCarter and Encizo confirmed this by exchanging nods with James. But the chattering of weapons continued as the defenders at the first limo battled the terrorists positioned at the truck blockade.

"Yakov and the others could use some help," James remarked and prepared to head back to the limos.

"Tell them to be ready to duck," Gary Manning announced as he stepped from behind Encizo and shoved his

Walther P-5 autoloader into shoulder leather. "They'll know when."

The Canadian walked to the fallen RPG rocket launcher and scooped up the Soviet-made blaster. The other three Phoenix pros understood what Manning had in mind. The demolition expert examined the launcher to be certain it had not been damaged during the battle and laid the tubular weapon across his brawny shoulder.

"Wait for us to pass the word," Encizo urged.

"Just don't chitchat too long," Manning replied.

James ran for the limousines, firing the Kalashnikov at the trucks as he rushed forward in a crouched stance. McCarter and Encizo swapped magazines to their subguns and reloaded the KG-99 and MP-5 before they charged back into battle. Manning remained at the van and sighted the confiscated rocket launcher at the terrorists' stronghold. He judged the distance with care. The Canadian had to get the target right the first time. If the shell landed too close to the limos, he might kill his own allies. If it sailed too far and exploded some distance from the truck blockade, the enemy would be virtually untouched by the blast.

Katz fired his SIG-Sauer at the terrorists, trying to make the most of each shot. Another ambusher had claimed the RPG that had been dropped by a slain comrade. He had reloaded the Soviet launcher, but had not been able to aim and fire because Katz and Mohammad forced him down every time he attempted to use it.

Ahmed and Brackman were relatively inexperienced with combat shooting. The Kuwaiti agent and his CIA counterpart simply fired their pistols at the enemy position in hope of keeping the terrorists busy while the better marksmen concentrated on actually shooting the ambushers.

Colonel Hillerman continued to use the door for shelter as he poked his pistol around the edge to squeeze off shots. Bassam helped the Briton and leaned from the open doorway to fire over the top of the car door. The increase of firepower from the direction of the second limo surprised

he defenders. Hillerman glanced over his shoulder and saw
McCarter and James headed for their car.

"Looks like things are shifting in our favor," Hillerman
declared with a tense grin as he began to feed a fresh magazine into the butt of his pistol.

A salvo of automatic fire raked the ground near the British officer. One 7.62 mm struck Hillerman's leg. The SIS
officer groaned and began to fall. Bassam quickly grabbed
the colonel and dragged him inside the car as another vol-
ey of enemy bullets hammered the open door.

"Oh, Christ!" McCarter exclaimed when he saw his former commanding officer hauled into the limo. He had seen
enough men stop a bullet in the past to know Hillerman had
been hit.

"Get down!" James shouted as he ran to the first limo.
The black warrior sprayed the enemy trucks with AK-47
rounds as he took cover behind the rear of the big black
auto. "Everybody down!"

"What does he mean?" Ahmed inquired, confused by the
demand.

"Just do it!" Katz replied sharply.

Gary Manning glanced at the limousines and saw his
friends and allies had ducked for cover, by or within the
government cars. The Canadian demolitions pro aimed the
RPG with care and triggered the Russian weapon. The
rocket streaked from the big muzzle of the launcher and
sizzled above the rooftops of the limousines. It crashed into
the center of the truck blockade and exploded.

The blast tore segments of the vehicles apart, ignited the
fuel tanks and detonated twin explosions a split second later.
Flaming shrapnel and jets of burning gasoline spewed from
the wreckage. Fiery remnants showered the limos.

Burning debris continued to litter to the ground, as Katz
and James raised their heads and advanced toward the
wreckage that had formerly been the truck barricade. Encizo and Omar followed, weapons held ready in case any
terrorists had survived the explosion. Rashid, the driver of

the second limo, held an Ingram M-10 machine pistol as he approached the flaming ruins. The site reminded them of a scene from the depths of hell itself. Twisted metal, ravaged corpses and chunks of burned flesh on splinters of bone lay among the flame-shrouded junk. None of the ambushers at the trucks survived.

McCarter remained by the limo, beside the open door. He gazed inside at Colonel Hillerman. The SIS man sat with his leg extended and rigid. A hole in the trouser at the shin revealed where the bullet had struck, but there was no blood. A piece of jagged gray plastic jutted from the tear in the pant leg.

"Bloody hell," McCarter said with a sigh of relief. "You were only shot in the artificial leg."

"Only the artificial leg?" Hillerman snorted gruffly as he pulled up the cloth to examine the damage to the plastic and metal limb. "You obviously don't know how much these damned prostheses cost, Sergeant."

"More expensive than a funeral?" McCarter asked with a sly grin, taking a pack of Player's from his shirt pocket.

"Somebody else would have to pay to bury me," the colonel muttered. He looked down at his leg with a scowl. "This damn thing is probably going to cost me about two hundred quid."

"Don't worry," Bassam assured him, placing a hand on his shoulder. "The government of the United Arab Emirates will pay for replacing your limb."

"The major is just letting off some steam," McCarter told the Arab agent. "SIS will cover the expense anyway. Right, Major?"

"I'm a bloody colonel now," Hillerman replied sourly. "If you were still SAS, I'd make sure you'd remember that."

"You're so tough," McCarter said with a chuckle.

Gary Manning shuffled backward toward the limos. He was dragging along two terrorists from the van to the gov-

rnment cars. Katz, James and Encizo walked back from the
hastly wreckage of the devastated trucks.

"These two are the only prisoners," Manning an-
ounced. "The others from the van are dead."

"There is hardly anything left of the ones at the trucks,"
ames replied, AK-47 canted across his shoulder. "They'll
ave to use a mop and a bucket to do any autopsy."

"Better them than us," Katz stated. He holstered his SIG-
auer and nodded at Manning. "You did well. All of you."

"We were lucky," Manning replied with a shrug. "The
errorists could have just waited for us and picked us off
vith rocket launchers without using the trucks to block us
ff first."

"Maybe this lot wasn't all that eager to be martyrs,"
ames suggested.

"Perhaps," Katz said thoughtfully. "Or Qabda may not
ave wanted them to sacrifice themselves tonight. But this
eally isn't the time or place to discuss it. Let's get out of
ere before the police arrive to ask a lot of time-consuming
uestions."

"What I'd like to have an answer to is how the hell they
new about us," James commented. "The mission is tough
nough already. If our security is blown, it's gonna be just
bout impossible."

"We'll talk about it later," Katz insisted. "Let's go."

13

The United Arab Emirates is a very wealthy nation, a small country with an estimated oil reserve of a hundred billion barrels. U.A.E. citizens enjoy one of the highest standards of living in the world, with an average annual income of approximately twenty thousand dollars a year—with government subsidized housing, food and utilities, free education and medical care, and no taxes. The prosperity of the U.A.E. was clearly visible in Dubai.

David McCarter peered out the window of the twelve-story office building the U.A.E. security service used as a safe house. Cars and buses traveled the busy streets below. The setting reminded him of Kuwait city, but there appeared to be even more evidence of Western influence. From the window, McCarter spotted an office building for Xerox, not far from a Safeway supermarket and a fast-food restaurant with distinctive golden arches.

"Hard to believe this is the Middle East," Rafael Encizo commented as he glanced over McCarter's shoulder to stare down at the street.

"It's sure different from battle-torn Lebanon, neurotic Libya, repressive Iran and just about all the rest except for the other progressive gulf nations," the Briton replied, taking a cigarette from a pack of Player's. "They don't want to wind up like the rest of the Middle East. Can't say I blame them."

"They've managed so far," Encizo stated. "Maybe their luck will hold out and they won't get mixed up in the wars and general madness that's become symbolic of the Middle East.''

"We wouldn't be here if they were immune," McCarter said, striking a flame under the cigarette. "No place in the bloody world is safe these days."

"There never was such a place," Encizo told his British partner and placed a hand on McCarter's shoulder. "And you'd be bored to death if the world was safe."

"Well, that's true enough," McCarter admitted as he turned away from the window.

The U.A.E. federation had supplied them with quarters which equalled the luxury and comfort of the Kuwaiti safe house. The spacious room was furnished with leather armchairs, sofas, television, VCR, stereo system and shelves of books. A hookah water pipe was placed on a glass-top coffee table. Three different blends of pipe tobacco were available. No hashish or opium. Despite popular misconceptions in the West, most people who smoke a hookah in the Middle East only use tobacco. Drugs are abhorrent to the followers of Islam.

The floor was multicolored stone tile with several beautiful handwoven rugs. Katz gazed at one of the rugs with interest, admiring the color and design. The Israeli sat in a chair, nursing a Camel cigarette and a cup of hot tea. Colonel Hillerman lay on a sofa, his cane propped against the backrest, the shattered artificial leg on the floor beside him. The torn and empty pant leg above the stump of his leg was knotted near the end of the abbreviated limb.

"You know what's really odd, Anderson?" Hillerman addressed Katz by his current cover name. "When I got shot tonight, the damn thing hurt for a moment there. Like it was still flesh and blood. That sort of thing ever happen to you?"

"Oh, you mean my arm?" Katz replied. He was so accustomed to being an amputee he seldom thought about it. Katz held up his trident hooks and puffed his cigarette. "Yes, I've had that sensation from time to time. I think they call it phantom pain. Sometimes I still feel as if my forearm itches, and I find myself scratching metal or groping at air if I'm not wearing the prosthesis.''

"How long has it been for you?" the Briton inquired.

"About twenty-five years," Katz said with a shrug.

"That's about twice as long as I've been without the leg," Hillerman said with a sigh. "Took me a while to accept being handicapped. Or do you call it being physically challenged?"

"I call it having one limb shorter than the other," Katz replied. "Physically challenged sounds like some idiot in a bar has threatened to punch you out. I regard it as more an adjustment than a challenge. You have to make some changes in how you live in order to fit the changes that have happened to your body."

"Well, I haven't run in many races lately," Hillerman said with a chuckle. "It can be a bloody nuisance at times."

"Yes, but you find that you can still do most things that other people can do," Katz stated. "It might be more difficult or take a bit longer, but you can manage if you really try. Of course, one has to be realistic. Some things simply require two arms or two legs. Still, you'll find those limitations are really fewer than you might imagine."

McCarter approached the pair. He looked down at Hillerman and smiled weakly. "You sure you're all right, Colonel?" he inquired.

"I'm fine, really," Hillerman assured him. "Just a bit annoyed about having my peg shot up. Had a nice chat with your mate here. I didn't get around to thanking him, but I'd like to do so now that I have an opportunity to do it face-to-face without jeopardizing national security."

"Thank me for what?" Katz asked, genuinely confused.

"The Mardarjan Embassy in London," Hillerman explained. "I know McCarter was part of that raid on those terrorist buggers three years ago, but I didn't have the privilege of meeting the other four gents who stormed the embassy until this mission."

"None of us said we were involved in that," Katz reminded him. "The U.S. government never sanctioned such a raid."

"I know," Hillerman said with a nod. "You fellows stuck your necks out with that one, besides putting your lives on the line. I also know you can't admit you did it. Not even now. Still, I want you to know I appreciate what you did for England that day, and I feel I can safely say the majority of Britain's population would thank you as well."

Katz smiled, but did not reply or even nod. He could not acknowledge Hillerman's thanks for the previous mission against the Mardarjan Embassy, but he did not want to lie to the colonel. The awkward silence was interrupted as Bassam and Ahmed approached the coffee table.

"More coffee, gentlemen?" Bassam inquired, indicating the silver coffeepot in his hand. He lowered it to the table and glanced at Katz. "I noticed you seemed interested in that rug. Excellent craftsmanship, is it not?"

"Lovely work," Katz confirmed. "Looks vaguely familiar, but I can't quite figure out why. Reproduction of a famous Arab tapestry?"

"Persian," Bassam corrected as he took a seat and raised a coffee cup to his lips. "In fact, that rug was actually made in Iran. I purchased it from an Iranian merchant just last year. Met him here in Dubai down at the docks."

"Iranians are coming to the United Arab Emirates to sell rugs?" Encizo asked with surprise. "You mean legitimate Iranian merchant ships still cross the Persian Gulf to do business here? I'm surprised they don't get blown out of the water before they can reach your port."

"They are aware of that danger," Bassam stated. "Yet some take the risk anyway. They usually trade with our people for household appliances and other items that are difficult to get in Iran these days."

"Hard to imagine somebody would risk his life for a toaster," McCarter commented. He scanned the tray and frowned. There was no Coca-Cola.

"They don't trade fine quality Persian rugs, carpets and other handicrafts for a toaster or two," Bassam assured him. "Such merchandise is quite valuable, not only here in my country but to collectors and lovers of fine things throughout the world. Of course, appliances are in great demand in Iran since such items are in short supply there. Personally I'm glad this trade still continues. It's a bit covert, of course. The Ayatollah doesn't approve of his people using Western technology."

"Evidently he doesn't object to using military hardware from the West to fight his holy war," Encizo snorted. "The Iranian air force uses American-made fighters left over from the Shah's time. They use automatic weapons of American, European and Soviet design. Last I heard, the Russians were supposed to be infidels as well. I guess it's okay to use modern technology to kill people, but not improve the quality of life among his own subjects."

"Something like that," Bassam confirmed. "Nevertheless, the trade between Iranians and Arabs continues. I like to think this suggests that not all the people of Iran are frothing at the mouth, brainwashed by the Ayatollah."

"They certainly aren't," Katz stated. "Iran is at war with Iraq, but it is also at war with itself. Iranians opposed to the Ayatollah's regime have formed the National Liberation Army. Last I heard, estimated forces of the NLA were approximately fifty thousand. That's just along the eastern borders. They're not very large compared to the Iranian military, but the NLA is well organized, well trained and highly motivated."

"They also tend to be left-wing," Hillerman added. "A lot of observers in the West have some doubts about who's really running the NLA. The Soviets might boast about *glasnost*, but I wouldn't put it past them to try to set up a puppet government in Iran, just as they've done so many other times in the past. There was an example of that in Afghanistan, which borders Iran."

"The Soviets will do what's in their own interest," Katz remarked with a shrug. "I'm not sure it's in their interest to try to seize more territory when they have so many economic and social problems in the USSR. However, I agree that it's naive to take *glasnost* on blind faith. Politicians aren't noted for their honesty, and there's no reason to think Soviet politicians are an exception to that rule."

"They certainly don't have a good track record," McCarter commented. "Of course, it is the politburo that really runs the Soviet Union. The secretary-general is powerful, but he has to try to get their backing."

"One world crisis at a time, gentlemen," Ahmed began as he handed McCarter a glass with ice cubes and a chilled bottle of Coke Classic. "We've still got the terrorists to deal with."

"Thank you very much," McCarter said, gladly accepting the cola. "You're a true humanitarian, Ahmed."

"I hoped it would please you, Mr. Stark," the Kuwaiti officer replied with a nod.

"All right," Katz began, crushing out his cigarette butt in a marble ashtray. "Mr. Washington is still with Omar, questioning the two captured terrorists with the aid of scopolamine. Maybe something of value will come to light, but I doubt such low-level stooges will know much of any value to us."

"I'd be satisfied if they just told us how they managed that ambush," Bassam stated, stuffing a special Turkish tobacco blend into the bowl of the hookah. "Apparently the Purple Warriors of Righteousness have either infiltrated my intelligence service or the Kuwaiti SIS or, Allah preserve us, *both* networks have been violated by terrorists agents."

"I don't think that is what had happened, Bassam," Katz explained. "I've thought about how we were ambushed on the road, and I don't believe it's evidence the terrorists have agents within any intelligence service."

"You're not just saying that to relieve our fears?" Ahmed inquired, hoping the Phoenix commander would answer in a positive manner.

"One doesn't deal with fears by rationalizing them away or minimizing a serious danger," Katz assured him. "I believe the terrorists in Kuwait must have contacted their superiors after our first encounter with the enemy. They no doubt mentioned that Western foreigners were assisting the Kuwaiti SIS. After Qabda or his subchief realized the base in Kuwait had been neutralized, they'd figure our next move would be to travel to another Arab gulf country where the Purple Warriors are active. Probably Oman or the United Arab Emirates, because terrorist attacks have recently taken place in those two countries. Then they simply had to station men at airports and border sections."

"And we arrived at an international airport on board a Kuwaiti Airways plane," Encizo added with a nod. "Might as well have carried signs around our necks telling the enemy who we were."

McCarter looked at Encizo in agreement. "That also explains why they didn't use cyanide gas," he stated. "I doubt if the terrorists have an unlimited supply of chemical warheads for their rocket launchers. Qabda wouldn't want to issue his most valuable weapons of terror to all those blokes hanging about waiting for us to show up at couple dozen different sites."

"But when the van followed us, we headed for a random dirt road where the enemy waited for us with the truck blockade," Bassam reminded the others.

"That simply proves the enemy guessed we'd try to avoid risking the lives of innocent bystanders," Katz replied. "After all, we didn't plan in advance to head down that road. It was the logical choice under the circumstances. Qabda or the local commander here in the U.A.E. guessed how we'd respond. Every good chess player tries to figure out what move his opponent will make in response to the other player's strategy."

"It does make sense," Ahmed agreed. "If only we could be sure."

"Well, we really can't be sure of anything just yet," Katz was forced to admit. "However, we haven't discovered any evidence that the Purple Warriors of Righteousness are sophisticated enough to infiltrate any intelligence agency with double agents. They appear to be fanatics, unreasonable extremists about politics and religion. I doubt that they would be able to slip through the screening process required before one is accepted into any sort of intelligence or security service. Ali Kamel succeeded to a degree with convincing his employers he was a former Shiite Muslim who was a Sunni Muslim convert, highly critical of his former faith. However, Kamel's devotion to the jihad proved to be less than total, and we didn't have much trouble seeing through his charade anyway."

"I think Anderson is right," Hillerman announced. "If these blokes actually had spies within our intelligence outfits, they would have been clever enough to concentrate on getting more information about us, to learn how much we knew about their terrorist activities instead of just trying to kill us."

"That is reassuring," Bassam said as he held a match to the bowl of the hookah and stuck the stem of the hose in his mouth. The U.A.E. agent puffed gently as the aromatic smoke rose from the water pipe. "Mr. Brackman and Mohammad are with the fifth member of your little group, Mr. Anderson. Unfortunately I wasn't told where they went."

"They're still in the building," Katz answered. "We mentioned earlier that Kamel came up with the names of individuals in the United Arab Emirates who belong to the Purple Warriors of Righteousness. Kamel only knew the identity of a few of his comrades in this country. Our friends are presently in the personnel information section, trying to learn about the whereabouts of the men Kamel spoke of."

"That's one thing I rather appreciate about this particular band of terrorists," McCarter declared. "They're all men. A lot of the terrorists we've encountered in the past have a fair number of female members. It still bothers me to have to shoot a woman—even in self-defense."

"I know what you mean," Encizo confirmed. "Some might accuse us of being chauvinists, but it is tougher to bring yourself to kill a woman than a man. When you're faced with an armed opponent, you don't have any choice. Kill or be killed. Females can be as dangerous as the males. Maybe that's a form of equal opportunity."

"That's the only agreeable thing about these bastards," Hillerman remarked. "Say, Bassam? You have any idea when you can see about replacing or repairing my leg?"

"I'll look into that in the morning," the Arab agent replied. "Perhaps we should take advantage of the opportunity to get some sleep. The pace you fellows have had since you arrived in the gulf area hasn't allowed much time for rest."

"That's a fact," McCarter said with a nod. He turned to Hillerman. "If our mates find any leads, we have to pull out in the morning."

"Even if they fix my leg I won't be charging off to battle with you, Sergeant," the British officer replied. "So watch your arse. I plan to get drunk with you next time you're in London."

"You take care, too, Colonel," McCarter said fondly. "It's been good working with you again, sir."

"If you'll follow me," Bassam began. "I'll show you where the sleeping quarters are."

Hillerman rose from the sofa and leaned heavily on his cane as he stood on his single leg. Bassam offered to help, but the British war-horse shook his head and hopped forward. McCarter stayed close to Hillerman in case his fellow countryman lost his balance. Encizo followed the two Britons as Bassam guided the visitors to a hallway.

"Just a moment, Mr. Anderson," Ahmed urged when the others had left the room. "Could I talk to you for a moment?"

"Of course," Katz replied, surprised by the request.

"Well, this isn't really important, but I am curious," the Kuwaiti agent began. "You're Jewish, aren't you?"

"I thought you suspected I'm a Jew," Katz said with a nod. "You remarked that you doubted my real name was anything like Anderson, and then you tried to prevent Bassam from criticizing Israel. I'm also curious about how you came to that conclusion?"

"You speak Arabic in the Northern Nile dialect," Ahmed explained. "The dialect spoken in the Cairo region of Egypt. However, your accent suggests you learned at least two European languages before you learned Arabic. Your English accent isn't quite British or American, so I guessed you're probably from Western Europe originally. Your age is right for you to have migrated to Palestine after World War Two. If you lost your right arm twenty-five years ago, it could have been during the conflicts between Egypt and Israel, which would explain why you speak an Egyptian dialect of Arabic."

"Impressive deductions, Ahmed," Katz said with a smile. "Sherlock Holmes would be proud of you. Does it matter if I'm a Jew?"

Ahmed interlaced his fingers and turned slowly to gaze at Bassam's Koran. The Islamic holy book sat on a lecture stand facing Mecca, almost identical to Ahmed's own private altar in Kuwait city.

"I believe I am a good Muslim," Ahmed began. "There is a passage in the Koran that warns Muslims not to take friends among the nonbelievers. The Christians and the Jews are to have their own friends. Yet, we are also supposed to treat others as our brothers. Even the nonbelievers."

"It seems to me some of us who are not Muslims are better friends to Kuwait and the other gulf countries than some of people who are members of Islam," Katz replied. "Your country has certainly made friends in the West."

"Yes," Ahmed said with a nod. "But you should know I don't agree with many of the actions Israel has taken in the past."

"I disagree with some of them myself," Katz admitted. "I'm not working for Israel now, my friend. True, we're here because of American interests, but you surely realize the mission is equally important to Kuwait and the other Arab gulf nations."

"Oh, I realize that," Ahmed assured him. "I believe Allah is a wise and merciful God. All-understanding and all-compassionate. I doubt that it is an accident that many non-Muslims are good people. I am certain that God would not object to a Muslim being friends with men as brave and noble as you and your four companions, regardless of your faith."

"Thank you, Ahmed," Katz smiled. "I appreciate that."

"I'm glad we had this talk," Ahmed stated.

"Perhaps the whole world would be better off if more people had such conversations," the Phoenix Force commander remarked. "I suspect if people paid more attention to what they have in common with others instead of concentrating on differences, and if they were a bit more tolerant of those who don't have exactly the same views in religion and politics, there wouldn't be nearly as much hatred and suspicion."

"And they wouldn't be killing each other in the name of God," Ahmed added. "That's an obscenity regardless of whether it is done by Muslim, Jew or Christian."

"The Bible warns not to take God's name in vain," Katz replied. "I can't imagine a worse form of profanity than using that name to justify murder."

"If there is justice, they'll pay for that blasphemy in the next world," Ahmed stated.

"There is justice," Katz assured him. "Not as much as there should be, but it still exists. And some of these vicious misguided ones will get a taste of it in *this* world."

14

Qabda stroked the blade of his *jambiya* across a whetstone. The leader of the Purple Warriors of Righteousness carried a Persian *jambiya*, the heavy curved blade nearly two inches longer than the traditional Arab *jambiya* fighting knife. Qabda admired the Persian culture and considered Iran to be the heart of the Shiite Muslim holy war. His choice of the Persian knife was a symbolic salute to Iran and the Islamic jihad. Qabda believed the holy war was the only just and sacred cause in the entire world. Tehran was thus the capital of Qabda's universe, and the Ayatollah was God's chosen supreme leader.

He gazed up at the silver crescent of the moon in the night sky. The crescent, an Islamic symbol, made Qabda smile. This was a good omen, he believed. Of course the moon in the last quarter phase was a natural cycle, but Qabda believed in mystical messages from nature, and he tended to interpret "signs" to fit his beliefs at the time.

The sky itself was a dark velvet sea adorned with countless stars, bright heavenly jewels in a beautiful cosmic display. Qabda considered that to be another good omen, encouragement from Allah that his cause was just and God would support their efforts with armies of mighty angels. Qabda had never seen an angel, but he had never seen God, either.

Qabda sat on the ground near the purple-domed mosque. Most of his men at the mountain base were asleep in their tents. The only sounds were the static of the radio in the

Gulf of Fire

communications shack at the summit of a nearby mountain, and the occasional yapping and howling of foxes that prowled the rocks after dark. Qabda tested the edge of his knife with a thumb. The blade left a hairline streak of crimson. He nodded with silent approval. The knife was sharp enough for any emergency, ready to shed the blood of the enemy.

He had many years of experience as a knife-fighter. During his wanderings as a homeless youth, Qabda had learned to defend himself with a blade. It had been a necessary survival skill. He still had more confidence in his ability with cold steel than firearms. Guns were products of the West, Qabda reckoned. The Islamic jihad had to use guns, explosives, rockets and bombs, all of which represented Western corruption to Qabda's mind. Eventually he hoped that the world would be able to abolish such weaponry, along with everything else associated with the infidels. The poison of Western literature, sciences, music, culture and vices had to be stamped out of existence before the revolution would be complete.

He saw Salim appear at the foot of the mountain where the communications center was located. The radio shack had to be positioned on a high point to transmit and receive beyond the mountain range. Metal ore deposits in the mountains and the sheer size of the great stone monuments of nature presented communications problems. The mountains helped conceal the secret base and the sacred mosque of the Shiite splinter group, but also hampered radio transmissions. Salim was one of Qabda's most trusted followers. A former radio engineer, Salim had been put in charge of the communications section. His expression seemed grim as he approached.

"We have received a message from our base in the United Arab Emirates," Salim began, shaking his sleek, ferrety head. "It is not good news."

"Allah gives us challenges, my brother," Qabda answered. "What test of faith must we face?"

"Our brothers in the U.A.E. attempted to kill the infidel Westerners who caused such misery for the Purple Warriors in Kuwait," Salim explained. "Apparently the foreign spawn of Satan slaughtered our brave holy soldiers. We don't have much detail about what happened, but there is no reason to believe any of the enemy were killed or that any of our people survived."

"They are martyrs to God's war, Salim," Qabda declared. "There is no need for us to mourn them. Their souls are now in paradise with Allah. Do not fear the infidels. They cannot harm us. God and His heavenly minions are on our side. You are familiar with what the Koran says about fighting the righteous battles?"

"Yes, Qabda," Salim answered, but he did not care to listen to a lecture about Islamic passages from his leader. He believed the foreigners presented a far more serious threat than Qabda seemed willing to recognize. "I am aware of these things, but our brothers in the United Arab Emirates are certainly in jeopardy. The enemy would not have arrived in the U.A.E. if they had not learned something about us in Kuwait."

"In two days it will not matter what the infidels know," Qabda declared, his eyes raised to the night sky. "Allah smiles on us. I have seen His signs this night. We shall be victorious. Only a lack of faith can stop us now."

"I realize that," Salim replied with a nod, then paused before continuing determinedly. "But there are also clear signs that the infidels may destroy our base in the United Arab Emirates and possibly even learn our location here."

"You must believe in the jihad, Salim," Qabda told him. "We must all have full trust."

"I do, Qabda," Salim assured him, worried that the leader of their movement might accuse him of treason against the Purple Warriors of Righteousness and thus against Allah Himself. Qabda had once stated that heretic traitors against the true Shiite faith should be burned alive. Salim did not wish to find out if his leader would carry out such a judgment. Qabda was not apt to say such things lightly.

"Of course," Qabda began. "The radio message may be a sign, as you say. Allah would not want His people to die in vain. Order them to leave the base and come join us so they can be part of the day of glory that will be ours."

"A wise decision, Qabda," Salim assured him with a sigh of relief. "One which may indeed be an insight from God."

"*May be* an insight?" the head of the terrorist cult replied, apparently offended. "There is *no doubt*, Salim. True believers have no reason for doubts."

"Forgive me for my poor choice of words," Salim said, beginning to fear for his life. A martyr's death was one thing, but to be executed as a traitor was quite another. "I will radio the base in the United Arab Emirates, Qabda."

Salim hurried back to the mountain. At least now he could safely order his radio operator in the commo center to contact the U.A.E. base and tell them to abandon their post before the infidels swooped down on them. However, it was not enough to ease Salim's concern about the well-being of himself and his friends at the Purple Warriors' mountain headquarters.

Worse, he was starting to doubt Qabda, and their entire organization revolved around the concept that Qabda was a prophet directly linked to Allah Himself. For the first time it occurred to Salim to wonder if Qabda was simply a madman, so strongly convinced of his own delusions of righteousness he had succeeded in convincing others of it. Salim considered himself to be a devout Shiite Muslim, and he believed in the Koran and God's unlimited power. Did this mean he had to also believe in the infallible ability of Qabda to interpret Allah's will?

Salim found it difficult to believe God was writing messages in the sky for Qabda's benefit. He had followed this man for years, trusted and believed in him, but now Salim feared Qabda might be just a man. Unfortunately it was too late to back away from the Purple Warriors of Righteousness. If Salim tried to leave, he would certainly be captured. He was a native of Iraq and had never ventured to this strange country before. Salim did not know the mountain range and could not hope to escape from the cult members who had been born and raised in the region. He had also heard gangs of hill bandits roamed the area. Even if he escaped from the Purple Warriors, the local mountain gangs would probably kill him.

Perhaps he would have a chance if he could convince others to accompany him. If enough of his comrades shared his doubts, they might even be able to mutiny against Qabda and overthrow the lunatic before more lives were lost. Yet how could Salim know if any of the other members shared his opinion? None of them spoke against Qabda. All seemed completely convinced that their leader was a spokesman for heaven and their cause was decreed by Allah.

Suddenly Salim was confused and frightened. He had been willing to die happily as a martyr for the jihad. Now he saw that if Qabda was not a prophet, then their cause was probably false as well. But the Ayatollah had declared the holy war, not Qabda. Was the old man in Iran a true prophet or another maniac? Would Allah reward them for dying as martyrs to the false claims of men? In every prayer, a good Muslim stated there was no god but Allah, yet they had regarded Qabda and the Ayatollah as gods. Salim trembled in fear for his soul as well as his flesh. Had their frenzied zeal to fight the alleged enemies of Islam turned them into heretics and blasphemers? Had they become soldiers of a holy war or murderers for Qabda? How would God choose to judge such men on the final day?

"Allah is all-merciful and all-compassionate," Salim whispered the familiar phrase which appeared so often in the Koran. He repeated it again and again, "Allah is all-merciful and all-compassionate."

Salim hoped deep in his heart that the passage was true.

SHORTLY AFTER DAWN Phoenix Force arrived at the home of Idris Rhamen. Rhamen was the man Ali Kamel had claimed was a top Purple Warrior subchief in the United Arab Emirates. Questioning the two terrorist prisoners who had survived the roadside battle near Dubai, the Phoenix commandos learned that Rhamen was a high-ranking member of the terrorist cult group and his house was often used as an improvised base of operations for the Purple Warriors stationed in the U.A.E.

Idris Rhamen was a respectable citizen of a good family, with a long history in an honorable and highly valued trade. Most Westerners seldom think of dates as a major cash crop, but it is one of the biggest exports from the U.A.E. A traditional desert food, date palms have been cultivated in the Middle East for centuries. Rhamen's family had operated a date farm not far from the Saudi border. His ancestors would probably turn over in their graves if their spirits knew what Idris Rhamen was doing with their property.

The five Phoenix commandos were accompanied by Ahmed, Bassam, Omar, Rashid and two dozen U.A.E. Marines. The latter were elite commandos, trained in a similar manner as the British Royal Marines. All carried assault weapons, side arms, grenades and an assortment of fighting knives. Once again each man was supplied with gas canisters and a protective mask. It was not known whether the enemy had cyanide gas tanks stored at the date farm, but they could not afford to take any chances.

However, they had not discovered any sentries among the date palm orchards. No booby traps, mines, surveillance cameras or listening devices for security. Workers were not visible in the orchards, but date palms didn't require much attention. The trees swayed slightly in the light breeze. The setting might have been exotic and pleasant under different circumstances. At the moment, the graceful motions of the slender trees seemed almost sinister in the otherwise undisturbed quiet.

No cars or trucks were parked by the stone-brick house. The strike team used the tree trunks for cover as they drew closer to the building. McCarter and Encizo headed for three aluminum silos, accompanied by three Arab marines. The others concentrated on the house.

"It seems unoccupied," Bassam remarked in a tense whisper. The U.A.E. agent clenched a submachine gun in his sweaty fists as he stared at the house.

"No vehicles," Omar observed. The intel agent would have felt safer if he were still working undercover as a double agent in Iraq. "That suggests there isn't a large group of people inside. Perhaps it is deserted."

"Let's not assume anything that might get us killed," Katz urged. The Israeli braced the Uzi across his prosthesis and raised the barrel toward the top of the palm he used for cover. "Watch the windows for movement."

"The only way we'll know if anyone is in the house is to go to the door and kick it in," Rashid announced in a firm voice. He was young, less than thirty, and still had the impatience of youth.

"Yeah," Gary Manning snorted. "I was with a guy who felt that way when we were checking out a farmhouse that was a former base for a group of terrorists back in the U.S. When he kicked in the door, he set off about a quarter of a pound of C-4 plastic explosive. Blew up half the house and splattered himself all over the state of Arizona."

"Speaking of which," Katz remarked, "this is your area of expertise."

"Right," the Canadian demolitions expert grunted. He slid the strap of his FAL over a shoulder. "I'd appreciate it if you fellas will cover me. If anything goes wrong, you might bury what's left of me in a nice shoe box."

"I'm coming with you," James announced as he slipped his arm through the shoulder sling to his M-16. "When you get that door open, you should have a backup."

"Your potential funeral," Manning replied with a shrug.

"Oh, thanks," the black warrior muttered. "I really needed to hear that."

Manning jogged toward the house, followed by Calvin James. The others watched the building warily, but nothing moved at the windows. The house was surrounded, and someone would have detected danger from any side of the building. The only other alternative was that the enemy was waiting for the ideal opportunity to make their move. Considering the suicidal nature of the Purple Warriors of Righteousness, the possibility was a very disturbing thought.

Gary Manning reached the door. He examined the framework and the narrow crack between the door and frame. The Canadian demolitions pro did not find any evidence of wires, pressure plates, spring detonators or miniature levers. This did not convince Manning the door was safe. He knew a hundred ways to booby-trap a door which would not be detectable from the outside.

Calvin James watched Manning remove a black metal disk from his pack. A small box was attached to the back of the disk, and a cord with an earphone extended from the device. It was a variation of the "hunter's ear," a listening device that amplified sound for the human ear. Manning prepared to plug the contraption in his ear, but James held out a palm and wiggled the fingers to urge Manning to hand him the amplifier.

Manning looked up at James's face. The dark ebony features were stern; the gaze was almost a silent command. The Canadian realized why James insisted he use the amplifier. Manning placed it in the black man's hand and stepped away from the door.

James plugged the device into his ear and placed the metal disk to the door. He listened carefully for the telltale ticking of a time bomb, the hum of an electric-powered booby trap and the labored breathing of a stress-racked opponent who might be waiting behind the door. He heard nothing.

Manning gestured toward the nearest window. James nodded and moved to the window, the listening device held ready. Both men stood clear of the window to avoid being seen by somebody who might be inside the house. James placed the disk close to the window frame. Sound causes vibrations and these would carry against the window pane to the frame. James listened for sounds of breathing, the rustle of clothing and the metallic *click-clack* of automatic weapon bolts being cocked. He heard no threatening noises and slowly leaned forward to carefully peer around the edge of the framework.

The curtains were not drawn, and James looked through the glass at the room within. The furniture appeared to be European, leaning toward Spanish decor. Two beautiful, multicolored crystal lamps stood on mahogany end tables by the sofa. A tear-shaped archway led to another room, but James could not make out any details beyond that. He did not see anyone in the front room, and he slowly changed position to try to get a look at the door.

He craned his neck awkwardly and finally managed a partial view of the door. He failed to spot sinister packages near the threshold, grenades wired to the doorknob, plastic explosive jammed into the hinges with pressure-activated detonators ready to ignite if the door opened. Even the bolt to the door was not in place. Possibly the door was not even locked, but James realized there were other ways to booby-trap an entrance which would not be obvious.

James moved away from the window and allowed Manning to examine the inside of the room via the window. The Canadian stared inside and looked at the door for a moment. From what was visible, he came to the same conclusion. There was no way to be absolutely certain, but Manning was reasonably sure the door was not rigged with any large explosive charges.

Manning tilted his head toward the trees. James nodded. They headed back to the date palms and took cover behind the nearest trunks. Manning pulled the pin from a concussion grenade, aimed carefully and lobbed it at the door. The blaster exploded and smashed in the door. There was no second explosion. The door was not booby-trapped.

"Go!" Katz shouted as he pulled on his protective mask.

The others followed his lead and donned their M-17 masks. James pointed his M-16 at the doorway and fired the M-203 attachment. The 40 mm shell rocketed across the threshold and exploded within the house. Columns of thick green tear gas rose from the doorway as the strike unit stormed the building.

More concussion grenades were used to blast the rear door, followed by tear gas that was lobbed into the doors and windows. The dense fog filled every room as the commandos searched the house. No terrorists confronted the assault team. The place was empty and deserted. Idris Rhamen and his followers had already fled.

"We're too late," Ahmed commented, his voice muffled by the rubber and plastic filters of his mask. "We should have made the raid last night instead of wasting time interrogating those stooges from the ambush on the road."

"What's done is done, my friend," Katz replied as he strained his eyes to see through the fogged lenses of his mask. The Israeli examined a room with several cots set up as improvised barracks.

"I would not have been able to get authorization for this raid if we had not confirmed Kamel's claims by interrogating the prisoners," Bassam nodded, his voice weary. "It also proved Mr. Anderson was correct with his theory about how the terrorists ambushed us on the road. It was a comfort to learn neither the Kuwaiti nor United Arab Emirate intelligence services had been infiltrated by Purple Warrior agents."

"I would have been far happier if we'd found a nest of enemy vipers here," Ahmed said, shaking his head with dismay. "Now we have reached what you Americans call a 'dead end,' and we don't have any leads left. We're no closer to finding Qabda's headquarters now than we were when this mission began.

15

"Who the hell are you people?" Captain Smith demanding, folding his hairy arms across his barrel chest. "Brackman tells me you're not CIA or NSA, but you've got top authority directly from the White House. I'd like to know what the hell that means."

Smith glared at Yakov Katzenelenbogen and Bassam. The Phoenix Force commander looked up at the U.S. Navy officer and sighed. He had had the very same conversation with dozens of members of intelligence and security organizations of several nationalities. The six-foot-seven naval officer was no doubt accustomed to giving orders and not taking them from anyone who did not wear the insignia of a rear admiral or above.

Many people would have found Captain Smith's appearance quite intimidating. He was an enormous man, and his strong lantern jaw and hard green eyes contributed to his formidable presence. The ONI officer had probably used his size and stern features to intimidate others in the past. Katz was not impressed. After all, Smith had not met with the Phoenix pro and the U.A.E. officer at the conference room of the U.S. embassy in Abu Dhabi to challenge them to a wrestling match. Katz had bested a lot of big men, so size did not physically worry him even if there had been a reason for such concern.

Smith was simply using tactics which had worked for him in the past. He was annoyed because civilians were intruding in his sphere of influence as a military intelligence officer. Katz understood that career military tend to distrust anything civilian. He was a retired full colonel with the Israeli Mossad himself. As far as he was concerned, though, there was too much at stake to worry about Captain Smith's sensitivity about the situation.

"Mr. Anderson and his people are in charge," Anton Brackman informed the captain. "Those were my instructions by the top section director of the CIA for the entire Middle East operations."

"CIA doesn't run the Organization of Navy Intelligence," Smith snorted. "You Company spooks..."

"Say what?" the black CIA agent asked, glaring up at Smith.

"I'm not using that term as an ethnic or racial slur and you know it, Brackman," the captain declared. "You fellows in the CIA are always trying to manipulate ONI and endlessly engage in secret political games. The navy has its own priorities here in the Persian Gulf."

"I would assume the survival of your men would be one of those priorities?" Katz remarked. "You must be aware of the number of sailors killed by terrorist attacks in the gulf waters off the coast of Kuwait and Iran. You know American personnel were killed when the oil platform was sabotaged here in the United Arab Emirates?"

"Of course I've been informed," Smith declared, his back stiff and the hairs on his neck bristling. "Goddamn Iranians. I don't know how much longer Washington intends to put up with this shit..."

"The Iranians aren't involved in the current round of terrorist actions," Katz told him. "It is the work of a terrorist group called the Purple Warriors of Righteousness. Sort of a Shiite extremist cult which is even more prone to violence than the Ayatollah's revolutionary groups."

"How do you know?" Smith asked suspiciously.

"It's the truth," Brackman said with disgust. "I was with these guys in Kuwait when they first arrived. Hell, Ahmed can vouch for them better than I can. He was part of the raid on the terrorist base in Kuwait. Got information about Idris Rhamen by interrogation—what was that fucker's name, Ali Kamel?''

"That's right," Ahmed confirmed. The Kuwaiti officer sat at the conference table, waiting for the right moment to speak. "If Captain Smith doesn't care to take the word of a wog, he might contact the British embassy in Oman and ask to talk to Colonel Hillerman."

"We don't have time for nonsense," Katz said in a hard, flat tone. He fixed his gaze on Smith. "A number of U.S. naval vessels are currently in the Arabian Sea and headed for the gulf. By this time tomorrow, they'll almost certainly be in the Gulf of Oman and on their way to the Strait of Hormuz. Then they'll move on to the Persian Gulf to escort three Kuwaiti supertankers. Correct?"

"That's not exactly a state secret," Smith said with a shrug. "Naturally, the safety of that convoy is a major concern for the ONI. We're trying to prepare for any sort of attack on the ships. That's why I'm here. I was told this matter concerns our national security and the safety of our naval fleet in this region."

"We're concerned, too, Captain," Bassam said dryly. "If the United States and Iran go to war in the gulf, my country and Ahmed's country will be in the middle of it. Geography involves us whether we like it or not."

"Americans are risking their lives to protect your tankers," Smith declared.

"And to protect American oil interests as well as the strategic advantage of having bases in the Persian Gulf on friendly soil," Ahmed replied. "Let's not argue about which country has the most to gain or lose at this point. None of us will win if the terrorists succeed."

"Why don't you just explain what's going on here and what you want from the ONI?" Smith asked, clearly frustrated.

"We're trying to close in on the terrorists' headquarters," Katz explained. "What we want from you and the navy is to keep the convoy away from the Strait of Hormuz as long as possible."

"Isn't that giving the terrorists what they want?" the naval officer demanded, hands held out in a palms-up gesture. "Keeping American ships out of the Persian Gulf?"

"You don't understand what we're talking about," Katz replied with a sigh. "The terrorists aren't motivated by international politics as it is generally understood in the West. They think they're fighting a religious war. These are Shiite fanatics who believe if they die as martyrs fighting the infidel Americans, they'll be rewarded in paradise."

"They've been making those martyrdom claims in Tehran ever since the Ayatollah took over," Smith said, unimpressed.

"But the Purple Warriors of Righteousness aren't from Iran," Brackman stated. "Most of them are Arabs and...hell, there's no point in talking to you. You don't pay attention anyway."

"He'll pay attention when he talks to Admiral Martin," the Phoenix commander announced, taking a pack of cigarettes from his pocket. "The admiral has already agreed to delay the convoy until he receives word to go ahead through the strait. He's also under orders not to use any Omani ports until told to do so."

"You've already talked to Admiral Martin?" Smith stared at Katz as if the Israeli had just announced he could raise the dead by spitting on graves.

"No," Katz corrected. "I didn't talk to him personally. The President of the United States relayed our message, and the admiral agreed to cooperate. I imagine the President gave him a direct order. He's Commander and Chief of the armed forces of the United States, you know."

"Holy!" Smith rasped. "Why didn't you mention it before?"

"Because we need your cooperation, Captain," Katz explained. "I wanted to find out a bit about you. What sort of man you are."

"I suppose I didn't make a good impression," the captain commented, suddenly concerned about the "civilian's" opinion.

"Well, I don't think we're going to become buddies," Katz replied with a shrug. "I suspect you're not popular with your men. You probably look down on enlisted personnel and officers of lower rank as if they were lesser life forms. That means you'd be apt to disregard their opinions, advice and information. A serious flaw, Captain. Sometimes the fellows in the trenches know more than those in command."

"I'll bear that in mind," Smith said solemnly.

"However," Katz continued, blowing a smoke ring at the ceiling, "I also suspect you're quite serious about your job. Serious about security and probably stubborn as hell. You're also suspicious and demanding. Necessary character traits in the cloak-and-dagger business."

"Okay," Smith replied, accepting the carrot after the stick. "So what do you want from ONI in general and me in particular?"

"This is eyes-only top secret," the Phoenix pro began. "In this case it's actually ears-only, because you're not getting any written details. The leader of the terrorists is a man who calls himself Qabda. We believe his main base may be located in Oman, possibly at the mountain range near the border."

"How'd you come up with this theory?" Smith inquired. "Got a good Ouija board or something?"

"We raided Idris Rhamen's date farm," Bassam supplied the answer. He stared figurative daggers at the ONI man. The U.A.E. intel officer had not liked Smith from the moment when he'd entered the conference room, and the naval officer had not done anything since then to change Bassam's original impression. "The terrorists had fled, but they left some evidence behind."

"A two-way radio," Ahmed picked up the story. "A large and very heavy radio. We found it in a compartment at the roof of a silo. Improvised communications room. Apparently the operator considered it too heavy to take, so he smashed it—or tried to. The speakers were damaged and the microphone was torn out, gauge shattered. Still, we have some idea of what frequencies they used.''

"They would not have such a bulky radio unless they needed to transmit beyond the United Arab Emirates," Bassam added.

Apparently Smith wasn't convinced. "That doesn't mean the enemy is in Oman," he stated challengingly. "They could be elsewhere in the country here or in Saudi Arabia or Kuwait."

"The Purple Warriors of Righteousness no longer have a base in Kuwait, and they wouldn't be able to set up a new one in less than forty-eight hours," Katz explained. "Rhamen and his group certainly would not have headed for Kuwait. They wouldn't stay in the U.A.E., either. This is a small country, and Rhamen is well-known here. He might decide to go underground for a while, but nothing about this terrorist organization suggests they're that sophisticated. These are fanatics, eager to fight and die for their cause. They don't seem to have safe houses, preplanned routes for emergency escape or secondary plans if things go wrong. They want to be martyrs, so such things would seem to have little purpose. Why run when you want to die?"

"You assume that to be true," Smith snorted as he placed his hands on his hips. "Didn't anyone ever tell you when you break down the word 'assume' it means 'ass-u-me' and makes an ass out of you and me?"

"I don't think that is a necessary process in your case," Bassam told the ONI man.

"Hold on!" Brackman urged, eager to prevent further hostilities. "Let's keep our tempers, fellas! Anderson, you didn't mention the trucks."

"That's another piece of evidence," Katz began. "We found tire marks of trucks which had recently driven away from Rhamen's property. The size of the tire prints and tread marks told us how many vehicles, general size of each rig and an idea of probably make of the trucks. With this information, we then checked with the vehicle records and learned Rhamen had three vehicles which fit the estimated descriptions of the trucks we believe fled the date farm less than two hours before our arrival."

"So you got the make, model and license numbers of these trucks?" Smith asked, showing some interest. "I assume...I would imagine that you contacted the border guards of Oman and Saudi Arabia."

"There aren't actual border guards, because the boundary areas of the United Arab Emirates, Saudi Arabia and Oman are not officially defined," Bassam explained. "All three countries are on good terms, and we don't worry about the borders because we're all pretty friendly. To a great extent the border regions are Bedouin territory. Bedouins don't care much for boundaries."

"However," Ahmed added quickly, guessing Smith would be impatient and in no mood to hear about details concerning relations between the U.A.E. and its neighbors. "The Saudies have military training bases near their boundary. Since they've had problems with terrorism in the past, these areas have armed guards on duty round the clock. The terrorists would certainly be aware of this and avoid going anywhere near the Saudi bases. Oman would be a more logical choice."

"Besides," Katz added, "the prisoners we interrogated never mentioned Saudi Arabia. Apparently the Purple Warriors of Righteousness are concentrating on the smaller gulf nations. I think they might be intimidated by the size of Saudi Arabia and the reputation they've acquired for dealing with terrorists quickly, efficiently and no-holds-barred. After the incidents at the Great Mosque and Mecca, terrorists have good reason to be reluctant to attempt to set up bases in Saudi Arabia."

"Our British SIS friend is in Muscat," Bassam began. "He left for Oman this morning with a new prosthetic device that he seemed quite pleased with. He hasn't been able to provide definite information, but the Sultanate Security Services agrees that it is possible the Purple Warriors of Righteousness could have a secret base in the mountain range.''

"This is where you come in, Captain," Katz declared. "My sources in the States informed me that the National Security Agency has been screening radio broadcasts in the Persian Gulf for the past eight years. NSA suspects the Iranians have been communicating with radical Shiite factions in the Arab nations by coded messages in civilian broadcasts."

"This concerns me?" Smith asked, genuinely surprised.

"You've been the OIC of the navy's radio scanners on board the USS *Pierce* and the two frigates, which I don't recall by name," Katz explained. "Well, all those radio broadcasts you've been recording, translating and sending off to ONI have actually been used by the National Security Agency."

"I've been working for NSA?" the captain was stunned. "How did you find out . . . ?"

"My chief of operations can find out almost anything that's going on with Washington," Katz answered. "What we need now are the recordings of radio transmissions detected in and around the Omani mountain ranges. Especially anything that suggests a conversation between Omani transceivers and radio operators in the United Arab Emirates. This should help us pinpoint the location of the enemy base—unless it turns out our entire theory is wrong."

"I'll get on it immediately, sir," Smith said with a solemn nod.

"Try to do it a bit sooner than that if you can," Katz said dryly.

16

The bus was a drab, ordinary-looking vehicle. A fifteen-footer, tan with a white roof, it was no different from hundreds of others that traveled to and fro across the borders of the United Arab Emirates and Oman. Its destination was the town of Dank. No great skyscrapers and office buildings probed the afternoon sky, but the houses and stores appeared to be well constructed and cared for. Several people sat on benches and watched a color television set mounted beneath a wood-and-canvas shelter. Outdoor public television was one of the sultanate's free offerings to the people of Oman.

The people in the town seemed reasonably happy with their lot in life. Oman, like the other progressive Arab nations of the gulf region, had used oil profits to improve the lives of its citizens. Shaped like a giant horseshoe around the great Arabian Peninsula, Oman was larger than Kuwait, the United Arab Emirates, Qatar and Bahrain put together, but its estimated oil reserves were much smaller than those of Kuwait and the U.A.E. Oman's estimated four billion barrel reserves were only slightly larger than that of the tiny nation of Qatar. Nonetheless, the sultanate provided its people with free education, medical care, telephone services and other advantages.

The Dank residents seemed to be representative of two separate cultures, and actually almost two different eras—one of the present and the other of the past. Some wore Western clothing and others were dressed in traditional

robes and headgear. Gary Manning noticed an elderly
woman clad in a long flowery dress with billowing sleeves
and cowllike head scarf as he peered out the tinted window
of the bus. The Canadian was startled when he saw her face.
The woman's features were covered by an odd device that
resembled a metal mask with a band around the forehead,
a narrow strip of vertical across the nose and a wide wing-
shaped lower band that concealed the mouth and jaw. Her
eyes were not covered, and she gazed up at the TV, barely
sparing a glance toward the passing bus.

"Jesus," Manning remarked. "Look at the woman.
What's she wearing? Some sort of punishment device to
keep her from talking? Looks like an iron muzzle."

"That's a *birkah*," David McCarter explained as he
leaned over the backrest of his seat on the bus to talk to the
Canadian. "It's not worn for punishment. It is the traditional type of veil worn by women in Oman. For the same
reason as the cloth veils worn by women throughout Arab
countries. It's made of leather, not metal, but at first glance
you can't tell for sure. First time I saw a woman wearing a
birkah it startled me a bit, too. Most Omani women don't
wear them anymore, but you'll see them from time to time."

"Women wearing veils is an Arab custom," Ahmed
added. "It is not required by the Koran or the Islamic faith.
The belief is that a woman's beauty is so great that she may
stir up carnal desires and sinful thoughts of adultery in the
hearts of men other than her husband. So traditionally she
only uncovers her beauty for her spouse in private."

"As you can see," Omar began a groan of disgust, "some
Arabs still haven't reached the twentieth century. You'll
probably find Oman to be a bit backward culturally. The
United Arab Emirates is a federation, and we have a prime
minister and a president. Kuwait is pretty much run by the
emir, but it also has a prime minister and a national assem-
bly. Oman is ruled entirely by the sultan and his advisors.
The government, if you can call it that, is based on Islamic
law and little else."

"That's a rather harsh evaluation, Omar," Bassam commented, a trace of disapproval in his voice. "Oman is our ally and a good neighbor."

"Yes, I know," Omar said with a nod, but the agnostic U.A.E. agent did not sound apologetic. "I suppose I shouldn't make such judgments. After all, our visitors from the West will see Oman for themselves and form their own opinion."

"I've been here before, mate," McCarter told Omar. "Personally, I rather liked the Omani people. They're hardworking, honest, reasonably charitable, and they'll fight like lions if they have to. You can bad-mouth the sultanate if you like, but the current leader has done a lot to unify and improve the standard of living for his people. There've been remarkable advances in Oman since 1970."

"Where's the guy from Muscat supposed to meet us?" James inquired as he watched two men dressed in traditional Bedouin clothing walk to a coffeehouse, leading a pair of camels by the reins.

"At a marble quarry outside of town," Ahmed answered. "If any Purple Warrior spies are in Dank, they'll probably think you gentlemen are foreign buyers. Marble is a big business in Oman."

"The geography of Oman is different from most Arab countries," McCarter declared, lighting up a Player's cigarette. "Among other things, there's not much desert. It's at the interior plateau. Lots of mountains and hills and miles of coast, which is used more for fishing than offshore drilling."

"I knew I should have brought my note pad," Manning said dryly. "We gonna be quizzed on this stuff later?"

"You're not interested?" McCarter growled. "Don't listen."

"Did you two reverse personalities today?" Rafael Encizo inquired with amusement. The Briton tended to be a "smart ass," and Manning was usually the most serious member of the Phoenix Force team.

"I'm sure it's just a phase they're going through," Katz remarked, not bothering to look up from a map of the Akhdhar mountain range.

Manning shrugged and headed for the rear of the bus to examine their gear stored there. James glanced back at him, and the Canadian jerked his head in a gesture that indicated he wanted James to join him. The black commando was not surprised by the request. He rose from his seat and walked back to the equipment.

"You want to talk, man?" James asked in a low whisper.

"When we were at the door of that date farm back in the U.A.E., you insisted on using the listening device because you didn't think I should do it," Manning replied in the same quiet tone.

"I figured I was better qualified to do it," James explained. "Because I'm not hard of hearing in one ear and you are."

"How'd you figure that out, Cal?" Manning asked, glancing down at the floor. "Was I that obvious?"

"Not at first," James explained. "But remember, I've had medical training. I noticed that you've started tilting your head so you can hear better with your good ear. I guessed some time ago you must have damaged an eardrum from all those explosions you've set off over the years. Your hearing is getting worse in that ear, isn't it?"

"You tell the others yet?" Manning asked tensely.

"Yakov already suspects it," the black commando answered. "You can't get anything past that old fox. I think Rafael and David do, too, but Hal doesn't seem to have a clue. We sort of figure you'll do something about it if it starts to get in the way of your ability to do your job."

"You'll help me?" Manning inquired, not looking at James's face.

"Shit, Gary," James muttered. "You need to ask?"

"Maybe I just need to be reassured," the Canadian said with a slight shrug.

"When we get back to the States," James promised, "I'll put you in touch with a guy I know in California who specializes in hearing disorders. He'll be able to tell you what you'll need. Hearing aid, operation, whatever. Don't worry about it, man. We'll take care of it."

"Thanks, Cal," Manning said with a nod.

"Friends help in other ways than shooting bad guys when your back is turned and you don't see the son of a bitch," James said with a grin. "Just be careful. Okay?"

"Okay," Manning confirmed.

THE BUS ARRIVED at the marble quarry at the outer regions of the Akhdhar mountain range. Blocks of the smooth stone had been stacked along the rim of the quarry pit. Cranes hauled heavy marble up from the gorge and transported it into company trucks. Workers, their heads covered by metal hard hats, labored in the quarry.

A pair of men dressed in white linen suits did not appear to be part of the working force. One man was portly, with a stubbly beard, dark glasses and a checkered *keffiyeh*, which made him resemble Yasser Arafat. His companion was slightly taller and clean-shaven, a white cloth hat pulled low on his forehead. Rashid drove the bus to the headquarters building where the pair waited patiently.

"Welcome to Oman, gentlemen," the tall man who was dressed like an English gentleman on a summer outing greeted, as Katz, Bassam and Ahmed climbed from the bus. "You must be Mr. Hillerman and his group?"

"Anderson," Katz corrected, but he realized the stranger had purposely used the British SIS officer's name to identify himself. "And you are?"

"Call me Khalifa," the man replied with a short bow. He gestured toward his companion. "This is Hussan."

The Arafat look-alike smiled and nodded.

"Shall we talk in the bus?" Bassam suggested.

"Capital idea," Khalifa announced. His clipped English and expressions indicated he had also been educated in Great Britain.

The bus rolled forward after the two Omanis joined the passengers. Khalifa and Hussan exchanged introductions with the others, which of course meant a round of cover names.

"Colonel Hillerman spoke with me in Muscat," Khalifa began, toying with a gold signet ring on the ring finger of his right hand. "You suspect these Purple Warrior terrorists are here in Oman. Yes?"

"We're fairly certain their base is only about sixty kilometers from here," Katz answered.

"The Akhdhar mountains?" Khalifa seemed surprised. "I think it more likely we'd find them in the Dhofar region. That's where terrorists in Oman have always run to in the past."

"Those blokes in Dhofar are Marxist rebels," McCarter declared, speaking from personal experience he'd acquired when he was stationed in Oman with the SAS. "The Purple Warriors are a different breed of terrorists."

"So I was told," the Omani agent admitted. "But I still suspect any terrorist group in my country will be linked to the Communists."

"Not this time," Katz insisted. "NSA discovered radio messages transmitted from the mountains, and the same frequency was also used by radio messages coming from the direction of the United Arab Emirates and Kuwait. The tracking devices used by NSA were employed only because the conversations seemed artificial, fabricated to relay information in code. However, the listening station did not have any reason to believe these broadcasts were communications by terrorists or espionage agents."

"Supposedly they thought it was some sort of smugglers' conspiracy," Manning remarked.

"Whatever the reason," Katz continued, "indifference, incompetence or ignorance—and with NSA it could have been a combination of all three—they didn't pay much attention to the radio messages, but they logged it in. Fortunately NSA loves stacking up information whether it seems important or not. We're lucky we've got what little they bothered with."

"What sort of messages were these?" Hussan inquired.

"Meaningless sentences, unless one understands the passwords for whatever code the terrorists are using," Encizo said with a sigh. "Don't worry about that. All we need from your organization is a guide who knows the mountains."

"I was born and raised in the Akhdhar range," Hussan said with a smile that intensified his resemblance to Arafat. "I can guide you, but we don't know the exact location of the alleged terrorist site."

"Wait a bloody minute," McCarter began, frustration in his tone. "You say you were born and raised in the mountain range. So you're from one of the villages. Right?"

"Of course," Hussan confirmed with a shrug. "That should be obvious..."

"Yeah, it should be," the Briton agreed. "You still have friends and family there?"

"I am a good Ibadhi Muslim," Hussan declared. "A good Muslim does not forget his family."

"Then they'll talk to you," Calvin James said. The streetwise tough guy from Chicago understood McCarter's plan and easily jumped in. "There can't be much going on in the area the locals don't know about. They probably don't realize these suckers are terrorists, but I bet they know when a bunch of outsiders move into their territory and set up camp there."

"Especially a bunch of outsiders led by a man who wears a purple turban," Gary Manning added.

"You gentlemen have good logic," Khalifa announced. "Perhaps the hand of Allah is also in our favor."

"I wouldn't count on that," Omar, the agnostic, muttered.

"Hussan is one of the best men in our service, but he is not the regular case officer for this area," Khalifa explained. "He happened to be in Muscat between assignments when I met with Colonel Hillerman. I needed a driver familiar with the area here, and that is why Hussan accompanied me."

"That's one hell of a coincidence," Encizo remarked.

"Allah provides," Ahmed declared. "However, I don't think He'll provide us with commandos to back us. Will the Omani military send us extra troops?"

"That may be difficult and time-consuming," Khalifa answered. "I'm not authorized to call in the military. However, we can go to Muscat and make arrangements. Under the circumstances, we can meet with the Sultan himself."

"That would be a great honor," Katz assured him, "but time isn't on our side. The Purple Warriors of Righteousness know we're stalking them. They know we've already located two of their bases in two separate countries. Qabda certainly realizes that one way or the other the end is near, or at least that a showdown is approaching. He must know we'll either close in soon or he'll have to act and carry out one final effort for martyrdom. Qabda will surely pick the latter choice of action. With a convoy of American vessels due through the Strait of Hormuz in less than twenty-four hours, it isn't hard to guess what target they intend to hit."

"You're not suggesting we do this alone?" Bassam asked, startled by the notion. "If everyone in this bus participated that would be eleven men total. There could be a couple hundred terrorists at that base."

"So the odds are less than fair," McCarter said with a wolfish grin. "Too bad for them. They shouldn't have started this fight."

"Could we hear a sane answer to Bassam's question?" Ahmed asked, turning toward Katz.

"We don't have time to get more men," the Phoenix commander replied. "The convoy won't be coming through the strait. The ships will stay in the Arabian Sea and perhaps the Gulf of Oman, but they won't move into the Persian Gulf or go to port along the coast of Oman. When Qabda learns the convoy isn't advancing, he'll realize they've been warned to stay back. He knows enough about basic strategy to understand we're playing for time. He'll either break up the base of set up elsewhere, or they'll attempt a massive assault against targets we can only guess at."

"We go in alone and we'll get killed," Omar stated the obvious concern every man shared.

"If we don't, hundreds or even thousands could die," Manning replied. "If we don't stop him now, it might take months to find Qabda again. By then it could be too late."

"You mean they'll all be dead from suicide missions?" Khalifa inquired.

"I mean it might be too late to prevent a full-scale war between the United States and Iran," the Canadian corrected. "The majority of people still think the Iranians are responsible for the recent terrorist attacks. If we don't put Qabda out of business, Nostradamus might be right about an anti-Christ in a purple turban who will start World War Three. The final war of mankind. Armageddon."

17

Twilight descended across the mountain range in northwest Oman as Phoenix Force and their Arab allies worked their way along a difficult pathway between two mountains. The surface was rough and cluttered with rocks of various size, from pebbles to boulders. They had been tumbling from the stone walls of the mountains for centuries without regard for any inconvenience to human travelers.

Khalifa did not accompany the Phoenix commandos. The tall Omani security service agent had a heart condition and wisely admitted he was not physically able to clamber about on the Akhdhar mountains or charge into combat. Khalifa had returned to Muscat to report to the sultanate and Colonel Hillerman. He would also try to get the Omani military to send a couple of platoons of commandos to assist the Phoenix Force group at the mountain range.

The Phoenix pros, Ahmed, Bassam, Omar, Rashid and Hussan were dressed in the style of the mountain tribes in the region. Each man wore baggy trousers and shirt, goat-skin boots, *keffiyeh* headgear and a sheepskin robe that looked a good deal like a vest that had sprouted knee-length tails. The garments seemed uncomfortable and awkward at first, and proved to be a particular hardship for Omar. Ironically the native of the United Arab Emirates had never worn such traditional Arab garb and had managed to avoid going into excursions in the desert. He had complained that he was about to pass out from the heat in such clothes.

Phoenix Force had carried out missions in various climates throughout the world. They had worn similar garments in the past, but the mountain garb took a while to get used to. Hussan seemed quite pleased to be clad in the manner of his mountain people. Katz was glad Hussan had changed his style of dress as well. The Omani agent did not resemble Arafat quite as much without the dark glasses and checkered head cloth.

Their costumes were dark and drab. Brown, green and gray. The bland colors served as camouflage among the rocks. Their weapons were not a problem. It was common practice for locals to go armed in the region because of the gangs of bandits rumored to prowl the mountain range. Even automatic weapons drew no more than an occasionally raised eyebrow. The robes concealed their pistols in shoulder leather. Grenades and other gear were carried in packs slung over shoulders.

The trek was difficult from the beginning, and most of the range had to be traversed on foot. Their first stop had been Hussan's village. To avoid suspicion, he had told the others to wait outside the village while he spoke with his people in private.

The village looked crude and thrown together. The people sheltered in rather flimsy huts and appeared to live in a manner similar to that of their ancestors. A few goats and some donkeys roamed the village, and there was no sign of any pens to contain the beasts. Apparently the domesticated animals chose to remain with the mountain tribe.

The men wore the garb of their people, *keffiyeh* and turban headgear, with *jambiya* knives thrust in sash belts. The women were dressed in long robes, heads and faces covered by scarves. They seemed reluctant to allow Hussan's companions to enter their world. They were a clannish lot who chose to keep to themselves and largely ignore the rest of society. Katz was surprised when he heard bits of conversation within the village. They spoke a language which sounded like a cross between Arabic and Turkish.

A superb linguist, and the son of an accomplished translator and language expert, Yakov Katzenelenbogen was intrigued by the village tongue. He had never heard anything quite like it before. He suspected Hussan's people might be descended of the Seljuk Turks, who in the tenth century had a large empire that included large portions of Iran, Iraq, Oman, besides other countries. If this theory was correct, Katz mused, it meant they had eventually developed a hybrid language. He wondered whether the culture of these mountain tribes had been studied, and whether there was anything written on the subject.

Hussan entered a large hut and visited with the occupants for almost fifteen minutes. Then he emerged and joined Phoenix Force and the other four Arab members of the unit. He smiled at them and announced that he now knew the location of the terrorist base.

The mountain people had seen the strange base of the outsiders who had come to the Akhdhar range more than a year ago. The strangers had set up tents in a small valley, surrounded by mountains in the heart of the region. They later built a mosque of brick and stone with a purple dome. The Ibadhi Muslim tribesmen did not understand the strange choice of color for the dome, and suspected it was some sort of splinter group of the Sunni or Shiite religion. The mountain people did not care to associate with such "cults," and steered clear of the strangers. They also suspiciously kept an eye on the strangers' camp from time to time.

They did not know much about the men stationed by the purple mosque, but they had observed that the strangers were well armed. There did not appear to be any women or children at the base. The villagers of the mountains had guessed the strangers were members of some sort of religious retreat, heavily armed due to fear of roving bandits. The isolated mountain people were only vaguely aware of the problems of international terrorism, so they did not realize what sinister purposes the purple mosque and base served.

The village chief had told Hussan where to find the camp set up by the outsiders. He relayed the information to Phoenix Force and the other Arabs in their improvised assault unit. There was little doubt Hussan had learned the location of the enemy base. Katz congratulated Hussan and told him to lead the way to the hidden fortress of the Purple Warriors of Righteousness.

Continuing their journey along the rugged path, they had to scale the rock walls of mountains, because the natural passage between the stony giants led to a dead end more than once. None of the mountains were particularly large, but they found few hand- or footholds on the relatively smooth rock surface. All the men of Phoenix Force were experienced mountaineers, but only Hussan and Rashid were veteran climbers among their companions. Not surprisingly, the majority of Arabs had little reason to climb mountains. The inexperience and hesitation of Ahmed, Bassam and Omar slowed down progress for the others.

Linked together by ropes, Phoenix Force and the experienced climbers virtually hauled the other three up the rock walls. The climb was still difficult, since darkness fell across the mountain range and they could not use flashlights or torches for fear they would be detected by the enemy. Nonetheless, they managed to scale the rock walls and descend to the next passage at the base of two mountains.

"We should be roughly three or four kilometers from the base," Hussan explained in a soft whisper, knowing that sound traveled among the echoes of the mountain range. "The purple mosque is said to be in the center of a junction at the base of four mountains."

"They'll have sentries posted on or near the peak of at least one mountain," McCarter stated. "The radio will be at an elevated position as well. Has to be to get decent reception or transmit with all these mountains about."

"Right," Encizo agreed, glancing up at the formidable, blank stone faces of the surrounding mountains. "One thing in our favor is the fact they won't have any vehicles. How the hell could they get them up here? No reason to anyway. What would they do with cars or trucks here?"

"They probably have cyanide canisters and explosives," Gary Manning said grimly. "These are the hard-core, totally dedicated fanatics of the Purple Warriors of Righteousness. They won't hesitate to blow up those canisters and release enough poison gas to kill everyone within a hundred kilometers of this site."

"All right," Katz began, his brow wrinkled in thought. "We have to get in position to observe and evaluate the enemy base. The sentries must be taken care of, and we'll need to determine where the gas canisters and explosives are stored."

"We may have to guess," Calvin James stated, glancing at his Seiko diver's watch. "I doubt they'll have labels on this stuff."

"So we'll guess," Katz said with a shrug. "Everyone bear in mind how dangerous these people are. We can't afford to let any of them get close to anything that even remotely resembles an explosive or a gas canister. Even if we have to kill every single individual at the base, we can't let that happen."

"Choosing between the lives of a bunch of murderous fanatics and hundreds of innocent people isn't very difficult," Omar said dryly. "We ought to execute the lot of them anyway. Do the world a favor, in my opinion."

"I wish we had some idea how many terrorists are waiting for us," Ahmed admitted as he screwed a foot-long silencer to the threaded barrel of his Sterling submachine gun.

"This way it'll be a surprise," McCarter commented. The Briton had removed his goatskin backpack and opened the flap to remove the Barnett Commando crossbow.

"I've never been very fond of surprises," Bassam muttered.

"Let's hope we don't have too many," Encizo replied. "Best if we split into teams and hit the place from four directions. The longest climbs should be handled by our best mountaineers. That would probably be Hussan and Stark."

"Agreed," Katz said with a nod. "We'll divide into four groups. Two two-man teams and two three-man. Ahmed was with us on a raid in Kuwait, so he knows a bit about how we work. However, his experience in the field is limited. Bassam and Omar are fairly new to this sort of mission as well."

"No argument about that," Bassam agreed. "You tell us what to do, Anderson."

"I wish I had the wisdom to make infallible decisions," the Phoenix Force commander confessed. "This is the sort of situation that requires flexible strategy. We'll plan this the best we can, but when we go in we'll have to improvise based on what we find."

"May Allah be with us," Ahmed said solemnly.

"And may we not screw up," Calvin James added.

RAFAEL ENCIZO, Omar and Rashid crept up the face of the mountain. The Cuban Phoenix pro gripped the rocks and pulled himself higher, boot groping the stone wall for a foothold. He felt Omar yank the rope attached to his waist. The tug threatened to break Encizo's grip on the rock wall. His fingers strained as his body jerked backward from the force pull. Encizo held on by his fingertips, and the edges of his boots scraped the stone surface.

His foot finally found support on a slight ridge. Omar stopped pulling the rope after Encizo managed to secure a firm grip. The Cuban wished he could turn around and tell the U.A.E. agent to take it easy on the goddamn rope. He wanted to remind Omar if one of them fell they all might follow, because the rope linked all three men together. The idea of smacking the Arab in the mouth fleetingly passed through Encizo's mind, but he was in no position to act on the notion, anyway. Silence and a cool head were vital if they intended to accomplish their mission—and survive.

Encizo continued the ascent to the peak. He reached the top, with Omar and Rashid behind him. The Cuban signaled to the others to stay put and disengaged himself from the rope. Encizo slowly crept along the rock wall toward the opposite side of the mountain. Hugging the wall, he shuffled along the narrow ridges very carefully. The sound of his own pulse sounded like a drum beat in his ears and seemed loud enough to warn any sentry who might be lying in wait on the rocks. He realized it was merely his imagination amplifying the sounds. Still, Encizo felt the tension in his spine, the rush of blood in his veins and the trip-hammer pace of his heartbeat as he moved around the peak.

At last he was in position and gazed down at the enemy base below. Although he expected to see the mosque, it still startled him. Two stories high, the second level consisting of the great purple dome, it stood by the base of another mountain to the east. Encizo was astonished that the Shiite extremists had gone to such effort to build the brick-and-stone building. The feat must have been extremely difficult, but the mosque was a handsome, well-made structure.

The Purple Warriors of Righteousness had probably used stones from the surrounding mountains. Nonetheless, hauling the heavy burden to the small valley without benefit of machines or even animals must have been a backbreaking chore. Encizo guessed the bricks were made of adobe clay, sun-baked as they had been for thousands of years in many cultures throughout the world. The terrorists had devoted months to the construction of this unique house of worship. Whatever else one could fault them for, the Purple Warrior sect certainly could not be accused of laziness or failing to take their religion seriously.

Cristo, Encizo thought. Phoenix Force would not be in the Persian Gulf region if the Shiite jihad members did not take their holy war seriously. The U.S. Navy would not be escorting supertankers or occasionally fighting Iranian forces in the gulf if this was not the case. A lot of killing would not occur if the jihad was not regarded with deadly earnestness.

The flickering glow of a camp fire illuminated the mosque and the other, more humble buildings below. The Purple Warriors had not spent nearly as much time or effort with personal dwellings as they had with the mosque. The camp consisted of several tents, each large enough to accommodate six men, and two simple wood structures draped in canvas for protection from the heat. The latter were like shacks, smaller than the average two-car garage back in the States. Encizo guessed one of the wood cottages was probably Qabda's quarters. The other? It could be a storage place for weapons and the other accessories of terror. They would want to keep these items in a fairly secure place with as much shelter from the merciless sun as possible.

Encizo also spotted the crude communications center near the summit of a mountain at the west side of the camp. It was another shack, smaller than the two below and covered by a gray tarp for camouflage as well as shade. The tall antenna of a radio extended from a hole in the canvas and betrayed the purpose of the little structure. A guard stood near the entrance, an AK-47 or a rifle of similar design slung to his shoulder.

The Cuban took all that in with little more than a single glance. He did not spot the terrorist sentry on a ledge beneath his position until he completed scanning the enemy site in general. The guard sat on a small boulder, his rifle propped against the rock wall beside him. The fellow was calmly smoking a cigarette, unaware an intruder lurked on the peak less than five feet above his head.

Encizo clearly saw the paisley headcloth of the guard's *keffiyeh* and the ammunition belts of 7.62 mm cartridges that crisscrossed his chest. Encizo spared another glance at the surrounding area. He spotted a third sentry on the rock wall of the north mountain, directly across from his position. The last guard seemed to be gazing up at the sky as if he expected to be attacked by helicopters or maybe flying saucers. Encizo saw another figure creep onto the ledge behind the star-gazing sentry. Even from a distance, Encizo recognized the heavy-set physique of Yakov Katzenelenbogen and the Israeli's prosthetic arm with steel hooks for a hand.

Time to act, Encizo realized as he slid his Cold Steel Tanto from its sheath.

The Cuban dropped down from the peak to the ledge. He landed sure-footed, face-to-face with the astonished sentry who had been sitting on the boulder, taking a smoke break. The man's eyes grew rounded in surprise and alarm as Encizo suddenly appeared in front of him. The guard dropped his cigarette and began to reach for his rifle. Encizo's arm snapped forward like the head of a striking cobra. The point of his Tanto knife plunged into the hollow of the sentry's neck. Encizo followed with a ruthless cut that sliced open the man's throat and severed the carotid and jugular.

Blood gushed across the sentry's shirtfront, and his body convulsed wildly. Encizo held the dying man down while the last struggles of fading life poured from the terrorist's body. At last the corpse went limp. Encizo removed the paisley *keffiyeh* from the dead man's head and discarded his own headgear. The Cuban donned the headcloth of the man he had killed. He was ready for the next step.

THE SENTRY by the radio shack had noticed sudden motion on the ledge of the south mountain rock wall. He had not seen it clearly, and when he turned his head for a better view he noticed a figure seated on a boulder. The paisley *keffiyeh* revealed it was the same man who was stationed there, but something about the figure made the sentry continue staring.

Then the slight tap of a pebble against stone drew the man's attention away from the south wall. He turned his toward the sound at a corner of the radio shack. Eyes fixed in that direction, he unslung his AK-47 from his shoulder.

When he heard something behind him and saw a cord flash before his eyes as it swung over his head, it was too late to defend himself. The wire instantly encircled his neck and snapped tightly around it like a steel noose. A knee slammed into the small of his back as the garrote bit into his neck and throat. It closed off his windpipe and carotid arteries. The wire loop crossed at the mastoid bone behind his left ear. A sharp twist snapped his neck and severed the spinal cord at the brain stem.

David McCarter held on to the garrote and dragged the sentry along by the neck. The man was already dead before McCarter reached the rear of the shack. The British ace deposited the corpse behind the building and gathered up his Barnett crossbow before he headed back to the entrance. Hussan was already there, and after they exchanged nods, McCarter kicked in the door.

A terrorist sat at a field table inside the shack, the headset to the radio transceiver clamped to his head. He whipped about in his chair, startled by the figure at the threshold. Yellow light from a kerosene lantern bathed the man's frightened features in a ghastly light. He opened his mouth to scream as McCarter triggered the Commando crossbow.

The bowstring hummed, and the steel-tip bolt shot into the radio operator's gaping mouth. The man's teeth snapped around the fiberglass shaft of the crossbow projectile. The point pierced vertebrae and punctured the back of his neck. Cyanide oozed from the split shaft to be rapidly absorbed from the wound. The man's body twitched, and slumped lifeless from its chair.

"That was quick," Hussan commented in a soft whisper as he joined McCarter inside the shack and closed the door.

"That's the idea," the Briton replied. He moved to the radio and switched it off. "I hope the others are on time."

"No shooting," Hussan observed. "That must mean the other sentries are gone."

He eased the door open and peered outside. Hussan recognized Encizo despite the new headgear. The Omani agent scanned the other mountains and saw a figure on a ledge at the north wall. A brief waving motion made Hussan smile. The man they called Anderson was also in position.

Hussan turned to face McCarter. "Allah smiles on us tonight," he declared.

A slight rustling suddenly announced Hussan's observation may have been premature. He gripped his Bren 9 mm submachine gun as the sounds grew stronger.

Salim, the communications expert for the Purple Warrior base, had made his way up the mountain to check on the radio operator. He was experienced with such duty and realized even the most devout soldier can start to drift off to sleep during such a boring assignment, so he frequently inspected the shack at various hours of the night and day. Salim was not surprised that the sentry was not outside the shack. Guard duty is also tiresome and dull. The sentry was probably inside the shack with the radio man, chatting over a cup of tea, or behind the building answering a call of nature.

Salim walked to the door and hesitated by the entrance. Something seemed wrong. He sensed danger, but could not understand why. Maybe Qabda's stories of mystical revelations had disturbed Salim more than he realized, or perhaps he was simply nervous because the following day they would all head into the gulf to seek out the American convoy and give up their lives in martyrdom for the jihad. A man had a right to be a little upset about dying. Since Salim had new doubts about Qabda, martyrdom no longer seemed as glorious as it had in the past.

He began to reach for the door, but pulled back his hand. Salim did not hear the static of the radio inside. He did not hear voices, either. Something was wrong. He reached for the pistol on his hip, then the door suddenly swung open.

Hussan charged from the doorway and quickly slammed the steel frame of his subgun into Salim's face. The unexpected blow sent the Purple Warrior hurtling backward. He stumbled to the lip of the ledge and desperately windmilled with his arms to maintain his balance. It was a vain effort, and he plunged over the edge. He screamed as his limbs thrashed wildly in midair, but there was nothing to provide support. He continued to scream until his body crashed into the roof of a tent at the base of the mountain. Canvas gave way under the impact of his hurtling form. The tent collapsed beneath him, and he smashed into the earth with bone-crushing force.

Shouts of anger and alarm erupted throughout the camp. The rudely awakened terrorists slithered beneath the fallen canvas of the tent, trying to untangle themselves. Other figures rushed from the open flaps of dwellings that still stood. Most already had weapons in hand.

"Well, hell," McCarter muttered as he joined Hussan by the ledge and looked down at the panicked activity below. "I think they might suspect something now."

18

The mountain headquarters of the Purple Warriors of Righteousness was more crowded than usual, because Idris Rhamen and a dozen other cult members had recently joined Qabda's secret base after they fled the United Arab Emirates. Rhamen charged from his tent, clad only in his underwear, a French MAB pistol in his fist. Two other U.A.E. fugitives followed him outside. They stared at the figures that groped and stumbled beneath the fallen tent. The canvas heaved awkwardly from the struggles of the men, and provided a sight that would have been comical under different circumstances.

But Phoenix Force was not amused, either. The five commandos and their Arab allies watched the terrorists swarm from the tents below. They were surprised by the number of opponents. There were more of them than the size of the tents suggested. Bassam recognized Rhamen among the terrorists. The U.A.E. case officer and Ahmed had joined Katz on the rock ledge of the north mountain.

"Traitorous illegitimate son of a she-pig," Bassam hissed as he aimed his Sterling submachine gun at Rhamen.

He opened fire and sprayed Rhamen with a volley of 9 mm slugs. Blood spurted from bullet holes in the renegade's back and chest. Idris Rhamen stumbled and fell to the ground face-first. Bassam fired another salvo and raked the twitching figure with more parabellums to be certain Rhamen would never endanger the United Arab Emirates or any other country or its people again.

Katz barely noticed. The Phoenix Force commander was concerned with dealing with the entire terrorist base and paid little attention to individual opponents. He had already opened his goatskin pack and removed an M-17 protective mask and several grenades. The Israeli pulled the pin from a concussion grenade and lobbed it into a cluster of confused and alarmed Purple Warrior fanatics.

The explosive egg landed at the feet of the disoriented terrorists. Panicked, they ran in all directions to try to get clear of the grenade. Some fired weapons at Katz's position, but the Israeli veteran had already ducked low behind the cover of the rock ridge. Ahmed had done likewise, but Bassam wasted a split second of vital time firing his subgun at Rhamen's already-dead body. Automatic rifle sounds and pistol bullets screeched against stone along the north wall. Two 7.62 mm slugs struck Bassam in the upper chest and face. The impact shattered bone and spun the U.A.E. agent about in a violent whirl that threw Bassam off balance.

Bassam shouted out as he began to topple over the edge of the ridge. It was the beginning of a traditional Muslim prayer, which stated one bears witness that Mohammed is Allah's prophet.

He continued to recite the prayer as he fell from the ledge and dropped more than a hundred feet to the hard ground below. Bassam did not cry out in fear, but called out his last words with the firm, loud conviction of a muezzin calling the faithful to prayer. His voice ceased abruptly when he crashed to earth, bones shattered and the life smashed from his body.

The concussion grenades exploded at the same time Bassam died. The blast hurled terrorists across the valley. Bodies slammed into tents and knocked down more canvas shelters. Some terrorists collapsed unconscious from the concussion blast while others fell to their knees, eardrums shattered by the explosion. They screamed in agony. Some passed out from shock, but the rest scrambled about for weapons to continue the fight.

Phoenix Force and their companions tossed more concussion grenades into the enemy stronghold below. The explosions erupted throughout the base. The ground trembled from the force of blasts, yet the concussion blasts lacked the deadly devastation of bulletlike shrapnel and blazing might of fragmentation grenades. They could not risk using fraggers because such explosions might detonate the terrorists' explosives or puncture the cyanide canisters, which were surely stored at the base. The concussion grenades were risky, but far less effective than fraggers.

Some terrorists were killed by the grenades because they were close enough to the center of a blast to suffer ruptured vital organs. They sprawled on the ground, overpowered by massive shock and internal bleeding. Other terrorists were rendered unconscious. Many suffered damage to one or both eardrums. More than half the Purple Warrior population were knocked down by the thunderous waves of concussion blasts. Many groaned in agony as they tried to rise and discovered bones had been broken.

A few terrorists managed to fire weapons at the figures on the surrounding rock walls. Phoenix Force and their allies returned fire with automatic weapons. The latter had a definite advantage becuase they had the high ground. The commando unit had also secured good cover at the rock ledges and boulders, while the enemy had virtually none. The Purple Warriors had relied on the mountains as protection. Now they were bound in on all four sides, and their strongest defense sheltered their opponents.

Calvin James and Gary Manning fired their rifles from the shelter of a cluster of boulders at the mountain to the east of the enemy base. Enemy bullets ricocheted against the stone cover and the rock wall beside the Phoenix pair. One projectile whined inches from Manning's right ear. The Canadian flinched and cursed under his breath.

"I sure as hell heard that," he complained.

James, however, did not hear his partner. The black commando had spotted two terrorists headed for the mosque, the only structure in the compound which was sturdy enough to block bullets. James hit the closest opponent with a trio of 5.56 mm slugs. The terrorist tumbled backward to the ground while his comrade raised a short-barreled machine pistol. James snap-aimed and triggered another three-round burst. The second Purple Warrior fell, a third of his skull shot off.

"Sons of bitches wanted to be martyrs," James muttered as ducked behind the boulders. "Hope they're satisfied."

"I'd say the survivors are pretty shook up," Manning commented, his eyes on the scope of his FAL rifle. "Let's give them something to weep over."

"They're not the type to appreciate a romance novel," James replied as he gripped the M-203 attachment under the barrel of his M-16. "Guess I'll have to give 'em something else."

Manning aimed his rifle at a terrorist who was about to fire an old British Enfield at the south rock wall. The Canadian wondered why the guy had such an out-of-date weapon. The man's forehead appeared in the center of the cross hairs of Manning's rifle scope. The Phoenix pro squeezed the trigger, and a 7.62 mm bullet smashed through the terrorist's skull.

"Guess there's no point in asking him about that Enfield now," Manning grunted as he watched the man fall dead.

James did not know what the hell his partner was talking about, but he did not have time to ask Manning for an explanation. He aimed his M-16 at the center of the enemy camp and triggered the M-203.

The 40 mm grenade hurtled from the big bore of the launcher and descended into the heart of the terrorist base. It exploded on impact and dense green tear gas spewed from the shell. Purple Warriors were quickly overcome by the fumes, and they staggered about, coughing and hacking helplessly.

Manning donned his M-17 mask and yanked the pin from a tear gas grenade. He lobbed it into the enemy base below and gathered up his rifle as more green fog filled the valley.

Other tear gas bombs descended as the rest of Phoenix Force responded to James's lead with the M-203 round. The black commando also pulled on his protective mask.

"That should've softened 'em up a bit," James commented as he peered through the M-17 lenses at the dazed, half-blind figures that reeled about in the waist-deep fog of noxious gas. "Kind'a hard to count them. Looks like a big green cloud down there."

"The gas is fairly contained within the valley," Manning observed with satisfaction. "It must be really affecting them. Kind of like the 'gas chamber' they put you through in basic training in the army."

"I was navy, remember?" James replied. "Figure there's about twenty-five or thirty terrorists left?"

"Sounds about right," Manning agreed as he hammered a piton into the rock wall. "Better figure there might be more than that. Ready to find out?"

"I can think of other things I'd rather be doin'," James admitted. He jammed the iron spike of another piton into a crack in the rock wall with one hand and took the hammer from Manning with the other. "But I can't think of anything I'd rather do right now."

James hammered the piton into place while Manning fed the rope through the eye of the first piton. He passed the line on to James who slid it through the eye of the second mountaineer spike. Both men hooked up to the line and knotted the rope securely to the pitons. Manning lowered one end of the line down the face of the mountain and slid his FAL onto a shoulder. He gripped the rope with both hands and swung over the ledge.

The Canadian braced his feet on the rock wall and began to "walk" down the surface, easing the rope through his hands as he descended. Manning heard gunshots snarl as he climbed. He realized the other members of Phoenix Force and their allies would continue to fire at the enemy to keep them busy while he and James descended the rock wall. Manning also knew the terrorists would continue to blast away as well. He hoped the enemy did not decide to throw lead in his direction while his hands were filled with the rope.

James watched Manning descend and prepared to follow. Before the Phoenix Force assault team launched the raid, they had made the decision that the members on the mountain near the purple mosque would be first to descend to the valley, since the building would provide some cover. It was unusual for the mosque to be at the east end because Mecca was actually northwest of Oman. However, Iran and the Ayatollah were east. Maybe the Purple Warriors of Righteousness faced Iran as well as Mecca when they prayed. Whatever the reason, James and Manning had won the honor of going first.

"Lucky us," James muttered as he glanced at the orange muzzle-flash of blazing weapons within the green fog in the valley.

Manning reached the base of the mountain behind the mosque. He dropped to the ground, relieved to be alive and in one piece. The Canadian moved to the wall of the mosque and unslung the FAL from his shoulder. Manning glanced up and saw James had begun to descend the face of the mountain.

Suddenly a figure appeared at the corner of the mosque. Manning swiveled around to face the enemy. The man's eyes were squinted into slits as he obviously struggled to recover. The tear gas had taken its toll, but he had managed to hold on to his Skorpion machine pistol.

Manning did not give the terrorist a chance to recover from the gas fumes. He lashed the barrel of his FAL rifle across the man's wrist and struck the Skorpion from his grasp. The terrorist's other hand snaked forward with surprising speed and grabbed the frame of Manning's weapon. The Canadian held on to the rifle with his right hand and jabbed his left fist to the Arab's breastbone. The man wheezed and weaved slightly. Manning hooked his fist into the terrorist's solar plexus.

The Purple Warrior doubled up from the blow and vomited on the ground. Manning easily wrenched the FAL from his opponent's hand and promptly chopped the stock across the base of the terrorist's skull. The man fell to all fours, dazed and semiconscious. Manning directed a blow to the head, his boot heel hitting the man hard at the left temple. It was a no-contest situation at that point.

Calvin James glanced down from the mountainside as he climbed along the rope toward the ground. He saw the Canadian clobber the terrorist with little difficulty. James hoped all the Purple Warrior followers would be as easy to deal with.

A burst of automatic rifle rounds pelted the rock wall above James's head. He instinctively froze and ducked his head, teeth clamped and fists clenched tightly around the rope. James glanced down and estimated the distance to the ground as he heard the high-pitched whine of ricochet bullets that sizzled all around him.

The black commando figured it was nearly forty feet to the base of the mountain. James realized he would probably survive a jump from this distance, but he would almost certainly break some bones. The ground below was hard, little more than layers of dirt over layers of rock. If James broke both legs he would not be any good to his companions in the battle. If he broke them badly enough, he would never be fit to participate in another mission with Phoenix Force.

Yeah, he thought grimly as he continued to climb down the mountain. *I won't be much good to anybody if I get a couple bullets in the spine.*

Another volley raked the rocks. Projectiles sparked on stone, and one grazed the rope overhead. Nylon cord snapped, and the line began to unravel. James saw the rope begin to give way and, cursing under his breath, he tried to scramble down to the ground before the rope broke.

A twang made by the rope fibers bursting apart announced he had not made it in time.

James felt himself plunge from the rock wall. He spun about in midair to face away from the mountain. The Phoenix pro planned to land on his feet, knees bent to absorb the impact. Then he would roll forward to break the fall...hopefully. He damn sure did not want to roll headlong into the mountain. However, a great purple sphere appeared before him. James hurtled toward the mosque dome as the roar of automatic fire rang louder and closer.

He landed spread-eagled on the curved dome. His belly and chest smacked into the stone surface hard. James's arm slapped the curved, bulb-shaped dome, hands clawing at the smooth stone. He slid down the dome, breath knocked from his lungs, limbs strained by the desperate effort to hold on.

"Oh, shit!" James exclaimed, voice muffled by the M-17. "I hate this kind a—"

The black warrior slipped off the bottom of the dome and dropped to the ground. The distance he had slid on the dome had effectively slowed his descent and allowed him to dangle for a split second by his hands, arms extended. Unable to hold on, however, he dropped to the ground, the sudden impact rattling his teeth. He nearly lost his balance, but slumped against the wall at the rear of the mosque to steady himself.

Gary Manning had aimed his FAL around the edge of the mosque and fired at the enemy gunmen who had tried to blast James. The Canadian triggered his rifle and pumped a trio of 7.62 mm slugs into the heart of the closest opponent. Literally dead on his feet, the man wilted to the ground while his comrade fired a hastily aimed salvo at Manning.

Bullets chipped adobe brick from the corner of the mosque above Manning's head. Clay dust showered down on his head and shoulders, but Manning paid no heed as he squeezed the trigger. The second terrorist gunman received a lethal dose of FAL lead poisoning and collapsed. The Canadian stepped back from the corner and turned to face James.

"You okay?" he inquired.

"I'm pissed off," James replied. "Let's go kick some ass."

He circled around the mosque and approached the terrorists at the center of the camp. Several of the terrorists,

who had been temporarily pinned under the canvas of their
fallen tents, had actually been protected against the most
savage effects of the concussion grenades and managed to
cover their faces with the scarf portions of *keffiyehs* before
they emerged. The cloth masks protected them to a limited
degree from the clouds of tear gas. Two of them saw James
approach.

They swung their weapons toward the tall black man with
the rubber mask and an assault rifle with grenade launcher
under the barrel. Calvin James seemed like a demon from
hell to the Shiite pair. A tall dark figure with an inhuman
face and a formidable weapon emerging from the swirling
vapors. They were taken off guard for a moment, and that
was all the advantage James needed.

The M-16 snarled, and three bullets tunneled through the
nasal cavity of the closest terrorist to punch into his brain.
James dropped to one knee and fired another burst into the
stomach of his second opponent. The man doubled up in
agony, and the hard-ass from the Southside dispatched him
with a final shot.

More men headed for James, armed with weapons that
ranged from *jambiya* knives to automatic rifles. Manning
fired his FAL rifle and took out one opponent with a well-
placed head shot. No sooner did he drop than a burst of
submachine gun rounds chopped between the shoulder
blades of another terrorist. The man moaned and fell forward to land lifeless on the ground.

A Purple Warrior fanatic whirled and fired a Turkish
autoloader pistol at a figure who had attacked the group
from the rear. At least one bullet struck the lens of the
commando's right eyepiece to an M-17 mask. Plexiglas
shattered, and the figure tumbled backward, blood already
pouring from the punctured eye socket to spill across the
rubber cheek of his mask. The man's Sterling submachine
gun roared as he began to fall. A trio of 9 mm rounds ripped
up the chest of the terrorist pistol man. With bullet holes in
his solar plexus, sternum and throat, the Purple Warrior was
no more.

Another blast of 9 mm slugs slammed into a fourth opponent and sent him hurtling in a cartwheel that deposited his bullet-ravaged corpse near James's feet. The black battle vet barely glimpsed at the fallen enemy as he triggered his M-16 and burned off the last rounds from the magazine. The last eager-for-combat terrorist spun about from the force of two 5.56 mm slugs to the torso and received an addition volley of 9 mm projectiles from the figure that closed in. The terrorist crumpled in a lifeless lump as the two Phoenix pros noticed the new arrival wore an M-17 mask and carried an Heckler & Kock MP5 machine pistol.

"Rafael," James sighed with relief. "Glad you made it."

"So far," Encizo replied. He glanced down at the still figure of the corpse with the M-17 mask. The Cuban saw the bullet-punctured eye beneath the shattered lens. "He didn't make it."

"Which one is he?" Manning inquired, looking down at the dead Arab ally.

"Rashid," Encizo answered. "Bullet tore through the eye socket to the brain. I hope it was quick."

"He took his assassin with him," Manning stated. "How we doing? Winning or losing?"

"Still fighting," Encizo replied. "Let's go."

HUSSAN WALKED to the two shacks at the west wall of the base. One building barely stood. Two walls had been smashed in by the force of the concussion grenades. The Omani agent stared through the lenses of his protective mask and examined the wreckage with interest. A single body lay beneath the rubble of flimsy wood boards and tattered canvas. Hussan pointed his Sterling chopper at the still form as he stepped closer.

The Omani agent was surprised to notice the man beneath the wreckage was fully dressed in white robe, red boots and sash. Most of the Purple Warriors had not had time to don any garments except a gun belt. Hussan saw a small field desk, a Persian prayer rug and a leather-bound Koran among the debris. He pulled back a strip of canvas to reveal the man's face. The motionless features resembled a desert falcon, and the green cloth of a *keffiyeh* surrounded it. A purple turban was bound to the top of his head.

"Qabda!" Hussan declared with delight. "You're finished, you Shiite glob of pig dung."

He spat on Qabda's face. The saliva oozed over the still figure's immobile features. Hussan was satisfied the man was dead and used the barrel of his subgun to pry loose rubble from the corpse. He discovered a Russian Makarov pistol by the cult leader's side. The Omani agent gathered it up and stuck the handgun in his belt. Qabda held a long-bladed *jambiya* in one hand and a small metal box in the other. Hussan knelt beside the dead man and tried to tug the box from the dead man's hand. The fingers did not move easily. Even in death Qabda had a powerful grip. However Hussan pried the fingers back and took the little box from its deceased owner.

"Shortwave radio transmitter," the Omani agent realized when he saw the stem of an antenna and a red button in the center of the box. "Curious . . ."

A sudden blur of motion drew his attention, and he turned his head to see a streak of steel rush forward. Hussan tried to pull away, but the long blade caught him in the side of the neck. The force of the heavy knife blade hacked into flesh and muscle to sever the carotid artery. The *jambiya* flashed in a deft backstroke and sliced open Hussan's throat with a swift, short movement.

Hussan tumbled to the ground, blood spattered across his shirtfront. He pawed at his slit throat with one hand and fumbled with the Sterling chopper with the other. The Omani agent knew he was dying, but he still intended to take Qabda with him before his life vanished.

The leader of the Purple Warriors of Righteousness rose from the rubble of his crushed shack and drove the point of his knife into Hussan's stomach. Qabda used his empty hand to press the Omani's Sterling across Hussan's chest to pin it down while he carved open the agent's belly. Qabda could have finished him off quickly, but chose to make Hussan's final moments of life as painful as possible.

He moved the knife between Hussan's legs, but the Omani's body ceased twitching before Qabda could cut open the trousers. The fanatic guessed the slit throat had caused a fatal injury and Hussan died before he could feel the next, most horrifying stroke of the knife. Qabda saw no point in mutilating the dead. He felt certain Allah would punish the intruder in eternal damnation anyway. The agonies of hell were surely worse than any injury endured by the living.

Qabda stuck his blade in the ground next to Hussan's corpse. He pulled the protective mask from the dead man's face and slipped it onto his own head. The terrorist leader's eyes burned, and his nostrils felt as if they were filled with hungry ants. Lying under the rubble, pretending to be dead had been very difficult, due to the effects of the floating mists of tear gas. Qabda was almost immune to pain, thanks to his years of self-abuse rituals to express his devotion to his religion. Nonetheless, the chemical assault had been a hard test of his physical endurance because it was unlike any of his previous self-inflicted ordeals of pain.

He was nearly blinded by tears and choked by the gas in his sinuses and throat. The protective mask did not seem to help. Qabda adjusted the straps to slip the M-17 over his turban and *keffiyeh*. It would have been more logical to remove his elaborate headgear, but Qabda clung to the symbols of his cult authority. He was not thinking clearly. The terrorist leader had been battered by the concussion grenades and falling wreckage. The tear gas had contributed to his dazed and disoriented condition. He had been only semi-conscious when Hussan spat on him and pried the transmitter from his hand—

The transmitter. Qabda recalled that he had the radio-detonator in hand when the shack crashed down on him. It was set for a shortwave frequency that would produce a single note that would trigger a radio-receiver unit in the storage shack. The receiver would switch on a mercury fuse to ignite a special blasting cap in plastic explosive. When the bomb went off, it would also detonate other demolitions in the shed and blast the cyanide canisters to bits.

Of course, Qabda would use this extreme action only as a last resort if the authorities defeated his men in conventional combat. Qabda intended to use the cyanide against American infidels, not the Omani military. He certainly did not want to waste his most vital weapons just to deal with a raid by mountain bandits—or sacrifice his life and the lives of his followers. So Qabda had hesitated to use the ultimate weapon until he was sure it was necessary.

Now he believed it was necessary.

The shooting had ceased, but he heard no shouts of victory and praises to Allah for allowing his men to defeat the invaders. This could only mean his side had lost the battle. Qabda walked to the bloodied corpse of Hussan. The transmitter lay next to the dead man. Qabda reached down and grabbed the handle of his *jambiya* with one hand and yanked the blade from the dirt while his other hand groped for the transmitter.

"Qabda!" a voice shouted.

He glanced up and peered through the unfamiliar lenses of the M-17 at a tall figure clad in peasant garb and a protective mask. Qabda wondered how the man knew his name. The purple turban must have told the stranger who he was.

"It's over, Qabda," David McCarter announced as he pointed his KG-99 machine pistol at the terrorist leader.

The Briton saw Hussan's corpse on the ground and the small metal box beside it. Qabda did not seem intimidated by McCarter's weapon. He hissed something in angry Arabic and quickly grabbed the transmitter.

McCarter opened fire. A trio of 9 mm rounds tore into Qabda's upper torso. A bullet smahed the bones at the fanatic's shoulder joint. His arm jerked uncontrollably from the sudden shock. His fingers loosened, and the transmitter fell from his hand. Qabda cried out and hurled his weapon at McCarter. The Phoenix pro ducked and raised his KG-99. The knife blade struck the steel frame of Mc-Carter's machine pistol and fell harmlessly to the ground.

He triggered the KG-99 once more. Another burst of death-dealing slugs smashed into the center of Qabda's chest. His heart and lungs fatally damaged, Qabda fell backward and landed on his back, muscles twitching in a final desperate effort to cling to a life that was already terminated. McCarter stepped forward and sprayed the body with a third salvo of parabellum rounds.

"David!" Rafael Encizo called out as he approached the British ace. "It's finished. What are you doing? He's already dead."

"Just making sure the anti-Christ goes back to hell and stays there," McCarter replied and turned to face the Cuban. "How'd we do?"

"The Purple Warriors of Righteousness have been wiped out," Encizo answered. "Some of them are still alive. They can be interrogated to find out details about other terrorists still at large. Without Qabda and the cyanide canisters, the cult is finished anyway. We lost three men—Bassam, Rashid and Hussan. None of Phoenix Force were injured. Omar and Ahmed are okay, too."

"Well, that's one less problem in the Persian Gulf," McCarter commented. "Too bad there are still so many others."

"We can't save the world by ourselves," Encizo replied. "The rest of the world has to put in a little effort as well. Come on, amigo. Let's go tell the others the good news."

"Able Team will go anywhere, do anything, in order to
complete their mission."
—West Coast Review of Books

SUPER ABLE TEAM #1
DICK STIVERS

The Desmondos, an organized street gang, terrorize the streets
of Los Angeles armed with AK-47s and full-auto Uzis.

Carl Lyons and his men are sent in to follow the trail of blood
and drugs to the power behind these teenage terrorists.

The Desmondos are bad, but they haven't met Able Team.

Phoenix Force—bonded in secrecy to avenge the acts of terrorists everywhere

SEARCH AND DESTROY $3.95 ☐

American ''killer'' mercenaries are involved in a KGB plot to overthrow the government of a South Pacific island. The American President, anxious to preserve his country's image and not disturb the precarious position of the island nation's government, sends in the experts—Phoenix Force—to prevent a coup.

FIRE STORM $3.95 ☐

An international peace conference turns into open warfare when terrorists kidnap the American President and the premier of the USSR at a summit meeting. As a last desperate measure Phoenix Force is brought in—for if demands are not met, a plutonium core device is set to explode.

Total Amount	$ _____
Plus 75¢ Postage	_____.75
Payment enclosed	$ _____